YOU HAD ME AT HOLA

A NOVEL

ALEXIS DARIA

AVON

An Imprint of HarperCollins*Publishers*

This is a work of fiction. Names, characters, places, and incidents are products of the author's imagination or are used fictitiously and are not to be construed as real. Any resemblance to actual events, locales, organizations, or persons, living or dead, is entirely coincidental.

HarperCollins books may be purchased for educational, business, or sales promotional use. For information, please email the Special Markets Department at SPsales@harpercollins.com.

FIRST EDITION

Designed by Diahann Sturge

Title page art © Daiquiri / Shutterstock, Inc.

Library of Congress Cataloging-in-Publication Data has been applied for.

ISBN 978-0-06-295992-8

20 21 22 23 24   LSC   10 9 8 7 6 5 4 3 2 1

YOU HAD ME AT HOLA

Also by Alexis Daria

To my own Primas of Power, who inspired this book.
And to Rita Moreno, for lighting the way.

In loving memory of Tara Lee
April 22, 1988–October 12, 2019

YOU HAD ME AT HOLA

Chapter 1

DUMPED!

The word glared at Jasmine in bright yellow letters, emblazoned directly beneath a picture of her own face. All caps, of course, and below it: *Exclusive details from soap star Jasmine Lin's humiliating breakup with rock star playboy McIntyre.*

"Who put this here?" Jasmine demanded, slapping her hand over the words, as if that could make them disappear, as if the whole embarrassing ordeal could be concealed so easily.

Avoiding the tabloids with her face on them had been hard enough in places like Target and the airport, but she thought she'd be safe in her grandmother's kitchen in the Bronx. But no, here was one of those blasted covers, stuck to the fridge with magnets shaped like a pan of paella and the Puerto Rican flag.

"We told Abuela to take it down, but she said it was a good picture of you," her cousin Ava said from behind her.

"Porque it *is* a good picture!" Over by the sink, Abuela Esperanza's voice spiked with indignation. She dried her hands on a dish towel and joined Jasmine at the fridge.

"A good picture?" Jasmine jabbed a finger at it. "I look like a deer in headlights watching a lifetime of breakups flash before its eyes."

"¿Que qué? No . . . You look beautiful, although you really should moisturize more." Abuela patted Jasmine's cheek.

Jasmine ignored the dig about her skincare routine and peered more closely at the magazine cover. A paparazzo had snapped the photo on a rare rainy day in Los Angeles as Jasmine was leaving the salon where she got her eyebrows threaded. Pairing that headline—DUMPED!—with that photo—bleary-eyed and frizzy-haired—made it seem like McIntyre had left her because she looked a mess, or she looked a mess because McIntyre had left her. Either way, it was unflattering and incredibly rude.

And on newsstands and refrigerators everywhere, for all to see.

"Just be glad you have an up-to-date photo on the fridge," her other cousin Michelle chimed in with an exaggerated shiver from over by the coffeepot. "My most recent is from sophomore year of high school when I still had braces and bangs."

"That's *also* a good picture," Esperanza protested.

The fridge was littered with photos of Esperanza and Willie Rodriguez's twelve grandchildren in various phases of childhood—never mind that all of them were adults now—held in place by a lifetime's collection of magnets from around the world. All of the grandkids were biracial, and Jasmine had often thought the range of skin tones on the refrigerator could've been used as a makeup foundation palette.

Jasmine, Ava, and Michelle were all brunettes, but that was

where the similarities ended. Michelle, whose father was Italian, had light brown eyes, a warm beige complexion, and straight hair. Jasmine had golden-brown skin, dark brown eyes, and thick wavy hair she usually straightened for roles. Ava, whose mother had been born in Barbados, was the tallest and naturally tan, with hazel eyes. Her dark curls fell to her shoulders, the result of a recent post-divorce chop.

But the surface differences didn't matter. They were family.

Jasmine gave the magazine cover one last scathing look, but didn't dare rip it down. Even at thirty, she still feared invoking her grandmother's wrath.

"Forget about the picture. Ven acá, nena." Abuela opened her arms and wrapped Jasmine in a hug.

Jasmine sank into the embrace, breathing in the sweet scents of vanilla and Esperanza's face powder. It had been too long since she'd last visited, too long since she'd spent time with this woman who meant so much to her. The signs of Esperanza's aging were clearer, although she still styled her now-gray hair in a short bob and wore red lipstick every day. *If you're not wearing lipstick and earrings, you might as well be naked*, Esperanza used to say. It wasn't until Jasmine was older that the true meaning sank in. Those things were armor against a world that had wanted to treat her grandmother as someone smaller and duller than the brilliant and beautiful woman she was. Looking after her appearance forced people to take her seriously.

Jasmine caught a glimpse of the magazine cover mocking her from over her grandmother's shoulder.

Never again, she promised herself. Never again would her

dating life give the national entertainment media machine a reason to shine a spotlight on her. Jasmine Lin Rodriguez was done with dating. She released her grandmother, who took Ava's spot at the stove, and joined her cousins at the kitchen counter where Michelle passed around steaming mugs of coffee. After a deep inhale of Café Bustelo mixed with the house's permanent scent of Sazón seasoning, Jasmine gulped the bitter black coffee, wishing it were a glass of wine.

Michelle jerked her head toward the kitchen doorway. "Basement?"

"Basement," Jasmine agreed. The three of them took their mugs and trooped downstairs.

The finished basement had long been their hideout, their refuge away from the rest of the family, where they could talk about their hopes, dreams, and dumb boys. McIntyre certainly fell into the latter category, although Jasmine had no interest in talking about him ever again. If she could erase him from her memory, she would. No, better yet, she'd erase him from everyone *else's* memories. Then he'd no longer be famous and no one would care that she'd dated him.

"Remind me where you're staying?" Michelle asked once they'd settled onto the old sofa. It had once lived upstairs under plastic, but after surviving twelve grandkids, the plastic had been removed and the couch relegated to the basement.

Jasmine sipped her coffee again. "ScreenFlix is putting me up at the Hutton Court. It's one of those long-term-stay hotels."

ScreenFlix, the number one streaming service in the country, had cast Jasmine in the starring role on the remake of *La patrona Carmen*, a Venezuelan telenovela from the 1990s. After the popularity of American remakes of telenovelas like *Ugly Betty*, *Jane the Virgin*, and *Queen of the South*, ScreenFlix had seen the writing on the wall. Telenovelas were where it was at.

For Jasmine, who'd made a name for herself on English soap operas and received a Daytime Emmy nom, headlining a show on ScreenFlix had the potential to be her big break. If it did well, it could lead to more ScreenFlix projects, or maybe even a big-budget cable show or primetime network program.

Michelle raised her eyebrows. "Ooh, fancy."

Jasmine shrugged. "Yeah, but it's in Midtown."

"East or West?" Ava asked.

"East."

Michelle wrinkled her nose. "Gross. There's nothing over there."

"Tell me about it. If it were any farther east, I'd be sleeping in the middle of the FDR Drive." Jasmine couldn't complain too much, though. ScreenFlix had a contract with the hotel company, and her agent had negotiated for her to stay in one of their one-bedroom units with views of the East River. And since it was an easy drive over the Queensboro Bridge to the ScreenFlix Studios production lot, the Hutton Court was where she'd be living for the next three months.

Ava and Michelle exchanged a look, making no move to hide it. Jasmine waited a beat, then caved. "What? What is it?"

"Jas." Michelle leveled her with a direct stare. "Just move back."

Jasmine slumped into the sofa. She'd known this was coming. Every time she returned to New York City for a visit or a gig, her cousins launched their campaign to persuade her to move back permanently. The three of them had been born just a few years apart and had been one another's constant companions, as close as sisters. Certainly closer to Jasmine than her own sister, Jillian.

Jasmine sucked in a breath to argue, but Ava leaped in before she could utter a word.

"Hear us out. There are plenty of shows filming in New York City now, and you'll be closer to us."

"Along with everyone else in our family." Jasmine shook her head. "No thanks."

Michelle shrugged. "A minor technicality."

"We've been over this. The remaining soaps film in Los Angeles, and there are tons of other opportunities there. I can't leave." As much as she might want to. "Anyway, I have a plan."

Michelle's eyebrows shot up. "Do tell."

"I love a good plan." Ava set down her mug. "Let's hear it."

"It's my Leading Lady Plan."

Michelle's eyebrows drew together. "What's that?"

"My roadmap for staying on track with my career goals." Jasmine pointed a finger at the ceiling, referencing her picture on the fridge upstairs. "One: Leading Ladies do not end up on tabloid covers."

"That's just not true," Michelle cut in. "Look at Jennifer Aniston. They put that poor lady on magazine covers for all sorts of made-up shit."

That was a good point. Jasmine didn't want to turn into

the next tabloid favorite, although she'd happily follow in Ms. Aniston's career footsteps.

"Can you give it a more positive spin?" Ava asked kindly. "Like saying what leading ladies *do* instead of what they *don't*?"

It was such an Ava thing to say, but she was right. They both were.

"Fine." Jasmine tore a sheet from the memo pad on the coffee table. The paper had beach details printed around the borders—sandals, an umbrella, a kid's plastic shovel and pail—and said "Esperanza" on top in elaborate cursive. "What should I say instead?"

"How about, 'Leading Ladies only end up on magazine covers with good reason'?" Ava suggested.

"That's not exactly catchy," Jasmine muttered, but she wrote it down with the tiny pen attached to the notepad.

"What was your second point?" Michelle asked.

Jasmine's cheek's warmed as she mumbled, "Two: Leading Ladies don't need a man to be happy."

Her cousins exchanged another look. It was the one they always shared when the subject of Jasmine's love life came up.

"What about, 'Leading Ladies are whole and happy on their own'?" Ava said, her tone gentle.

Jasmine doubted that, but since this plan was also supposed to keep her from getting derailed by romance, she wrote it down.

"What's the third one?" Ava asked.

Shit. Why had she mentioned this stupid plan in the first place? Jasmine thought fast. "Um, Leading Ladies take their careers seriously."

Michelle rolled her eyes. "You just pulled that out of your ass."

"Fine." Jasmine tossed the pen onto the table. "Three: Leading Ladies don't sit home crying over their exes."

Ava rubbed Jasmine's shoulder while Michelle took the pen and wrote something down. When she was done, she slid the paper over to Jasmine.

Leading Ladies are badass queens making jefa moves.

"I almost wrote *boss queens* but with *jefa* in there, it would have been redundant," Michelle explained.

Jasmine gave a small smile and spoke around the lump in her throat. "Thanks."

They were all silent for a moment, sipping their coffees, and then Ava set her mug down and folded her hands on her lap. In a quiet voice, she asked, "Do you want to talk about it?"

It was the closest she would come to asking outright about McIntyre. Subtlety and patience were Ava's tools of choice, which made her a great teacher. Michelle, a high-level corporate marketing consultant turned freelance graphic designer, was less likely to beat around the bush, but she'd follow Ava's lead when it made sense to her.

"You've seen the tabloids, so you know the gist of it." Jasmine heaved a deep sigh. "Obviously, I'm not dating McIntyre anymore."

"We know that's not the full story," Ava said at the same

time that Michelle said, "He was a tool anyway," but then Jasmine's phone rang. *Saved by the bell.* The last thing she wanted to do right now was rehash the painful and embarrassing experience of being publicly cheated on by a rock star.

"It's my agent," Jasmine murmured, answering the call. "Hi, Riley."

"Hey, Jasmine." Riley's chipper tones filled her ear. Riley Chen was young and friendly, but when it came to making deals, she was a pit bull, latching on to negotiations with a ferocity that had made her a rising star in the agency. "Did you get into New York okay?"

"I did. Dropped my luggage off at the hotel and now I'm visiting my family."

"I won't keep you, then. But I wanted to call because I figured you hadn't seen your email yet, and I know you don't like surprises."

A shimmer of dread threaded through Jasmine's gut. *Now what?* Aware that her cousins were watching with undisguised interest, Jasmine kept her expression bland. "No, I haven't checked my email."

"It's not a big deal," Riley said quickly, as if reading the apprehension in Jasmine's voice. "Just a casting change for the love interest."

"Oh?" That kind of *was* a big deal. She'd already done chemistry reads in LA with the guy she thought she'd be kissing on-screen.

Riley continued. "The actor who was supposed to play him broke his leg in Aspen."

"Oh, damn. Was it a skiing accident? It's June." And since they'd already signed their contracts, he shouldn't have been doing something dangerous, like skiing. Not when they were due to start production in a few days.

"Well . . . not exactly." Riley lowered her voice. "Apparently, he was meeting someone there, and he tripped getting out of his car. It looked like he was trying to be stealthy."

Jasmine's brows creased. "How do you know all this?"

"Someone caught the whole thing on their phone and sold the video to *Buzz Weekly*."

Jasmine groaned. *Buzz Weekly* was the tabloid news source that had taken the McIntyre story and run with it, thus making Jasmine a household name. *But not for a good reason*, she thought, recalling the first point on her new Leading Lady Plan.

"I know," Riley said. "We hate *Buzz Weekly*. But I watched the video, and the guy did a pirouette thing before toppling down a few steps. Only, like, three of them, but they were brick. He broke his leg and scraped up his face too."

"Yikes. That sounds pretty bad."

"Don't feel too sorry for him. A girl in a bikini came running out to get him, and it turns out she's only nineteen, whereas he's almost forty."

Jasmine pressed her fingers to the bridge of her nose. There was always some scandal in Hollywood. And while it would be nice to think this one would take the place of her own, she doubted it. McIntyre was just too famous.

And now, by extension, so was she.

Riley wasn't done, though. "All that to say, he's off the show. You'll have a new costar for *Carmen in Charge*."

This was a big change. "Do you know if we'll be doing chemistry reads, or is this a done deal?"

"Done deal," Riley said, sounding sympathetic. "The producers don't want to delay production, and he's finishing up a pilot, so there's no time for a chemistry read."

"Who is it?"

The phone connection broke for a second. "—shton Suarez."

Jasmine blinked. "Wait, did you say Ashton Suarez?"

On either side of her, Ava's and Michelle's eyes widened.

"Yes," Riley said. "Have you heard of him?"

"Um . . . yes." Holy shit. Of course she had. Ashton Suarez was her grandmother's favorite telenovela star. Esperanza had watched every show he'd been on for almost a decade. She was going to flip when she found out.

"Oh, good, that'll make intros easier. You'll meet him at the table read. Anyway, I'll let you go now. Have fun with your family!"

Jasmine murmured a farewell to Riley and slowly lowered her phone to the table. It had been completely stupid to say his name out loud in front of her cousins. *Cue overreaction in three . . . two . . .*

Michelle grabbed Jasmine's wrist in a tight grip, her brown eyes wide. "Ashton. Suarez," she repeated. "Ashton *Fucking* Suarez . . ."

"He's el león dorado!" Ava squealed.

Michelle flung her head back and pressed the back of her hand to her forehead, adopting a dramatic tone. "And el matador!"

"El hombre seductor!"

"El duque de amor!"

"I know, I know," Jasmine cut in. The guy had been on something like twenty different Spanish soap operas, and they'd be here all day if her cousins continued to spout his various character names.

"I think the one where he played the Golden Lion was my favorite," Ava mused. "It was like *The Godfather* meets *Indiana Jones*."

"I liked the one where he was an old-timey sheriff." Michelle fanned herself. "He cut quite the dashing figure in that uniform."

"Okay, that's e—" Jasmine began, but Ava cut her off.

"He played a villain recently, and I liked his beard. But I thought they killed him off too soon."

"Ava!" Michelle's jaw dropped, aghast. "Spoilers!"

Ava shrugged, entirely unapologetic. "If you spent more time with Abuela, you'd be caught up."

While they went back and forth about Ashton's best roles, Jasmine mulled over this latest news. Ashton Suarez was a solid fixture in telenovelas, and even though Jasmine's Spanish wasn't good enough for her to follow them fully, she'd seen him on Esperanza's TV plenty of times over the years. He was a good-looking man, even if he had a tendency to overact sometimes.

Not that Jasmine was one to talk. Her role on *The Glamour Squad*, a newer soap centered around a modeling agency, had required a level of melodramatics even her telenovela-loving abuela found a little ridiculous. Still, Jasmine's back-from-the-dead trophy wife character, Cordelia, had stolen the show.

Fans had loved Cordelia's forbidden romance with Keane, the fashion photographer with a gambling addiction. For Jasmine, Cordelia would always hold a special place in her heart—the character had earned her a Daytime Emmy nom and won her the role of Carmen.

Never mind that she didn't speak Spanish. Jasmine's accent was perfect, even if her conversation skills left something to be desired. The last time she'd tried to gossip with her grandmother in Spanish, Esperanza had complained Jasmine was hurting her ears.

Her younger brother, Jeremy, had teased her when he found out she had to speak Spanish for the role, but he shut up real quick when Jasmine pointed out he knew even less of the language than she did. While Spanish had been Jasmine's father's first language, her mother, who was Puerto Rican and Filipina, knew very little Spanish or Tagalog, so English had been the main language in their home. Working on this show was going to be like a crash course in language immersion, and Jasmine sincerely hoped she was up to the challenge.

Michelle raised a hand, breaking into her thoughts. "Hold on. I'm getting an idea."

Jasmine groaned. Michelle's ideas were often brilliant but just as often got the three of them into trouble. Like the time they'd snuck out to a concert in New Jersey on a school night and missed the last bus back. They'd had to call their oldest cousin, Sammy, to pick them up. His silence had been expensive.

"I want to hear this idea," said Ava.

Of course she did. *Enabler.* Jasmine made a face at her. "I don't."

But Michelle was not to be deterred when she was in possession of an idea. "Abuela's eightieth birthday is coming up. If you could get Ashton Suarez to come to the party as your guest, Abuela would be over the moon. She'd make enough pasteles to last you the rest of your life."

Biting her lip, Jasmine couldn't disagree. It wouldn't just make her grandmother's year. It would make her whole *decade.*

"And if you bring him, I absolve you of party-planning duties," Ava added.

"I didn't realize I had any party-planning duties."

"Of course you do. Everyone does."

"What about Tony? He's in London."

Ava shrugged. "Don't worry, I'll find something for him to do. All the cousins have to help."

How many times had Jasmine heard those words? "Everyone has to help" had been one of the guiding forces in her life for as long as she could remember, going back to before she was born. Despite whatever fights or petty squabbles might be going on among the members, when the time called for it, the Rodriguez family banded together. And Esperanza's birthday was going to be an event the family would be talking about for years to come.

All the more reason not to bring an unknown entity into the mix. But for her abuela, Jasmine was willing to do just about anything. Including asking her new costar for a potentially embarrassing favor.

Maybe Ava and Michelle were right. Maybe it was time to move back.

The ceiling creaked, followed by the sound of steady footsteps overhead, moving toward the stairs.

"Don't tell anyone," Jasmine hissed. "I haven't even met the guy yet. He could turn out to be a total asshole." So many guys in the entertainment industry did, after all. Like McIntyre.

"Rumor has it he's kind of full of himself," Ava mused. "But professional. Easy to work with."

"Don't let that stop you from inviting him." Michelle clapped a hand on Jasmine's shoulder and shot her a raised-eyebrow look that said, *You better figure out a way to bring this guy to the party.* Jasmine waved her away.

Someone opened the basement door and tromped down the stairs. Their cousin Sammy came into view and Jasmine quickly shoved her Leading Lady Plan into her jeans pocket. She wasn't in the mood for his teasing.

"What do you want, Sammy?" Michelle called out.

"Well, well, if it isn't the Bochinche Brujas," he said, striding over to them.

Jasmine rolled her eyes. Sammy had been using that tired old nickname for at least fifteen years, and it was never funny. Especially since they weren't even the biggest gossips in the family.

Sammy grinned. "You made me lose a bet, you know."

Jasmine didn't like where this was going. "How's that?"

"I figured you and McIntyre would last at least three months, but you had to join the Sisterhood of the Single Ladies over here, huh?" He gestured at the three of them on the sofa.

While Michelle and Ava shouted at Sammy to get out, Jasmine groaned and covered her face with her hands. Had she really just been thinking of moving here permanently? Forget it. She was booking her return flight to Los Angeles the second the show wrapped.

Chapter 2

The elevator doors pinged, then opened with a whoosh, and Ashton Suarez stepped into ScreenFlix's Midtown Manhattan office for the first time.

The ScreenFlix office decor was trendy and spacious—glass walls, leather armchairs, lots of plants. The orange and dark gray ScreenFlix logo was everywhere, along with posters from some of the streaming network's hottest original shows, like *The Clandestine Cases of Detective Yang, Showbiz, Party All Night*, and *The Dreamers*. Wide windows overlooked Bryant Park's expansive lawn.

It had been years since Ashton had worked for a new production company. The studio lot in Miami where he filmed telenovelas was so familiar to him, he barely even noticed his surroundings there anymore. And while he wouldn't be filming here—ScreenFlix Studios was located in Queens—he paused to take it all in.

And to give himself a pep talk.

Get your act together, pendejo. You wanted this.

The first time meeting a new cast always brought on a case of nerves, and it didn't help that this particular production had the chance to make or break his career. ScreenFlix was a whole new ball game.

The production assistant waiting nearby gave him a friendly smile. "Hello, Mr. Suarez. I'm Skye. I'm here to take you to the conference room."

Skye had close-cropped brown hair and porcelain skin, wore a "they/them" button on the lapel of their peach linen blazer, and carried a tablet tucked under one arm.

"Thanks." Ashton stuck his hands in his pockets before he could pick at his nails. He needed a prop, something to hold. "Do you know where I could get a cup of coffee?"

"I'll take you to the green room first," Skye said, gesturing for Ashton to follow. "You can chill there before the table read."

As Ashton followed them, he mentally ran through the show notes he'd been sent by the producer the night before. Even though he'd read them countless times already, it made him feel prepared and more in control. Plus, it gave him something to think about other than the spiraling state of his acting career.

Carmen in Charge would follow the love life and professional pursuits of Carmen Serrano, a public relations manager working for a firm that specialized in booking events for Spanish-speaking stars during their trips to New York City. Ashton had been cast to play Victor Vega, a famous singer. Originally, Victor had been one of Carmen's clients. But the writers had made a big change—Victor was now going to be Carmen's ex-husband.

An ex-husband was a completely different dynamic than a new love interest. There would be an immediate level of familiarity between the characters, a sense of emotional baggage and underlying sexual tension. The whole show hinged on the developing romance between Carmen and Victor. Not only had he not done a chemistry read for the role, Ashton had never even met his costar, Jasmine Lin. Yeah, he'd played the romantic lead dozens of times, but he already knew most of the Miami-area actors pretty well and felt comfortable around them. Jasmine was an unknown entity.

The stakes had never been this high. In the world of telenovelas, he was well-known, ever since his star turn on *La maldición del león dorado.* And up until a few months ago, he'd felt steady in his position there. Then *El fuego de amor* had given him a villain narrative, and while it had been a refreshing change of pace from his typical macho hero roles, the writers had then written him into a love triangle and *killed him off.* Well, killed his character off. But the shock and betrayal had felt the same. On the show, he'd lost his life and lost the heroine to the other male lead—Fernando Vargas, a Chilean actor ten years Ashton's junior.

Ever since Ashton had played el león dorado five years earlier, he'd always made it to the finale episode. Despite being shot, stabbed, and thrown from cliffs, his characters had always survived, and in some cases, gone on to happy endings. Now, that streak was broken, and he was terrified about what it meant for his career.

His agent had spoken with the writers and producers, bringing up various options for keeping him involved with the show. Evil twin, back from the dead—any number of tried-and-true tropes could be used. None of it had made a difference. They'd felt his character's death was the best story arc, and anyway, he was only missing out on a few episodes before the show ended. What was the big deal?

The big deal was that Ashton was almost forty, and after fifteen years, he was spinning his wheels in the telenovela landscape because he believed it would eventually catapult him beyond. He was waiting for the chance to prove himself and instead, he'd been removed from the show early.

He still had no idea if he'd done something to piss off an exec or if the viewers were just tired of him. There'd been a minor outcry on social media when the episode aired, but by then it had been too late. In the meantime, he'd only managed to book a couple of pilot episodes that didn't seem likely to get picked up.

So when the call came in for *Carmen in Charge*, Ashton had leaped at the chance. He was a last-minute replacement, scooped up by the casting gods thanks to a taped audition his agent had sent on a whim. Even though it was a telenovela remake, ScreenFlix would get him in front of a broader audience, and hopefully on the path to becoming the next Javier Bardem.

In the back of his mind, though, he worried this would be his last shot. If this didn't work out, where would it leave him?

Carajo. So much for not thinking about it. On the outside, he was cool and collected as he followed Skye through the office space, passing glassed-in offices and open-plan desk areas where people worked at their computers. No one even looked at him—they were probably used to actors walking through here all the time—but he still felt exposed.

On the inside? He was struggling not to think about all the ways this could go wrong.

Skye stopped in front of an open doorway and gestured with a flourish. "Your coffee awaits," they said, and Ashton pulled himself together long enough to smile and thank them.

The green room had a small kitchenette attached to it, with three different kinds of coffee makers. Even though it was just after eight in the morning, his first cup had been over three hours ago, and he needed the pick-me-up. And since he was feeling stressed, he opted to indulge his sweet tooth with one of the French vanilla coffee pods in the basket.

Once it was brewing, Ashton checked his watch. He'd meet Jasmine for the first time in twenty minutes, at the table read. It was stupid to feel so nervous. She worked in soap operas, which had a grueling production schedule similar to that of telenovelas, where they could sometimes film an episode a day. That meant she likely had a good work ethic and would be totally professional—traits he could admire in a scene partner. He'd do his best to be charming and make sure they got off on the right foot. It would be fine.

Except for one thing.

After getting the role, Ashton had googled Jasmine, expecting to find the usual—a Wikipedia page with her headshot and birthday, an IMDb listing with all her acting roles, her social media accounts, maybe some YouTube clips. Instead, he'd been surprised to see the first results were recent news stories about her breakup with some musician he'd never heard of who only went by one name.

McIntyre, a lanky guy with greasy hair, tattoos, and a guitar, was known for his disaffected attitude and crooning vocals. Ashton's first thought when he'd seen pictures of the guy was "cut your damn hair," and then he worried that meant he was getting old. He also wondered what Jasmine had ever seen in the guy, then chastised himself. He had no business wondering or judging.

The tabloids were having a field day with the story. And as much as Ashton sympathized with Jasmine, he didn't want to get dragged into the media circus surrounding her. He already struggled to keep his personal life out of the Latinx entertainment news, and he'd have to be extra careful not to do or say anything that would give English-language tabloids reason to pay more attention to him. Being costars was often enough to start rumors, and Jasmine was stunningly beautiful, which already made them prime bait for a behind-the-scenes romance rumor. Not her fault, but people often looked for stories that weren't there. Truth was, Ashton had no time for romance, behind the scenes or otherwise. But the press didn't care about what was true—only what sold magazines or got clicks. Aside from work, he would have to keep his distance from Jasmine.

With his cup filled with sweet, caffeinated nectar, Ashton took his time adding more sugar and cream. With as much energy as he put in at the gym and monitoring his diet, fixing his coffee just the way he liked it was one of his only remaining vices. Once he was done, he stepped back from the table, intending to find his new costar to introduce himself.

Instead, his heel landed on something that wasn't linoleum, and someone behind him let out a high-pitched yelp.

Ashton spun in surprise, colliding with a body. There was a splash, followed by a clattering sound. The smell of coffee intensified. And he stared in horror at the sight of a woman wearing a white blouse and soft pink slacks, now splattered and dripping with foamy brown stains. Ice cubes scattered on the tiles around her stiletto-clad feet.

It would have been bad enough to spill coffee on anyone during his first day on the job, but this was not just any woman. It was Jasmine Lin, his new costar. She was gorgeous—her golden skin glowed against the white of her wet shirt, now clinging to her torso and breasts—but at the moment, she looked like she wanted to murder him. Her dark brows set in a fierce scowl, and her full lips parted over clenched teeth. The nerves he'd battled all morning took over and came out of his mouth.

"Um, hola." Trying for a joke, he gestured at the half-empty cup in her hand. "Supongo que no te ibas a beber eso."

When she just stared at him, mouth hanging open, his stomach sank. So much for getting off on the right foot.

Chapter 3

The combination of ice-cold coffee, unexpected Spanish, and the full force of Ashton's famously handsome face stole Jasmine's voice. Her silk shirt clung to her chilled skin, thanks to the faulty lid that had leaped off her cold brew the second Ashton had backed into her.

Ashton. She drank him in as if he were a steaming cappuccino on a cold day, her body warming from the inside despite the inadvertent ice bath. Dark curly hair, the shadow of a beard, tan skin, and sexy dark brown eyes. He seemed even taller in person, and more magnetic, like a behemoth of a planet tugging her into his orbit.

She felt drawn to him in a way that made no sense, but that was the magic of TV—it made you feel close to people you'd never met, through familiarity and carefully crafted characters designed to make you root for them, fall in love with them, or love to hate them.

And here he was, in the flesh, and somehow even hotter in person. The Golden Lion. She'd watched some episodes at Michelle's urging, and Ashton's command of the viewer's attention was masterful.

In an effort to ignore the way her heart pounded at his nearness, she focused on what he'd said.

Since she didn't want to admit just yet that she wasn't fluent in Spanish, Jasmine picked over the words, replaying them in her mind and translating each one.

Hola. Those first deep, fluid syllables of his greeting had sent a thrill through her.

Supongo que no te ibas a beber eso.

I guess you weren't going to drink that.

Wait, was he being sarcastic? Or serious? Shit, she couldn't tell.

Jasmine narrowed her eyes at him just in case. "Was that meant to be a joke?"

His eyebrows twitched, like maybe he was surprised she'd answered in English. She was used to that.

"Uh . . . yes. A joke. But not a funny joke, I see." In English, his deep voice was accented and smooth. He grabbed a handful of paper napkins from the table and thrust them at her. "I'm Ashton Suarez."

"I know who you are. My grandmother absolutely adores you." God, had she really just said that? Jasmine patted her torso with the napkins, which did little to sop up the dark coffee soaking her shirt. Even worse, although it was hard to tell from her vantage point, she was pretty sure the white silk had become see-through. She tried to pull on the wet fabric so it didn't cling to her like a second skin, but it just slapped back onto her boobs. *Awesome.*

"I'll take care of the dry cleaning." His expression was contrite, and the worry in his eyes made him look younger, more boyish.

"Don't bother. They're probably ruined." It came out bitchier than she meant it to, so she added, "Anyway, they're just clothes."

Just clothes she'd spent two hours selecting, with her cousins' help. She bit back a sigh. She didn't want to make him feel bad, but fuck, this was inconvenient.

"I'm sorry for stepping on you," Ashton said in a rush, as if belatedly realizing he hadn't yet apologized. "And bumping into you. And spilling your coffee."

She shrugged and sent him a rueful smile. "It was an accident. But I could have used the caffeine."

He held up his own cup. "Do you want mine?"

Had he drunk from it yet? Didn't matter. She'd soon be locking lips with this guy. And it would be rude to turn down his olive branch.

"Sure, thanks." Their fingers brushed and she sucked in a trembling breath. To cover the blush rising in her cheeks, she quickly brought the cup to her lips. Took a sip. And gagged.

"*Jeez*, how much sugar did you put in there?"

He grimaced. "A lot?"

Jasmine shoved the cup back at him. "Thanks but I think I've had enough coffee for today." She gestured at her shirt and his eyes followed her movement. Damn it, she'd drawn his attention back to the now-sheer blouse clinging to her breasts. Just brilliant.

With what seemed like great effort, Ashton dragged his gaze away from her chest and back to her eyes. His expression was bland, but she caught the ripple of his throat as he swallowed.

Her skin grew hot with embarrassment and, damn it, attraction. This was so not how she'd imagined their first meeting unfolding. She had to get out of here.

Jasmine waved a hand toward the green-room door. "I'm, ah . . . I'm going to go change."

Into what, she had no idea.

He nodded. "Claro."

"Um, bye." Jasmine hurried out and hobbled to the bathroom.

A glance at her phone showed she had less than ten minutes before the table read began, and she was drenched in super strong coffee and coconut milk. Not wanting to be late on the first day, Jasmine flagged down an office assistant. The woman had shoulder-length blond hair and a nervous tilt to her eyebrows.

"Hi. I'm Jasmine Lin. What's your name?"

"Penny." Penny's rosy skin paled as she took a horrified look at Jasmine's coffee-splattered attire.

"As you can see, I'm having a wardrobe emergency." Jasmine shoved all the cash in her wallet—a whopping thirty-four bucks—into Penny's hand. "Can you please run down to the nearest store and buy me a change of clothes? I seem to be in need of a new outfit."

Penny's light eyebrows drew together. "What kind of outfit?"

"Whatever you can bring back in the next five minutes." Jasmine gestured at the restroom door. "I'll be in there cleaning coffee out of silk."

With a nod, Penny hurried off, and Jasmine poked her head into the restroom. An older woman with smooth brown skin was washing her hands at one of the sinks. She wore a sharp gray bespoke suit and a patterned head scarf. She did a double take when she saw Jasmine's clothes, then jerked a thumb at the accessible stall.

"That one has its own sink," she said. "Looks like you're going to need it."

Jasmine thanked her profusely and locked herself inside the big stall. She stripped off the wet, clammy clothes and ran them under cold water in the sink.

She hated to admit it, but the coffee spill had been a welcome distraction. The quick flash of alarm at being soaked in ice-cold liquid had been easier to deal with than the equally quick jolt of desire when she'd laid eyes on Ashton, so she'd clung to it. Because in that moment, McIntyre and his stupid, soulful green eyes had also disappeared from her mind, along with all the anxiety and despair she'd carried since spotting a tabloid cover photo of him kissing another woman in Mexico.

Ashton's horror at spilling coffee on her had been genuine and kind of adorable, but she had no business whatsoever noticing her new costar's magnetism. This was her MO, after all. A spectacularly messy breakup—although this McIntyre thing was even messier than normal—followed by a stars-in-her-eyes crush on yet another emotionally unavailable man. Rebound, relationship, breakup—rinse and repeat.

Well, not this time, thank you very much. She was a Leading Lady now. *Carmen in Charge* was a big step up for her, and she wasn't going to let an inconvenient attraction get in the way of making this role a success. No matter how sexy her costar might be.

ALONE IN THE green room, Ashton cleaned up the ice cubes from the floor, then slumped into a chair and scrubbed a hand over his face. Well, *that* had been a fucking disaster. He'd never forget the sight of Jasmine limping away with a crushed foot and a soaked blouse. She would forever think of him as the guy who'd ruined her first day on the job.

He sipped the coffee Jasmine had returned to him, although he was so tense, maybe more caffeine and sugar were a bad idea. When he saw her next, he would apologize profusely. He'd find some way to make it up to her . . . while also keeping his distance. Maybe they'd be able to laugh it off at some point. Before the table read started would be ideal, but that seemed like too much to hope for.

Still, he'd ruined her outfit, and should try to make it right.

But first . . . Ashton shut the door to the green room and pulled out his phone to FaceTime his father in Puerto Rico.

It rang a few times before Ignacio Suarez's lined brown face appeared on the screen. "Hola, mijo."

The words, a rushed baritone rumble, were the same greeting Ashton had heard from his father every day of his life, and they brought a smile to his face. "Hola, Pa. ¿Cómo estás?"

He listened while his father rattled off a report about Abuelito Gus and Abuelita Bibi's health. Ashton's mother had died ten years earlier, but Ignacio's parents had always been a big part of

Ashton's life. They were in their eighties now, and their well-being was a major concern and a driving factor behind Ashton's work ethic.

Another driving factor popped up on the screen, his messy hair and big brown eyes peeking out at Ashton and making his heart swell.

"¿Es mi papá?" a squeaky voice asked, and Ashton laughed.

"Sí, mijo, es tu papá," he said.

On-screen, Ignacio backed away to make room for Yadiel, Ashton's eight-year-old son.

Ashton listened intently as Yadiel filled him in on the last TV show he'd watched (*Teen Titans Go*), the video game he was currently obsessed with (*Minecraft*), and the comic book he was in the middle of reading (*Spider-Man*). Most of it went over Ashton's head, and he wished, not for the first time, that he could be there with his son, to watch, play, and read with him.

Yadiel finished off with, "Papi, when are you coming back to Puerto Rico?"

"Not yet, Yadi." Ashton didn't have a better answer. Yadiel lived with Ignacio y los bisabuelos in Humacao while Ashton lived in Miami for most of the year. When Yadi had been born, he'd lived in Miami with Ashton. But after the Incident, Yadiel had gone to live with Ignacio, and Ashton had sold the house and moved into a high-rise condo instead.

When Yadiel was younger, Ashton had been able to spend more time at home with him in Puerto Rico. But as his career had taken off and Yadi started attending a private school, there'd been less time for making the two-and-a-half-hour flight from Miami to San Juan every weekend.

After Hurricane Maria wreaked havoc on the island, the federal government's absolute failure to provide resources and aid and unwillingness to treat the people of Puerto Rico as the American citizens they were by right of birth had prompted Ashton to move his family to Miami for a time. He'd loved having them closer and being able to see Yadiel nearly every day. But the whole time, he couldn't stop remembering what had happened when Yadiel had lived there before. Once Yadiel's school reopened, they'd gone back.

Ashton missed his son with a depth that had no end, but growing up on the island, away from the chaos of the entertainment industry, was what was safest for the boy. Ashton would have loved to spend the summer hanging out with Yadiel in Puerto Rico, but bills had to be paid, and now that Ashton was financially responsible for four generations of his family, there were a lot of bills—especially after making repairs to the family restaurant, which now served half the customers it once did.

"Has anything funny happened on set?" Yadiel asked. He enjoyed hearing behind-the-scenes stories "from Papi's work."

"Well, it's only the first day, but . . . yes, something happened."

Yadiel's eyes went wide as Ashton told him about spilling coffee on Jasmine. Ashton mimed the movements, added sound effects, and cast himself in the role of the bumbling idiot for his son's amusement. Yadiel was chortling with laughter by the time he was done, and Ashton's spirits lifted. He loved making his son laugh. Maybe someday he'd have the opportunity to do more comedy in his career.

A knock sounded on the door. "Ashton? Are you in there?"

Uh-oh. Yadiel was the reason Ashton kept his private life locked away. He wanted his son to have as normal an upbringing as possible, even if it meant spending time apart. Ashton had experienced some alarming moments with fans early in his career—he'd never forget the terror of hearing glass breaking in his son's nursery—so he did everything in his power to keep Yadiel safe, protected, and secret.

Ashton blew a kiss into the phone and dropped his voice to a whisper. "Ciao, mi amor."

"Bye, Papi."

Disconnecting the call, Ashton called, "Pase," then repeated it in English, just in case. "Come in."

Marquita Arroyo, the showrunner and a fellow Boricua, stuck her head inside. She was tall, with fair skin, a mass of spiraling curls, and a big smile. "Hey there. We have some people who want to meet you before the table read begins."

Ashton took a final swig of coffee, then set it aside. Showtime.

JASMINE STOOD IN the empty ladies' restroom in her underwear, trying to dry her bra under the hand dryer while she was still wearing it, when someone knocked on the outer door and called out, "Hello? I have your clothes."

"In here!" Jasmine scurried back into the stall and stuck her head out. Penny rushed in and handed her a plastic "I Heart New York" bag with folded items inside.

"I hope these work," Penny said, sounding uncertain. "There weren't a whole lot of options, and you'd be surprised how much tourist wear costs."

Jasmine clutched the bag to her chest and eased back into the stall. "I'm sure they're fine. Thank you so much!"

Jasmine tore into the bag—and froze. Shit, maybe she should have been more specific about *what kind of outfit*.

The nylon running shorts were black, at least, and devoid of any logo. They were shorter than she would have liked, but not the shortest thing she'd ever worn in a professional setting. She'd make them work.

The T-shirt, on the other hand . . .

Jasmine unfolded it and stared. It was fuchsia with black trim, a hood, and NYC emblazoned across the front in sketchy white block letters. Tacky, yes, but that was to be expected when buying clothes in a souvenir shop. More worryingly, however, was that it was very, very small.

Jasmine took a closer look at the tags and sighed. It was a size medium . . . for a child. Both articles of clothing had clearance tags, and still came out to thirty-three and change. Apparently thirty-four dollars hardly got you anything these days.

She stuck her head out of the stall, but Penny was long gone. Probably scared Jasmine would bite her head off or ask her to switch clothes. Which, in hindsight, might have been a better idea. Too late now.

She glanced at her blouse, which was currently soaked and still bore faint brown stains, and then her watch. She was out of time.

Jasmine wrestled herself into the shirt, which fit—just barely—like a crop top. The material was thick but stretchy. It was especially tight in the shoulders, but it covered her boobs more than a wet white silk blouse would. She shoved her wet clothes into the plastic bag and exited the stall, then caught sight of herself in the bathroom's full-length mirror.

Between the child-sized shirt, the gym shorts, the black heels, and her sparkly gold jewelry, she was certainly rocking *some* kind of look, albeit not one that said *Leading Lady*. More like Sporty Spice on a hot date. Maybe coffee-splattered wouldn't have been so bad, but she didn't have time to dry everything with the bathroom's weak-ass hand dryer.

Then she remembered her grandmother's adage: *If you're not wearing lipstick and earrings, you might as well be naked.*

After freshening up her dark magenta lipstick, Jasmine snapped a photo of her reflection, then sent it to Ava and Michelle in their Primas of Power group text. Time to call in the hype squad.

Ava answered first.

> **Ava:** Um, what are you wearing?

Michelle's reply came a second later.

> **Michelle:** Hawt.

> **Jasmine:** I had a run in with an iced coffee.
> Quick, tell me I'm still pretty.

Michelle replied with an animated GIF of Natalie Wood in *West Side Story*, twirling and saying, "I feel pretty!"

Ava added one of Barbra Streisand in *Funny Girl* saying, "Hello, gorgeous."

It would have to do. Jasmine tossed her hair, squared her shoulders, and cocked a hand on her hip. "Make jefa moves, remember?" she told her reflection.

Inside, she didn't believe that for a second, but she was a good enough actress that her embarrassment didn't show on her face.

Then she exited the bathroom and strutted into that table read like she was on a motherfucking runway.

Chapter 4

Between the chat with Yadiel and a series of increasingly positive interactions with the showrunner, the first assistant director, and the director for episode one, Ashton's confidence came roaring back. After working in TV for more than fifteen years, the bustle felt like home, more so than his apartment in Miami or his suite at the Hutton Court did. Sure, there was a lot riding on this role, but he could do this. He was one of the best in his industry—no, not one of the best, *the* best—and he was here to show American audiences—plus the casting agents and producers—what he could do. No sweat.

He followed Marquita to the conference room where the table read would be held. Tons of people milled about in the hallway, including ScreenFlix execs, producers, writers, and a few of the actors Ashton recalled from the show notes. It had been a long time since he'd joined a new cast where he didn't know a single person. All he wanted to do was slip into the room and find his seat, but he introduced himself to Peter Calabasas, a longtime TV actor who'd play Carmen's father. Peter, a barrel-chested Afro-Latinx man with a dark beard, was easy to talk to, and they quickly struck up a lively conversation about baseball.

Then Jasmine strolled in and Ashton did a double take.

She was still gorgeous and mouth-wateringly sexy, but . . . what the hell was she wearing?

She'd gotten a new outfit from somewhere, and while her hair and makeup were still flawless, she looked like a fitness model who'd wandered into the wrong room, not the star of a show about a fierce PR exec.

Guilt washed over Ashton. How would he feel if he had to show up on his first day in gym shorts? Sure, some actors dressed casually for table reads. Three of the others were wearing jeans. But being the title character carried a sense of leadership. It wasn't uncommon to make more of an effort at the beginning, to put on professional airs, at least before the fourteen-hour work days had everyone battling exhaustion. Ashton wasn't the title character, but as one of the leads and the show's love interest, he'd dressed up in a crisp blue button-down shirt and black slacks with Italian leather loafers.

Jasmine, as he'd seen her that morning, had shown up looking her very best. Even covered in coffee, it was clear her outfit had been stylish and sophisticated. She'd even said as much, but he'd been so mortified, it had gone right over his head. Because of his mistake, she now looked like she was on her way to the gym . . . in high heels.

He felt like an ass all over again. Had he really only offered her his coffee and a half-hearted attempt to pay for her dry cleaning? What the hell was wrong with him? She was never going to forgive him, and he couldn't blame her.

"All right, let's begin!" Marquita clapped her hands.

Everyone quieted and crowded inside to find their seats

around the conference table. Tented white card stock with the actors' names printed on them marked the assigned seats. At each spot, there was a script, a short stack of index cards, a cup, and a glass carafe filled with water and lemon slices.

As one of the show's main characters, Ashton was seated right next to Jasmine—something he'd been too preoccupied to even think about before this moment.

He slid into the uncomfortable metal chair and busied himself with flipping through the script, his whole body on high alert as Jasmine took her place beside him. He snuck a glance her way, noting the slide of her long—bare—legs as she crossed them under the table.

"Sorry again," he muttered under his breath, but she didn't look at him. A shrug of one shoulder was the only clue she'd heard him.

The other show regulars took their places around the table. On Jasmine's other side was Miriam Perez, the actress who would play her mother, and Nino Colón, the trans actor who'd play Carmen's assistant. Miriam was lightly tanned with dyed blonde curls, and Nino had rich brown skin and a stylish haircut. To Ashton's right sat Peter Calabasas as well as Lily Benitez, who'd been cast as Carmen's sister. Lily had a mane of dark waves and wore bright red lipstick that complemented her bronze complexion.

Before they started, Marquita introduced herself and welcomed everyone with a short speech. Then she had all the actors introduce themselves in order. Ashton struggled to concentrate, but he noted the range of different entertainment backgrounds among the actors. He'd done telenovelas. Jasmine's background was in soap operas. Lily had started out as a plus-size lingerie model. Nino had been a dancer on Broadway. Miriam had done stand-up and sketch comedy in the 1980s and 90s. And Peter had been working steadily in TV for thirty years, from sitcoms to police procedurals.

The script began with Carmen discussing her goals for the family business with her sister before leaving for work. This section was in English, and while Ashton's eyes followed along on the script, he'd be lying if he said he was paying attention. Instead, his mind took him on a downward spiral that started with spilled coffee and ended with tanking his career.

The next scene showed Carmen at work, interacting with her assistant, and then her father. Ashton tuned in enough to catch his cue from Peter, then sat up straight, calling on all his years of experience to speak his lines while mentally beating himself up for blowing his first impression with Jasmine.

They got through the reunion scene, but a later part called for an argument in Spanish.

"You have a lot of nerve coming back here to ask for my help," Jasmine said from beside him.

Ashton was so attuned to her every movement, he didn't miss his cue. His character shot back a retort, which he delivered in strong, rapid Spanish. He paused at the end of his lines, waiting for Jasmine's response. It was supposed to start with, "¿Y quién diablos piensas que eres?" A sort of, "Who the hell do you think you are?" And then she would put him in his place.

Except Jasmine stumbled over her lines, messing up the vowels. She paused, stared intently at the script in front of her, and he imagined her repeating the words in her head. She started again and made it through the entire passage, albeit slowly, and without the fierceness she'd displayed when speaking her lines in English.

They finished the scene, but Jasmine's difficulty with Spanish puzzled him. Ashton replayed the coffee moment over again in his head, recalling her long pause and the way she'd stared at him after his poor attempt at a joke . . .

Wait, was it possible she didn't speak Spanish?

Carmen in Charge had a bilingual script, cast, and crew. It was a big part of the promo for the show. How was this going to work if the lead actress wasn't fluent?

He listened to Jasmine work her way through a scene in Spanish with Miriam Perez. Maybe he wasn't being fair. Jasmine's accent was spot on, even if her pronunciation was a little inconsistent.

It was something he particularly worried about for himself. While his English was good, he still had an accent and sometimes came across idioms he didn't immediately recognize or that didn't translate easily to Spanish. Would wider American audiences accept a new leading man with a Puerto Rican accent? A few Spanish-speaking actors had achieved success— guys like Javier Bardem, Diego Luna, and Gael García Bernal. Was there still room in that lexicon for Ashton Suarez?

The sudden silence made him blink. Jasmine stared at him expectantly. No, not just Jasmine. *Everyone* was staring at him. Puñeta. It was his line.

In his rush to flip the page, Ashton knocked over his drinking glass. Lemon water splashed all over his script and the table.

He shoved back his chair before it could get on his pants. To his left, Jasmine leaped out of her seat like she'd been stuck with a pin.

Ashton imagined a sinkhole opening beneath him and swallowing him up. That would be preferable to whatever was happening to him today.

"Did it get on you?" he asked under his breath.

"Not this time," she answered.

It was amazing how much mortification could feel like heartburn.

A pair of PAs rushed in with paper towels to sop up the mess, and Ashton leaned back to get out of their way. "Sorry," he muttered. "Too much caffeine."

Jasmine turned a laugh into a cough.

She was laughing at him. Was it a good laugh? Like a *haha, we have a shared joke about coffee* kind of laugh? Or a bad laugh, like, *you clumsy idiot, always spilling drinks*?

He didn't dare look at her to find out, and everyone was waiting for him. His neck felt hot. Another PA handed him a fresh script. This time, he would give it his complete attention. Something he should have been doing anyway. On any other set, on any other day, he would have.

But today . . . today sucked.

Somehow, Ashton got through it. Even though nerves made his skin feel too tight, and he couldn't stop fidgeting. He was like Yadiel trying to sit through Sunday mass. It was the most awkward table read he'd ever participated in.

Marquita made her closing speech, and this time, Ashton listened.

"That was a great start, team! I'm so excited to be embarking on this journey with all of you. Now, enjoy the rest of the weekend, and I'll see you at the studio Monday morning, bright and early."

Before Ashton could turn to Jasmine to apologize for almost spilling *another* drink on her, she slipped out of her chair and rounded the table to chat with Lily Benitez.

No problem. He'd catch her before he left. He felt terrible about ruining her outfit, and he couldn't end this day without trying to make things right. This entire production hinged on the two of them selling the audience a romance between their characters. If she thought he was a fool, this would never work.

And he really needed it to work.

As Ashton was saying goodbye to the others, his ears picked up Jasmine's voice somewhere behind him.

"Oh, the outfit?" She gave an easy laugh. "Spilled a giant coffee on myself right before we started. Had to make do with what was available, you know?"

The person she was talking to chuckled and said, "The show must go on?"

"Exactly."

Ashton turned his head to catch a glimpse of her out of the corner of his eye. She was chatting with one of the Screen-Flix VPs, but standing with them was someone else—someone wearing a visitor's badge and recording their conversation with a phone.

A reporter.

Ashton did a sharp about-face and made a prompt exit. Peter called his name, and Ashton waved, but kept going. Farther down the hallway he encountered Skye, and asked them to show him back to the elevators.

Once the doors shut behind him and he was on his way down, Ashton was finally able to take a deep breath.

He *hated* talking to the press. While the Miami-based entertainment reporters were used to his standoffishness and had reached the point of joking about it good-naturedly, he was in New York now. He had no idea what to expect from the media here. And the last thing he needed was for a reporter to record him apologizing to Jasmine. It would spark curiosity, and he couldn't afford rumors or invasive questions. His son's safety was too important.

Later. He'd talk to Jasmine later.

The awkward table read set the tone for Jasmine's first week on *Carmen*.

Not that she had trouble adjusting. If anything, the production pace was leisurely compared to what she was used to from working on soaps, where they filmed over one hundred pages per day and were expected to nail the shot on the first take. Having more than a week to shoot an episode felt positively decadent.

She assumed it must be the same for Ashton, coming from telenovelas, but she couldn't know for sure because the man was never around to ask.

After the table read, he'd taken one look at her and left without even saying goodbye. And sure, he showed up when it was time to rehearse, and he was of course there while they filmed, but as soon as the scene wrapped, Ashton disappeared again.

Hell, he would barely even *look* at her unless the script called for it.

Jasmine tried not to take it personally, but taking things personally was one of her greatest skills. Fortunately, the first episodes called for some awkwardness between them.

Carmen Serrano, Jasmine's character, worked at a public relations firm owned by her family in New York City. She was a tough, take-no-shit kind of woman. A real Leading Lady type. Jasmine could stand to take a few lessons from her.

The show started with Carmen getting the rug pulled out from under her—not only was the family business in trouble, but their latest client, the one who could get them back on top? None other than her ex-husband, Victor Vega, an international pop star.

Jasmine could sympathize with Carmen. She had a problem with exes too.

Most of the scenes Jasmine had already filmed involved the actors who played Carmen's family members. They were all lovely people, and Peter Calabasas, who played her on-screen dad, Ernesto Serrano, reminded Jasmine of her grandfather, Willie Rodriguez. She felt so at ease with him and Miriam Perez, who played Carmen's mom Dahlia, she took them up on their offer to run through the Spanish dialogue together, and Jasmine aced the scenes when they filmed them.

So far, she hadn't had too much interaction with Ashton on set, but that would be changing soon. Today, they were filming Carmen and Victor's reunion scene. After spending the morning drinking way too much coffee in hair and makeup, Jasmine was ready to get it over with.

Ashton showed up on set looking sleek and sexy. For Victor, they'd given him a fresh shave and slicked his dark curls away from his face. Jasmine wished they'd left something to distract from his extreme handsomeness . . . like a mask, or a paper bag.

Wardrobe wasn't helping either. They'd outfitted Ashton in tight black chinos and a gray V-neck T-shirt with a black leather jacket to complete the musician look. His cologne was a delicious combo of sweet and spicy, somehow sexy and comforting at the same time.

Jasmine turned away and gulped water from a stainless steel bottle. She had to pull herself together.

A member of the makeup team approached to blot away any shininess from her face. With her eyes closed and the scent of powder soothing her nerves, Jasmine gave herself a mental pep talk.

Come on, jefa, you can do this. Let Carmen take over and nail your lines. It's just acting. You've done this a million times.

Jasmine took three deep, slow breaths. She tapped into the part of her that connected with the character, the part of her who owned her power and knew her worth. It was a small part, but it was there, deep inside. She was a Leading Lady, damn it. A Leading Lady who had her shit together.

When she opened her eyes, she thanked the makeup artist then sashayed over to Lily Benitez, who played her on-screen sister, Helen. Lily just happened to be standing within earshot of Ashton, so Jasmine called on Carmen's bravado and draped it around her like her great-grandmother's wedding mantilla.

"Ready to get your ass beat at dominoes?" Jasmine said, referring to the game they had going in Miriam's dressing room.

Lily, who was fiercely competitive, snorted in disdain. "You wish!"

As they went back and forth, Jasmine watched Ashton from the corner of her eye. He was listening—he had to be, there was no way he couldn't hear them—but he never turned their way.

It was on the tip of Jasmine's tongue to call out his name. She didn't know what she'd say, exactly. *Do you play dominoes?* No, that was a stupid question. He probably did. *Why do you smell so good?* Um, no. That was totally inappropriate, even though it was true. *Hey, pay attention to me!* That one was pure middle-child id, and Jasmine didn't want to think too deeply about where the impulse came from.

Instead, she said nothing to him at all. Just kept chatting with Lily. A minute later, the first assistant director, Ofelia Gomez, called them all to their places, and there was nothing else to do but begin.

Chapter 5

Scene: Carmen and Victor reunite for the first
time.
INT: Carmen's office—DAY

"Action!"

Carmen bustled into her office—a chic workspace decorated in white with gold accents—and picked up a tablet from her desk. Her father followed her in, albeit more slowly.

"So who's this big new client we've signed?" She tapped the tablet screen. "I haven't gotten any paperwork yet."

Her father ducked his head, like he was afraid to meet her gaze. "He's a singer. And this one might be a little . . . difficult."

Carmen looked up from her desk and flashed him a fierce grin. "Papi, there's nobody in this business better than I am. Come on, what's the catch?"

With a resigned grimace, Ernesto leaned out the glass door of the office and called, "Déjalo pasar."

The man who strolled into the office made Carmen's confident smile drop. A myriad of emotions raced through her, all visible on her face. Shock, hurt, and then—anger.

But he . . . he was all smooth and secure, as if he had every right to be here. His lips curved in a sexy smile and he gave a little nod. "Hola, Carmen."

His voice was silken and deep, wrapping around her, urging her to loosen up. Instead, Carmen steeled her spine. With tight, controlled movements, she set the tablet down, lest she throw it at him, and pressed her hands to the cool surface, letting it ground her. Her lips compressed into a thin line as she glared from the newcomer to her father.

"Really?" she said in a harsh tone, breaking the silence but not the tension. "My ex-husband is our new client?"

On a network show, this would have been a prime commercial break, but since this was being filmed for a streaming service, the scene continued.

Ernesto rushed over to Carmen, his tone conciliatory. "Mija, óyeme—"

"No, I will not listen." Carmen slashed her hand through the air. "The answer is no. I won't work with him."

Her father didn't give up. "Like you said, you're the best in the business at rehabbing celebrity images. If you can turn Victor's career around, we'll have clients knocking down our door. Come on, mija. Do it for the family."

Carmen pinned Victor with a glare. "What. Did. You. Do?"

Victor had the grace to look slightly abashed. His throat

worked as he swallowed, and he lifted a hand to scratch the back of his neck. "Ah . . . I might have . . . canceled a world tour."

Carmen nodded and slowly let out a breath. "I probably would have known that if I hadn't so thoroughly scrubbed you out of my life."

Victor pressed a hand to his chest and winced. "Ouch. Direct hit."

"Basta," Ernesto said, getting between them. "You're both grown adults. Can't you work together?"

Carmen sucked on her lower lip, as if she were thinking about it, then she shook her head. "No, Papi. I can't. I *won't* work with him. Now, if you'll excuse me, I have more important things to do than to waste my time talking with this piece of basura." She raised a finger and pointed at the door. "Victor, *out*."

Victor and Ernesto exchanged glances, but Victor raised his hands in surrender and left the office.

With a heavy sigh, Carmen dropped into her desk chair. When she looked up at her father, betrayal was etched all over her features. "Papi, how could you do that to me?"

"Lo siento, querida. Pero . . ." Her father sat in the chair on the other side of Carmen's desk, shoulders slumped. "Pero Victor es nuestra única esperanza."

Carmen's brows creased, and her tone was pleading. "No entiendo. Why is Victor our only hope?"

"Porque . . ." There was a hitch in his voice. "Porque, mija, we are on the verge of losing the business."

Carmen let the shock of his words show on her face. "But . . . I thought we were doing well. You never said . . ."

"I know. Ever since your tío Fredo died, we've been struggling. He was the strong one, the smart one. I was good with people, but Fredo was good with numbers."

"That was three years ago . . ." Carmen shook her head, still not comprehending. "Why didn't you tell me? I could have helped."

"You and Victor were having trouble, and I didn't want to worry you, or give you more work. Anyway, now . . . it looks like signing Victor is all we can do to save the business."

Carmen clasped her hands together on the desk and shut her eyes for a moment. When she opened them, she met her father's gaze, and it was as if she had suited herself in armor. Eyes cold, shoulders squared, voice sharp.

"I will work with Victor under two conditions," she said, and held up a finger before her father could rejoice. "One, I take over the financials for the business."

"Pero you'll be so busy—"

"Not too busy to get the firm back on top. Serranos do it better, remember?" A ghost of a smile played on her lips, but she squashed it and held up a second finger. "Two, no one gets any ideas about me and Victor, got it?"

Her father's expression was all innocence. "¿Qué quieres decir? *Ideas?*"

"You know exactly what I mean," Carmen said, getting to her feet. "Just because I'll be working with him does *not* mean that Victor and I will be getting back together. So get that out of your head. Same goes for Mom."

Her father held up his hands. "Okay, bueno. I believe you."

"Now call him back in. I know he's still out there. He only

leaves when it's convenient for him." Carmen came around from her desk and waited with her hands on her hips.

Victor returned, shit-eating grin firmly in place.

"I knew you couldn't resist me."

"You'd be surprised what I can resist," Carmen replied through gritted teeth. "Right now, I'm resisting throwing a paperweight at your head."

"I'm not worried." He smirked and gestured at her minimalist desk space.

Carmen raised her chin and lobbed the ball back into his court. "You want to tell me why you canceled a *world tour*?"

His expression shuttered, dark eyebrows creasing as his gaze slanted away from hers. "No."

"Of course not." Carmen turned to her father. "So what's the plan? What's our goal here?"

Victor answered instead. "There's another tour coming up, with a few other Latinx singers. I want in on it."

Carmen eyed him up and down. "We have our work cut out for us if you want someone to give you a spot on a tour so soon after you canceled another one."

Her father spoke up. "Especially since they're also looking at giving the spot to Dimas del Valle."

"Dimas?" Carmen's gaze shot back to Victor. "You hate that guy."

Victor's expression turned thunderous and he muttered a string of Spanish insults under his breath.

"Oye." Carmen snapped her fingers and strode over to Victor, getting all up in his personal space, closer than she would with a typical client. Close enough to catch the heady scent of his cologne. She jabbed her finger in his chest to get his attention. His hard, firm chest. "They're going to make a decision soon, and if you don't clean up your image and make yourself visible, they're going to pick Dimas for the tour. Is that what you want?"

Victor scowled, his eyes darkening. "You know it isn't."

Carmen gave a cocky little head shake. "Then you need to stay out of trouble. That means no parties, no drinking, and no messing around with your stupid friends. Where are you staying?"

When the corner of his mouth ticked up, Carmen narrowed her eyes. "Whenever you make that face, I know I'm not going to like whatever you say next."

Victor's grin turned mocking. "Well, if I have to stay out of trouble, there's only one place that's perfect for that."

Carmen scoffed. "Where, a monastery?"

His smile was slow and devious. "No, even better." He waited a beat for effect, then said, "Your parents' house."

Carmen sucked in a breath. "Ay, puñeta."

"Cut!"

Chapter 6

Jasmine turned to the director, who wore a big grin.

"That was perfect," he said from his chair, looking up from the playback screen. "We'll get the shot of Victor walking in again, but then we'll go to the next scene."

Jasmine moved off to the side and gratefully accepted the bottle of water handed to her by a PA.

"Great work, Jas." Peter Calabasas joined her, trailed by two makeup artists who immediately set about touching up the actors' faces. "You're a natural."

"You make it easy, *Dad*," Jasmine said with a grin. "Are you joining us for drinks Friday night?"

"I wouldn't miss it," he said. "Thanks for organizing that."

"A cast is a family." She hadn't asked Ashton yet, but she hoped he would join them.

"Eyes closed, Jasmine," the makeup artist said, and Jasmine complied. When she opened them, her gaze landed on the set. As expected, Ashton had already disappeared.

A pang shot through her. Was it her fault?

It had been a week, and she had yet to have a real conversation with Ashton. Well, aside from their disastrous first encounter. Her white blouse from that day had been ruined, but her grandmother had worked some laundry magic with the pink slacks, and they were good as new.

This whole thing would be easier if she could run lines with him, like she did with Lily, Miriam, and Peter. But Ashton had made himself clear. He didn't want anything to do with her—or the rest of the cast, if her observations were correct. Her cousins had been right—he was unapproachable and kept to himself. She should just leave him to it.

Still, it didn't feel right not to invite Ashton out for drinks. She'd let him know, and if he said yes, then great, and if he said no . . .

She hoped he didn't say no.

The reunion scene had gone well because Carmen was supposed to feel thrown off balance by Victor's appearance. Not hard to manage, since Jasmine was still a bundle of nerves around Ashton. But as Carmen and Victor began to grow more comfortable around each other? Jasmine dreaded those scenes.

Especially the kiss in episode three.

Marquita had told Jasmine that the production would be bringing in an intimacy coordinator, someone who helped direct physically intimate scenes between actors to ensure everyone was comfortable, to choreograph Carmen and Victor's first on-screen kiss.

Jasmine had filmed more than her fair share of kisses and sex scenes during her career, and it hadn't really been an issue before. But then, she'd also never worried that her costar actively hated her. Usually she was able to develop a good rapport with someone before getting intimate on camera. Ashton, however, was making that impossible.

If she were being honest, she was curious what it would be like to kiss Ashton. His lips were just so . . . *sensual.* Smooth and full, with a defined dip in the top lip. He used them to great effect while he was acting, along with his dark, facile eyebrows and expressive eyes.

It was totally possible to develop a crush on someone's acting ability, and Jasmine already had it bad. She'd taken to watching an episode of *La maldición del león dorado* with subtitles before bed each night to better understand Ashton's performance technique, although it was a fun story too. She could see why Ava liked it. The key was to make sure she only admired his acting, and nothing else.

Well okay, she could appreciate his sexiness, too, but that was it. Purely objective.

Except the thing that always toppled her headlong from crush into infatuation wasn't just good looks or competence—it was attention.

So maybe it was better that Ashton was ignoring her. Because if he suddenly gave her the time of day . . .

Remember McIntyre, she told herself.

Jasmine had gone to his concert on a whim, accompanying a friend in Los Angeles who had VIP seats and backstage passes. His music was fine—not for her, but she could get why other people liked it. The problem started when Jasmine went backstage to meet him. McIntyre was a dynamic performer, but he was also an incorrigible flirt. That was his superpower—when he turned on the full power of that green-eyed gaze, it made you feel like the only person in the room. Like somebody important. Somebody who truly mattered.

Classic middle child that she was, Jasmine had eaten that up with a spoon.

And look where it had gotten her. Splashed across magazine covers. Unable to check her social media accounts. Hounded by paparazzi on the way to ScreenFlix's production lot.

She'd had enough. And if she'd learned anything from a string of shitty exes, it was that she was better off alone.

If only she could make herself believe that.

A PA approached her, double-checking a clipboard. "They want you to film some B-roll in the office before we move on," he said.

Jasmine followed, taking three deep breaths to shake off her gloom. She had this. She was going to shoot this footage, and then she was going to ask Ashton to join the rest of the cast for drinks. Piece of cake. Absolutely nothing to be scared of.

Nothing at all.

IN THE SAFETY of his dressing room, Ashton could finally breathe.

You wanted this, cabrón, he reminded himself. This job was the next step in his career plan, the thing that would move him closer to his goals. He could imagine being interviewed on the red carpet, replying to the interviewer with, "And everything changed with *Carmen in Charge*."

But only if the show went well. And it wouldn't go well if he couldn't get his head out of his own ass.

He started brewing coffee, the familiar scent and sound of the single-cup coffee maker soothing his frayed nerves. The room itself, done in ScreenFlix's signature orange, charcoal, and white color scheme with blocky modern furniture, wasn't so calming. But it was spacious and clean, and the sofa was comfortable enough to nap on, if not exactly long enough for someone his height.

As much as he'd wanted this career upgrade, he missed Miami. He missed the other local telenovela actors and regular crew members. He missed his bright, spacious apartment and the trailer he'd personalized over years of working with the same production company. No pictures of Yadiel, of course, which weighed on him, but his phone camera roll was filled with photos of the two of them with silly animal filters over their faces. He missed being able to see Yadiel more easily.

And if he were being honest with himself, he missed being a big fish in a small pond. He'd built up his career over fifteen years in the telenovela scene and achieved a modicum of fame. Yet it hadn't felt like enough. Despite his intense need for privacy, he wanted *more*.

But now that he was on the verge of having it, he felt like he was drowning. It didn't make any sense.

Maybe it was just that he didn't like being so far away from Yadi. Ashton worried about him constantly, and he was sure he was annoying his father with his frequent check-ins. His last text to Ignacio had been met with an all-caps "ESTAMOS BIEN," and he could just imagine his father typing it with flared nostrils and thinly veiled irritation.

Maybe it was that he didn't know anybody here. He knew

how he came across—cold, aloof, reserved. It was a carefully crafted persona that made it easier to shut down intrusive reporters and impromptu interviews. If he kept people out, they didn't look too deep, and therefore didn't learn about his life. It was something he'd adopted with his coworkers, too, but he'd gradually felt more comfortable around his telenovela costars after being part of the industry for many years. Here, working on *Carmen*, he felt like the new kid all over again, and his walls were up.

And then there was Jasmine.

As a scene partner, he couldn't have asked for anyone better. She was open, giving, and vulnerable. And when she was out of character, her humor and lightheartedness drew his attention, despite his best efforts to remain ambivalent.

Everyone loved her. And while Ashton could play that kind of open, carefree character, he could never really be like that.

When his coffee finished brewing, he added a ton of milk and sugar from the mini-fridge and stirred. The smell comforted him, reminded him of the way his mother had brewed her morning cafecito. Maybe he should order an espresso machine for his dressing room. He'd just taken his first sip when someone knocked on the door.

"It's Jasmine," came a voice from the other side.

Heart pounding, Ashton set down the mug, just in case. He was still mortified about their first encounter. For a split second, he thought of pretending not to be in, but that was stupid. He got up and opened the door.

Jasmine greeted him with a brilliant smile that made his pulse beat even harder. She was so fucking pretty, and she'd been so forgiving after the coffee thing, even when she would have been totally justified in chewing him out.

"Hey, Ashton," she said. "I just wanted to let you know a bunch of us are going out for drinks after we finish on Friday. We have a reservation at a tapas bar that Miriam recommended. Do you want to come with us?"

"Ah . . ." Ashton's mind ricocheted between yes and no. He should say yes. What was the harm? But some unidentified anxiety held him back. It was that damned pond metaphor. This was a bigger pond, and he was scared to dip his toe in.

"Gracias, pero no," he finally said. "Para la próxima."

"Okay." Jasmine's smile tightened, and her voice was brittle. "Maybe next time."

Closing the door, he shook his head at himself. What the fuck was wrong with him? Why couldn't he bring himself to trust these people enough to go out for one night?

Because you don't trust anybody, a little voice whispered in the back of his mind.

It was true. He didn't. His father and grandparents, yes, but that was it. Over the years, he'd grown more and more withdrawn.

He hadn't always been this way, damn it. In his twenties, he'd relished his budding fame, partying and clubbing with his actor friends and enjoying everything the Miami nightlife had to offer.

But then he'd become a father, and everything changed.

When Yadiel had been born, his mother—another telenovela star Ashton had a short-lived fling with—had handed the baby over, along with a list of terms. As a devout Catholic, she'd done her duty by giving birth, but she had no interest in ever being a mother. It would ruin her career. Ashton could have full custody, provided he kept her identity secret and paid for the cosmetic surgery treatments to get her body back to what it had been pre-pregnancy. Not only that, she never wanted to work on a show with Ashton ever again.

For Ashton, who'd grown up as an only child, the prospect of being a dad had been scary, but exciting. The first time he'd held Yadiel in the hospital in Orlando, his heart had broken and reformed into something stronger than he'd ever imagined, forged in the purest love someone could feel. His son was everything to him, and Yadiel's happiness and well-being was worth any price. Yadiel's birth had brought joy back to Ignacio, too, who'd struggled to find his balance after losing his wife.

But that didn't mean there weren't sacrifices, or stress. Every time hurricane season rolled around, Ashton bit his nails and sweated while he watched the weather reports, ready to hop on a plane to evacuate his family at a moment's notice.

And the bigger his career grew, the more he worried about how his visibility would affect his son. He still had nightmares about being awakened by a sound in the middle of the night. Of getting up, as he often did since becoming a father, to check on his little boy as he slept.

Of finding a shadowy figure outside Yadiel's broken window.

Everything changed after the night an overzealous fan-turned-stalker, angry that Ashton hadn't been replying to his letters, tried to break into Yadiel's nursery. It happened after a local Miami newspaper ran a story on neighborhoods where telenovela stars lived. Ashton hadn't even been that famous then, living in a modest residential neighborhood on a typical telenovela actor's salary, which wasn't as high as people thought. But that had been enough for the man to find his home.

Even though Ashton moved his son to Puerto Rico after the Incident, as he called it, it had taken a long time to feel safe again. Ashton still pursued his career, but he did it with his walls up. The Latin American media could be merciless, so he did everything in his power to keep his son safe and hidden. Even if it meant spending time away from him.

Even if it meant closing himself off from everything and everyone else. Including his new costars.

Just thinking about the Incident made him antsy, and being far away from home didn't help.

He drank a big gulp of coffee, then picked up his phone and shot another check-in text to Ignacio.

Chapter 7

CARMEN IN CHARGE

EPISODE 2

Scene: Carmen and Victor attend a red-carpet event.
EXT: Red carpet—NIGHT

At the edge of the red carpet, Carmen adjusted the bodice of her dress, making a show of looking uncomfortable in the strapless blue-sequined getup. "I still don't understand why I have to be in the photos *with* you."

Victor grinned down at her, and butterflies fluttered in her belly, spurred to action by the full, stunning force of his attention. "Because you're my date."

"No, I'm not." *Go back to sleep, butterflies. This isn't real.* "I'm your publicist. Babysitter even. Not your date."

Victor lowered his head and his voice. The dulcet tones shivered over her skin. "Once upon a time, you loved being on my arm on the red carpet."

"Yeah, well, once upon a time I was your wife," Carmen

retorted, the words coming out harsh as she tried to ignore the delicious things his voice was doing to her. "And now I'm not."

Victor straightened, his expression hardening. Carmen tried to ignore the prick of her conscience, letting her gaze drift over to the carpet, where other beautifully dressed people posed for pictures while flashbulbs popped. The lighting and set designers had outdone themselves with this one.

"We're next," Victor said, his voice cold.

Yep. She'd hurt his feelings. But he'd hurt her too. There were lots of reasons why they'd gotten divorced, and one of them was that they just couldn't stop hurting each other.

Or at least, that was the back story she'd come up with on her own while reading the script.

Carmen took a deep breath, fixed a smile on her face, and stepped out onto the carpet, clinging to Victor's arm.

Lights flashed. Extras milled around silently. The hum of the crowd would be added in later. Carmen smiled, awash in nerves and the need to appear professional. She wasn't here as his date, but his publicist. Her only goal was to help repair Victor's image so she could save the family business. She was *not* here to have fun, or to enjoy being close to him.

Even though she did enjoy it.

As they moved to their mark, Victor spoke out of the corner of his mouth. "This isn't so bad, is it?"

"It's terrible," Carmen said through a tight smile. But she didn't mean the lights or the people. She meant the closeness, the scent of his cologne wrapping around her like a comforting cloud, his hard body warm at her side.

It was all so terribly . . . wonderful. She wanted to shift closer, to lean into him, to wrap herself in his warmth and the feel of his skin against hers.

Focus, Jasmine.

"Cut!"

Oh, thank god.

Chapter 8

Despite his bone-deep exhaustion, Ashton caught a late flight to San Juan after the second episode wrapped. The final scenes had called not just for physicality, thanks to Victor's drunken outburst and shoving match with a rival singer, but emotion, as the complications of Victor and Carmen's relationship reached a new low.

The fight had required multiple takes to film, to the point where Ashton regretted insisting that sure, he could absolutely do his own stunts. Not that the actual stunt guy he acted opposite had hurt him, but stage combat could be grueling work. Another concern had been Jasmine's presence in the scene, since Carmen's character was called upon to break up the fight. The last thing he'd wanted to do was accidentally hurt her, so Ashton had been aware of her every second, from the moments she was glued to his side on the red carpet, to the way she banded her arms around his torso to pull him out of the fight, to the way she tenderly cupped his cheek to check for bruises.

Acting was reacting, and they'd taken their cues from each

other, even as Ashton had dug deeper and deeper into himself to pull out Victor's pain. Jasmine matched him beat for emotional beat as Victor had raged himself into exhaustion. The quiet moments between them after the fight were probably some of the best acting he'd ever done.

But by the end of the week, he was ready to drop, and homesickness was like a lead weight in his gut. On Friday night, he went straight from the studio to the airport, and from the airport to the apartment he kept in San Juan, where he caught a few hours of sleep. In the morning, he drove to Humacao, to the condo where his son, father, and grandparents lived full time in a secure gated community.

Keeping an eye out for any suspicious figures, Ashton parked in the driveway, then let himself into the blocky peach and terra-cotta house. Even though his family had moved after the Incident, his sense of safety had never fully recovered. Inside, Ignacio approached him with una taza de café con leche while Ashton reset the security system. Ashton greeted his father and gratefully took a sip of the coffee.

"¿Yadiel está durmiendo?" Ashton asked, following Ignacio into the kitchen.

"Sí." Ignacio sat at the table and put his reading glasses on to resume his perusal of the newspaper. "He'll be happy to see you when he wakes up."

Ashton took a seat, but he felt jumpy. "Everything's okay? Nothing weird?"

Ignacio put down the paper and sent Ashton a bland look over the top of his glasses.

"If there were something weird, don't you think I'd tell you?"

"Of course." Ashton didn't fully believe that, but no point upsetting his father this early in the morning.

"When did you arrive?"

"Late last night."

"Ah. You stayed in the apartment?"

"Yeah."

Ignacio just raised his eyebrows and kept reading about the latest political protests. He didn't have to say anything, because they'd already had this conversation multiple times. He thought it was silly for Ashton to pay for two homes in Puerto Rico and an apartment in Miami, but he knew why Ashton didn't feel comfortable sleeping in the house.

"And how long are we supposed to have Yadi's teachers and friends sign NDAs?" Ignacio asked pointedly.

Ashton just sighed. "Stop exaggerating."

"You've kept him secret this long," his father went on, his tone mild. "But you can't do it forever."

Ashton knew that, but he'd convinced himself it was possible. He was saved from having to come up with an answer by the sound of feet on the stairs. Setting his cup down, he stood as Yadi entered the room in his Spider-Man pajamas.

"Papi!" the boy screeched, then launched himself into Ashton's arms.

Ashton picked him up and held him close. Yadi was small for his age, and Ashton wouldn't be able to do this for much longer. He wished, not for the first time, that he could be here every day when his son woke up.

Yadiel clambered down and greeted his grandfather, then went to pour himself a glass of juice.

"Well, since you're here, I'll go get an early start at the restaurant," Ignacio told Ashton. He set down the newspaper, open to the entertainment page. "Looks like your friend Fernando Vargas is doing well."

Ashton glanced at the paper and groaned. His "rival" from *El fuego de amor* had booked a big role in a movie Ashton hadn't even been called to audition for.

Yadiel drained his juice and grabbed Ashton's hand with sticky fingers. "¡Ven, Papi! Come look at the castle I built in *Minecraft!*"

Ashton let his son consume his thoughts that weekend. They spent every waking minute together while Ignacio and Abuelita Bibi and Abuelito Gus were at the restaurant. Ashton even kept Yadiel home from Sunday mass, which did not thrill Abuelita Bibi.

Ashton set up a badminton net in the backyard, and they played for hours until they were both sweaty and hot. They swam in the pool, with Yadiel showing off how he could pick up brightly colored rings from the bottom. And they watched countless animated superhero movies, with Yadiel helpfully filling in any character backstory Ashton might be unaware of.

On Sunday night, after Ashton put Yadiel to bed, Ignacio pulled him aside before he left for the airport.

"The show is going well?" Ignacio asked.

Ashton shrugged. "Well enough." He'd spent the whole weekend trying not to think about it.

"Ah. Does that mean you're pulling your usual disappearing act behind the scenes?"

"Pa, enough."

"You never used to be that way, is all I'm saying."

Ashton lowered his voice. "That was *before*."

"It was years ago."

Ashton shook his head and reached for the door. "I have to go."

Ignacio caught his arm and looked him dead in the eyes. "This is what you wanted, mijo. Don't screw it up."

In the car, Ashton reflected on his father's words. Why had he even come here this weekend? Yes, he'd loved spending time with his son, but he would have been better served resting and memorizing his lines for the third episode.

Part of him had wanted to get away from the stress of it all. Another part had wanted to see for himself that Yadi was safe and happy. But even though he'd confirmed that everything was okay, he still felt unsettled.

Well enough, he'd told his father. Deep down, he knew he could be doing better as Victor. Ashton was too much of a perfectionist to ever feel like he'd done a *great* job, but he knew when he was holding back. If this show was going to catapult his career, he needed to give it his all.

It was with this thought in mind that he ran into Jasmine entering the Hutton Court late that night.

She did a double take when he approached her at the elevator bank, where she'd just pressed the up button.

"You're out late," she remarked, giving him a once-over

while he did the same. She looked tired, but gorgeous in a floaty purple dress that showed off her shoulders and arms.

"I could say the same to you," he quipped, exhaustion loosening his tongue.

"Just getting back from the Bronx. My cousin Ronnie's daughter turned one." She rolled her eyes. "Nothing says 'baby's first birthday' like an open bar."

"Your family lives in New York?" he asked, more curious about her than he should be.

The elevator arrived and the doors whooshed open. They both stepped in, and she leaned a shoulder on the elevator wall.

"Yup. And since I'm here, I'm expected to visit my parents, siblings, nephews, aunts, uncles, cousins, etcetera." She ticked them off on her fingers. "Why the hell is my family so damn *big*?"

"I was just visiting my father in Puerto Rico," he said, even though he definitely hadn't been planning to tell her that.

"Really?" Her expression softened. "How was it?"

"Great." The elevator dinged and stopped at her floor. If they were on TV, it would malfunction, trapping them in together and then . . . what? The doors slid open. He'd never know.

Jasmine straightened and Ashton pressed a hand to the frame to hold it open for her. "Well, I'll see you tomorrow morning."

"Right. We have the intimacy coordinator meeting before we start filming episode three."

Episode three. The one with the kiss.

Maybe Jasmine was also thinking about the upcoming kiss, because she bit her lower lip and ducked her head, like she was suddenly embarrassed to look at him. "Um, good night."

"Buenas noches," he murmured as she brushed past him, leaving a sweet citrusy scent in her wake. He held the elevator open, watching her as she walked down the hall. When she looked back over her shoulder at him, he let go. The doors shut, blocking his view of her.

Chapter 9

Jasmine had a hard time falling asleep after her encounter with Ashton in the elevator, but she'd eventually managed to nod off, and only hit snooze twice the next morning when her alarm blared. Curse Ronnie and her Sunday night open bar.

At the party, she'd filled in Ava and Michelle on Ashton's behavior, and they'd assured her she should *not* take his reclusive behavior personally. Ava had even looked up some Spanish-language gossip sites, which all confirmed Ashton's rep for being easy to work with but kind of a diva.

While Jasmine couldn't deny his acting ability, his disappearing acts were annoying. But when she *did* manage to catch him—like in the elevator and after he'd spilled coffee on her—he seemed normal. Down to earth, a little awkward, sweetly endearing. And sexy as hell. Whatever cologne he wore was really doing it for her, and she didn't even like men's cologne.

Worse, while their performances were fine, she was convinced they could bring even more to the characters if he would just freaking *talk* to her for more than two minutes.

Before they got to the kissing scene, Jasmine and Ashton were instructed to attend a meeting with the episode's director, Ilba Montez, and the intimacy coordinator, Vera Parks. Marquita Arroyo, the showrunner, was also in attendance.

Since they hadn't hit wardrobe yet, Jasmine wore cutoff shorts and a white T-shirt, her hair pulled back in a ponytail. Ashton was dressed in faded jeans that made his legs look a million miles long and a beige guayabera shirt, like the kind Jasmine's grandfathers wore.

Ashton had no right to look so sexy in an old man's shirt, but he apparently hadn't gotten that memo.

The five of them gathered in a small conference room, sipping coffees from to-go cups.

Vera wasn't what Jasmine expected. For one thing, she was young. Younger than Jasmine, anyway, maybe midtwenties. She had straight dark hair, a creamy complexion, and striking green eyes. She was dressed in olive cargo pants and a double layer of distressed tank tops. But when Jasmine met her gaze, she was struck by the intensity she saw there. When Vera looked at her, it was with her full attention. Her smile was warm and genuine, and Jasmine instantly felt at ease with her.

"Hi, Jasmine," Vera said, shaking her hand. "It's really nice to meet you."

Despite the early hour and Jasmine's worries about Ashton, she felt herself relaxing. "Thanks, Vera. I'm excited to work together."

Vera went to say hello to Ashton, and Ilba Montez took her place in front of Jasmine.

Ilba was a petite woman, around fifty, with luminous brown skin, big brown eyes, and a ready laugh. Her wavy black hair was cut short and she dressed casually in jeans and a *Doctor Who* T-shirt.

"My wife and I loved you on *The Glamour Squad*," Ilba confessed when she introduced herself. "I'm a big fan of soaps. Such creative storytelling techniques. I hope they make a comeback."

"Me too," Jasmine said with a laugh, but Ilba shook her head.

"Nah, this show is going to catapult you. Just watch." She winked, and they took their seats around the table.

Only Vera remained standing, with her hands resting on the back of her chair.

"Welcome, everyone." She flashed a grin around the room. "Thanks for bringing me in. I've read the scripts, and I'm excited to assist with this production. Have any of you worked with an intimacy coordinator before?"

Jasmine would have thought the question was aimed at her and Ashton, but Ilba and Marquita responded too. Marquita was the only one who answered yes.

Vera nodded like she wasn't surprised. "It's a newer part of production, although it shouldn't be. To give some background, it's a role that started in theater, and is now being used more in TV and film. How about stage combat? Do either of you have experience with that?"

Both Jasmine and Ashton murmured their assent. Jasmine had filmed a few "catfights" while working in soaps. She'd also taken some fight choreography classes in drama school and, more recently, before auditioning for a couple of superhero roles. She'd been passed over for them, but she was holding out hope.

"So you know the importance of choreographing close movements for maximum safety," Vera continued. "My goal as an intimacy coordinator is to make sure the performers, directors, and crew are all on the same page, and that clear consent is being given at all stages."

Well, this was a welcome change. Jasmine couldn't remember ever having been asked if she explicitly consented to something—or didn't—while filming.

"One of the first things we have to do is determine the context," Vera went on. "By that I mean, why is this scene here? Does it make sense for the story and characters?"

"The last thing we want is to put the actors in uncomfortable situations for scenes that don't serve the story," Marquita agreed.

Vera turned to Ashton. "Ashton, why do you think this episode needs an intimate moment between the characters?"

Jasmine watched him from the corner of her eye. Oh, she couldn't wait to hear his answer to this.

CoÑo. Ashton swallowed hard as all the women in the room turned to look at him. "Ah . . . you mean the . . . kissing?"

What the hell was wrong with him? He was acting like Yadiel, who gagged every time people kissed in movies, even animated ones.

Vera's smile was patient, but he got the feeling she'd caught his embarrassment at saying the word *kissing*. "Yes, Carmen and Victor share a very passionate kiss in this episode. Do you think it's necessary for the story?"

Ashton supposed it made sense to ask these questions. Granted, most of his acting roles to date leaned heavily in favor of gratuitousness, but it was nice to have someone on the team who would focus on the integrity of the story. It wasn't something he'd ever considered in his telenovela roles, which often had him kissing, fighting, yelling, and sometimes even crying in the same episode. *Necessary* didn't cover it. If it added to the drama, it stayed in. High emotions plus high drama equaled higher ratings.

But while *Carmen in Charge* was based on a telenovela, the tone was different from the original show, *La patrona Carmen*, which had been more of a workplace drama between rival execs. Ashton considered the third episode's storyline, which focused on Carmen's continuing efforts to improve Victor's reputation after the disastrous red-carpet appearance in the previous episode.

"Talk us through it," Vera urged.

He was starting to dislike this process, but he complied. "Well, Carmen books Victor on a cooking competition show to raise money for charity."

Vera turned to Jasmine. "Anything to add, regarding context?"

Jasmine answered readily, like a dutiful student. "It's a good publicity move, but Carmen knows Victor is a terrible cook. He's her ex-husband, after all. She'd know that about him."

"Cooking, food, the closeness of a kitchen—it can create a very intimate environment," Marquita added. "That's what we're going for with the scene—pushing Carmen and Victor closer together."

"But Carmen doesn't really cook either," Jasmine jumped in, her tone rising with excitement. "She enlists her mother to teach Victor how to make the dish before he goes on the show."

"So do you think it makes sense, within the context of the story, for Carmen and Victor to kiss in this episode?" Vera asked.

Jasmine pursed her lips and her gaze drifted up to the ceiling as she thought. Ashton found he was holding his breath as he waited for her to speak, curious about what she would say.

Then Jasmine's gaze flicked to his. She caught him staring at her, but that wasn't the worst part.

The worst part? There was heat in her eyes. He felt it in the split second before she directed her attention back to Vera.

No wait, that wasn't the worst part. The actual worst part was the answering flash of heat in his own body. The look in her eyes kick-started his system, sending a bolt of desire through him, making him harden. He shifted uncomfortably as Jasmine answered Vera.

"Carmen and Victor have a history," Jasmine explained. "Yes, they're divorced, and there's pain and hurt there, but there's still love and attraction too. They're fire together, and like Marquita said, the heat and closeness of the kitchen . . . it sets them ablaze."

Her gaze shot to Ashton again, then dropped to her hands on the table. Was he imagining things, or had Jasmine's voice gone the slightest bit . . . breathy?

"The attraction part is easier for them to deal with," she went on. "The other stuff . . . well, it's messy. So they give in to the—oh god, this is a bad pun, but the *heat of the moment.*"

Marquita and Ilba laughed, and Vera grinned. Ashton was glad for the break in tension. Had Vera noticed the looks Jasmine was shooting him? He hoped she wouldn't call them out on making eyes at each other like a couple of horny teenagers.

Vera looked to Ashton then. "So, it makes sense for them to kiss in that moment?"

Without meaning to, Ashton replied, "He still wants her. He never stopped."

Silence fell, as the others nodded their agreement.

Jasmine watched him from the other side of the table. Her expression was intense and unreadable. He didn't know what it meant. But he wanted to.

"It's also the first time they're alone together," Marquita pointed out. "We've purposely built the tension between them over the first two episodes. By the time Carmen's mother leaves them alone in the kitchen, they've built up a lot of *steam.*"

Everyone laughed and continued to toss out bad kitchen puns until Vera brought the meeting to a close.

"It's incredibly important that we maintain open communication," she said. "I'll loop in future directors, but I want all of you to feel comfortable coming to me with any concerns. We'll check in and obtain permission from all parties at every step."

"We've built extra time into the schedule to rehearse scenes where we need Vera's help," Marquita explained to the others. "She'll work on the choreography then."

"The last step is a moment of closure," Vera said. "At the end of each scene, I encourage the actors—in this case, Jasmine and Ashton—to develop some sort of ritual to help you both break the spell of the work and transition back to real life."

Ashton exchanged a glance with Jasmine. Actors had all sorts of rituals and superstitions, but his mind went blank when he tried to think of what they could do.

"That's all I have. Thanks for being so open to this process." Vera's eyes landed on Ashton when she said "open" and he got the feeling she knew he was holding back. "I'll see you tomorrow for rehearsal."

THAT NIGHT, JASMINE met Michelle for dinner at a wine bar in Greenwich Village. After two glasses of wine—and forty-five minutes spent on party-planning details—Jasmine loosened up enough to approach the sexy elephant in the room.

"I think I like Ashton," she mused.

"I thought you said he doesn't talk to you." Michelle's voice was direct, but not unkind. She topped off their glasses from the bottle of Merlot on the table.

Jasmine scowled. "He kinda doesn't?"

"So how do you know you like him?"

Jasmine blew out a breath and slumped back in her seat. "Fine. I'm attracted to him. Plus, he's a good actor. And when I get little glimpses of him . . . I like what I see."

"Where are you on the scale?"

Years ago, Michelle had created the four-point Jasmine Scale to track Jasmine's progression—or descent, as Michelle called it—into love.

The first point on the scale was Attraction. It was the curiosity phase, where Jasmine started to wonder about the guy and noticed all the cute and charming things about him, usually while ignoring glaring flaws and red flags.

Next came the Crush. In the Crush phase, Jasmine amped up the flirting, getting physically closer and making it obvious that she was interested.

The third phase, Infatuation, was where she started to lose her sense of self and all good judgment. She made herself too available and did too many favors for the guy in question.

After that, there was only one more step left: Falling in Love, where she threw herself headfirst into the emotional abyss.

"I think I'm still on the first point," Jasmine said. Michelle was right. Jasmine hadn't actually spent enough time around Ashton to reach Crush levels yet.

"Then there's still hope for you." Michelle grinned, then popped a french fry in her mouth.

Jasmine stole some of Michelle's fries. "Hooray for me."

Michelle reached across the table and patted her arm. "Look, Ashton is super hot. If you *were* going to rebound with someone, you could do a lot worse than him."

"I'm trying not to rebound *at all*."

"Remember your Leading Lady Plan."

How could she forget? And while she was thinking about it, Jasmine mentally added a fourth point: *Leading Ladies do not rebound with their costars.*

Speaking of . . .

"We film the kissing scene tomorrow," she blurted out.

Michelle's eyes went wide, and then she laughed her head off while Jasmine stewed.

"You are toast," Michelle said, then raised her glass. "Here lies Jasmine. We loved her well. Cause of death: crushing on her costar."

Jasmine grabbed her own wine and gulped down half of it. "What is so wrong with having a crush?"

"Oh, now it's a crush? Are you at the second point on the scale?"

"No." *Not yet.*

"There's nothing wrong with a crush," Michelle said, her tone gentle. "But you don't do crushes."

Jasmine wished she did crushes. How much easier would her life be if she could find someone appealing, never act on it, and then forget all about them? But she just wasn't wired that way, and she didn't want to be. Was it so much to ask for a loving, committed relationship with someone who unconditionally loved and accepted her for who she was?

Apparently so, because she'd kissed a lot of frogs over the years, and all of them had broken her heart.

"I'm not going to rebound with Ashton," she said firmly, more to herself than to Michelle.

Her cousin raised a skeptical eyebrow, then lifted her glass again. "Cheers to that," she said, although she didn't sound convinced.

"Don't tell Ava."

"Oh, I'm *definitely* telling Ava."

Jasmine let out a sigh. "Fine. Tell Ava. Saves me the trouble of bringing her up to speed."

Michelle chuckled while Jasmine drained her glass.

Chapter 10

Vera was waiting when Ashton arrived on set for private rehearsal early the next day. These scenes would be shot in a working kitchen that was normally used for talk shows but was now outfitted to look like the basement-level kitchen of the Serranos' East Harlem brownstone. The crew had dressed it in dark wood with warm yellow lighting and copper pots and pans hanging from a low ceiling. Three walls had been built around the kitchen appliances—a sink on one side, a stove on the other, fake stairs in the back, and a wood-topped island in the center.

Since they were just rehearsing, Ashton was still in the jeans and T-shirt he'd dressed in after his five a.m. gym session. Jasmine arrived just behind him, looking fresh and sexy in a floral romper. She wasn't tall, but she was all legs, and it took everything he had not to stare like a creep when she strutted around in shorts.

"Morning," she said, sending him a sleepy little smile. Damn, she was adorable.

"Buenos días," he replied, then reminded himself to stick to English. "Tired?"

She nodded. "No coffee yet. I didn't want to—you know, drink coffee and then kiss. It's kinda gross."

He couldn't help but smile, since he'd considered the same thing this morning—brushing, flossing, and rinsing his mouth three times after drinking his own coffee.

Ilba and Marquita strolled in then. It was only the five of them on set to practice. Vera's orders.

They sat on folding chairs while Vera reviewed the points she'd made the previous day regarding communication and consent.

"Did you two come up with some sort of closure ritual?" Vera asked, turning her bright, intense gaze on Ashton and Jasmine.

Carajo, he hadn't even thought about it, but Jasmine raised her hand tentatively, like they were in school.

"I had an idea," she said, her voice unsure as she met Ashton's eyes. "What if we . . . high-fived? After Ilba yells 'cut.' To, you know, snap us out of character."

Ashton's mind flashed back through eight years of high-fiving Yadiel every time the kid nailed his goals—walking, tying his shoes, adding numbers, flipping his skateboard and landing on it. He still couldn't remember what that move was called, but Yadiel had been so proud of himself when he'd stuck the landing that first time. It had warranted a double high five, using both hands. A "high ten," Yadiel called it.

Everyone was waiting for him to reply, so Ashton nodded. "Okay. Yes, a high five."

With Jasmine it would be an innocuous move, the sound

and motion of their slapping palms serving to break them out of the awkward haze of kissing on camera.

Because it *was* awkward, no matter how many times he did it.

The last woman he'd kissed on camera had been a seasoned telenovela actress on *El fuego de amor*. In fact, they'd both starred on another show together, maybe six years earlier, where they'd had to kiss. They'd cracked jokes leading up to the moment, teasing each other about how much older they were now. But Ashton didn't have that rapport with Jasmine. All he had was a feeling like electricity singing through his veins when she was near.

It was his own fault. He should have worked harder to get to know her before this moment. Media attention and social anxiety be damned, this was his *chance*. And he was on the verge of blowing it because he'd spent too much time hiding in his dressing room.

"So we have a passionate, heat-of-the-moment kiss between two ex-lovers," Vera went on, oblivious to Ashton's inner turmoil. "There'd be some reluctance there, too, right? But also surrender. They're finally giving in to what they both feel."

Ashton glanced at Jasmine. Giving in? That wouldn't be too hard to pretend. But feeling real attraction for the other actor often made the whole thing even more awkward. He had to shut those feelings away and focus. This was *work*.

Ilba spoke up. "I'm thinking more clutching, less groping."

Vera nodded. "Yes, these are two people who once loved each other enough to get married. They've spent years apart and they're desperate to revisit what they once had. But also, it's a stolen moment in the family kitchen, and Carmen's mother could come back at any time. They're holding each other, not tearing off clothing." She turned to Jasmine and Ashton. "How does that sound to you two?"

Jasmine agreed. "It's a release of tension too. They've been snapping at each other since he returned, but the anger and teasing mask the real feelings underneath—both the hurt and the lingering love."

The others nodded approvingly, then Ilba turned to Marquita. "How hot are we making this? Like, tongue? Or—"

Vera took one look at Jasmine, and whatever she saw on her face had her interrupting quickly. "No tongue. It won't be necessary."

Now Ashton wanted to know what Jasmine was thinking. He preferred not to use tongue on-screen. It was weird, and kind of jarring. There was already too much to think about without bringing tongues and saliva into it. What had Jasmine's experiences been? She must have had plenty of on-screen kisses. It was too late to ask her, however. They were getting ready to begin.

While Marquita and Ilba discussed something in the script, Vera took Ashton aside.

"Is there anything you're uncomfortable with?" she asked in a low voice. "Doing or receiving. Or anywhere you'd prefer not to be touched?"

It was the first time anyone had asked him that. He'd thought to ask some of his female costars in the past, but it wasn't something the production team usually took into account, especially for a male actor. Everyone had always assumed he was perfectly comfortable touching women he didn't know, or being touched by them.

When he didn't answer right away, Vera gave him a reassuring smile. "I've done my research. I know you're a pro. But still, if there's anything that makes you uncomfortable, or you don't want to do, please tell me. This is a safe space for you too."

"Um, thank you," he said, not sure what else to say. In truth, he didn't mind being touched within the context of a scene. He certainly didn't mind the thought of Jasmine touching him, although having an audience changed the dynamic significantly. But he liked that Vera had thought to ask. "I just want to make sure she—Jasmine—is comfortable."

"I want that too." Vera left him to go speak to Jasmine. While they talked, Jasmine's gaze lifted and caught Ashton's across the set. She said something to Vera and gave a little shake of her head. He would have given anything to hear what she was saying, but then again, maybe he was better off not knowing.

And then . . . there was nothing more to do but rehearse the kiss.

Ilba handled the first part. "You'll both be standing here," she said, pointing. "Working together at the kitchen island, cooking a meal."

"Will we have food on our hands?" Jasmine asked, sounding dubious as she joined Ashton at the counter.

Marquita and Ilba exchanged a look, and the showrunner shook her head.

"No, it's not a messy make-out session," Marquita said. "You're admiring the plated dishes."

"What does the script say?" Ilba asked, flipping pages.

"'They kiss,'" Jasmine and Ashton replied in unison. He caught her eye, then looked away. It was something he'd noticed while memorizing his lines. No stage direction except *They kiss*. There was a world of possibility in those two little words.

Vera reviewed her own copy. "Okay, Carmen's mother gets a phone call, says, 'It's Tía Jimena. Un momentito,' then leaves the room. Carmen rolls her eyes and says—"

Jasmine spoke her line right on cue. "She'll be gone an hour."

"This is where Victor takes the opportunity to move a little closer," Ilba said.

Ashton sidled closer to Jasmine, but Vera shook her head.

"Ashton, let's have you be a little smoother. What if you do it like this?" Vera stood next to Ashton, mimicking his pose—right hip leaning on the counter, head turned toward Jasmine, who was to his left.

"Instead of just leaning down, how about you . . ." Vera slid her hip along the edge of the counter toward Ashton. In one smooth move, she shifted closer, her body now facing his, and she'd never dropped eye contact.

Ashton nodded, impressed. "I can do that."

He tried it a few times until the move was as easy as breathing.

"What should I do?" Jasmine asked.

"Can you lean your elbows on the counter?" Ilba suggested. When Jasmine had to lean down too far, Marquita shook her head.

"You're too tall," the showrunner said. "Take off your shoes. We'll get you chancletas to wear during the shoot."

Jasmine kicked off her platform sandals and repeated the casual pose. The other women nodded.

"This is the lead in to the moment that becomes a kiss," Vera explained. "Your characters are both very comfortable right now. Their defenses are down, and they're remembering what they like about each other. Ashton, start with the slide, getting as close to Jasmine as you can without knocking her over. You're opening up your body to her, but subtly, not overwhelmingly."

"What do I do with my arms?" he asked.

They explored a few options—hands on the counter, in his pockets, on his hips—and settled on having him cross his arms as he turned toward Jasmine. But he was instructed to make it look "relaxed, not defensive."

Then they set to work on Jasmine—her reaction, her pose, her eye movement and facial expressions. It was almost like a dance, and Ashton understood why this was called choreography. They broke down the scene into steps of emotion, and attached those feelings to a movement, a look, a stance. Then they ran through them, adjusting and perfecting each piece until it created the whole of the interaction.

It had been a long time since he'd workshopped a scene with such deliberate attention to detail, and he'd forgotten how much he enjoyed this aspect of acting. Most of the shows he'd been on adopted a quick and dirty approach to getting the footage, relying on heightened emotion and over-the-top theatrics.

This was . . . nice, he decided. More calming, despite the awkwardness.

"Let's take it through with the lines," Vera told him, and he took his spot at the counter.

When Ilba gave the signal, Ashton slid closer to Jasmine. With his arms crossed over his chest, he tapped into Victor's easy charm—something he wished he could employ more in his real life—and grinned. "Do you think I have a chance at winning?"

Jasmine looked up at him from under long lashes. She pursed her lips before she answered, like she was thinking about what he'd said.

"I think so. *If* you remember every step of the recipe, execute it all perfectly, and finish on time."

He raised his eyebrows. "No pressure."

She softened then. Nothing obvious, but still, a noticeable easing of her stance, her tone, her expression. Her words were serious, not sarcastic, as she repeated, "No pressure."

This was it. Time for him—Victor—to make his move. Uncrossing his arms in a slow movement, Ashton raised his hand.

Suddenly, Vera was there, close to them.

"Stay in the moment," she said in a hushed voice. She took Ashton's hand and gently brought it to Jasmine's cheek.

Ashton positioned his hand on the side of Jasmine's face the way Vera directed it. His fingers slid over Jasmine's jaw to curl around the side of her neck, under her ear. Her skin was so warm. He had a flash of pressing his mouth there. How would she feel against his lips?

"Say your line." Vera's words were faint, barely interrupting the tension spinning out between the three of them.

Ashton dropped his voice. "You have something here." With Vera's hand over his, Ashton's thumb came to rest on the curve of Jasmine's cheekbone. Vera gave the digit a little nudge, and Ashton stroked Jasmine's cheek in a soft, gentle glide. Then Vera shifted, resting her hands on Jasmine's upper arms. Slowly, Jasmine rose up from her elbows. Her dark eyes stayed locked on Ashton's, even as Vera moved her like a doll, or a puppet. But Vera wasn't controlling them—no, she was guiding. They'd given her permission, given each other permission. They'd consented to this, and there was power in that. Vera was part of this.

And damn if it wasn't incredibly intimate.

Jasmine's lashes dropped a fraction, and Ashton marveled at how easily she turned on the bedroom eyes. Then the corner of her full lips pinched into the barest trace of a smile as Carmen called Victor's bluff. "No, I don't."

Ashton was struck by the mixture of humor, lust, and . . . trust in this moment, between the characters. It formed a heady swirl of emotions that the viewers would eat up. But he had to nail this next part.

"You're right," he said, still stroking her cheek languidly, speaking with naked honesty. "You don't. I just . . . wanted to . . ."

He trailed off, leaning in. Jasmine tilted her chin up toward him.

"Hold it," Vera said, her face inches from theirs.

They both froze. Ashton's gaze shot to Vera, questioning, but the intimacy coordinator was smiling.

"That was great," she said. "Did it feel okay to you two?"

Easing back, Ashton nodded, and Jasmine gave a hum of agreement.

He'd been nervous about this process, but now that they

were in it, he was a little startled at how much more than okay it felt to him. From an acting standpoint, he'd been completely in tune with Jasmine, more deeply connected than any of their other times on set together. Already, he could see that their performance was improving.

Once Ilba and Marquita had signed off on the choreography, Vera clapped her hands together. "Great. Let's choreograph the kiss!"

KISSING A STRANGER was weird.

Kissing a stranger while another person hovered around them, adjusting their body parts and giving direction, was also weird. But Vera was so quirky and genuine, Jasmine couldn't help but love her a little. She also truly seemed to understand the characters, which was more than Jasmine could say for many directors she'd worked with.

At every step, Vera asked if they were comfortable and if the moves made sense for Carmen and Victor. To Jasmine's surprise, Ilba and Marquita stayed off to the side, offering comments and suggestions when asked, but for the most part, letting Vera do her thing. There was no ego here, and wasn't that a rare thing in this industry?

Vera was clearly good at her job. This kiss was going to look *hot* once they filmed the whole thing together. So far, they'd just done bits and pieces, choreographing it like a dance or a stage fight.

And strictly speaking, Ashton wasn't a complete stranger, but it was still weird. The first time he touched his lips to hers, it was as unsexy as you could get. They were both looking at

Vera, not each other, and balancing awkwardly, with his lower lip pressed to her top one. Vera had instructed them not to kiss so much as touch their mouths together while they perfected each part before moving on to the next.

It was going well, and everyone was behaving like a consummate professional, but Jasmine was used to laughing through love scenes, finding common ground in how weird and awkward the whole thing was. With Ashton, it was like all the strangeness of what they were doing was being filtered through Vera. Which was good, but . . . when were they going to connect?

Finally, Vera seemed satisfied with the rehearsal. "Do you two feel comfortable running through the whole scene now?"

Ashton nodded, but Jasmine's "yes" was interrupted by a jaw-cracking yawn.

She clapped a hand over her mouth. "Sorry. No coffee yet."

Ashton shot her a look, and was it her imagination, or was he fighting back a smile?

Marquita checked her phone. "Uh-oh. The crew is waiting to come in."

Vera looked troubled as she addressed Jasmine and Ashton. "I don't want to rush you through this now, but I also don't want the first time you run through the whole thing to be with the entire crew present."

Before Jasmine could say anything, Ashton shrugged. "We'll be fine. We don't want to get too far off schedule."

He raised an eyebrow at Jasmine, like he was asking her to agree, so she nodded. The impulse to not waste the crew's time was ingrained in her from her time on soap operas, and she couldn't stand the thought that people were waiting on them to finish.

"Yeah," she said, giving Vera a reassuring smile. "We'll be fine."

"Don't forget to high-five," Vera told them.

Ah yes. The closure ritual. Jasmine looked to Ashton, who wore an unreadable expression. Without a word, they raised their hands and slapped them together.

Except their timing was off. She'd started too early, and he hadn't put enough force into it. Probably trying not to hurt her. Either way, it was a pretty poor showing as far as high fives went.

"Awesome." Ilba grabbed her things. "Let's get you two into hair and makeup."

Jasmine followed her out. Maybe the makeup brushes would wash away the feel of Ashton's strong fingers on her skin. The last thing she needed was his phantom caresses plaguing her all day.

The man was an enigma, albeit a sexy one. If she were smart, she'd keep her distance.

Too bad Jasmine had never been smart when it came to men.

Chapter 11

CARMEN IN CHARGE

EPISODE 3

Scene: Carmen's mother teaches Victor to cook.
INT: Serranos' kitchen—NIGHT

Carmen staggered into the basement-level kitchen of her parents' Spanish Harlem brownstone, loaded down with heavy shopping bags. Victor and her mother, Dahlia Serrano, stood at the kitchen island calmly chopping vegetables together.

"Didn't you two already go to the grocery store?" Carmen complained. "Why did I have to make another trip after work? The lines were unbelievable."

"We want Victor to win, no? Pues, necesitamos un side dish."

Carmen rolled her eyes, but began unloading the groceries into the fridge. "What are you making?" She made a show of sniffing the air. "It smells like a garlic farm exploded in here."

"We're making mofongo," Victor replied with a grin.

"Ah, your favorite." Carmen pulled an open bottle of white

wine from the refrigerator and poured herself a glass. "I can't count how many times you came to bed reeking of garlic after eating Mami's mofongo."

"I can't help it if Dahlia is an amazing cook." He shot his ex-mother-in-law a dashing grin, which Dahlia totally fell for. She trilled a little laugh and patted the side of Victor's face.

"Ay, muchacho, we missed you around here," she said, then snapped up a spare apron and tossed it to Carmen. "Póntelo, nena. Those plátanos aren't going to peel themselves."

"Isn't this cheating?" Carmen grumbled, but she tied the apron on over her dress. "Victor's going to have to do all this himself during the competition."

"It's not like you're a master chef either," Victor pointed out with a smile. "You could also stand to learn."

"Oh, I know *how* to make mofongo," she retorted. "You think I could get away with not helping my mom cook? In *this* house?"

"So what happened?" He leaned in closer while Dahlia rinsed greens in the sink. "You never cooked for me."

Carmen gave a sassy little shrug. "Not the best use of my time," she said primly. "Some of us had to work."

He leaned his hip on the counter and ducked his head closer to hers. "That's not fair," he said in a low voice. "I didn't become an international pop star by accident. I had demands on my time too."

Carmen stilled. She set down the plátano in her hands, and with a deliberate movement, turned her face toward his. Their gazes locked, and all traces of teasing and frustration melted from her expression.

This was a big moment. They'd practiced it multiple times during rehearsal, and Ilba had told them it would be a big close-up: the moment when Carmen and Victor connected emotionally. Again.

"I know," Carmen said in a soft voice. "You're right. We were both . . . unavailable."

The moment stretched between them until a loud clang made them both jump. With perfect timing, Dahlia had plunked down a giant soup pot onto the stove.

"Time to start the broth!" she called out cheerfully, oblivious to what she'd interrupted. Eyes on their work, Carmen went back to peeling plantains and Victor resumed crushing garlic.

"Cut!"

Chapter 12

With the help of a real chef from a Caribbean restaurant uptown, they filmed the cooking montage, which involved a lot of chopping, laughing, and tasting. Ashton had grown up in his family's restaurant, so this was nothing new to him. If anything, he was more comfortable in a kitchen than anywhere else, surrounded by the scents of garlic and cooked plantains.

This part was being filmed MOS—a motor only shot with no sound—so nothing they said would be included in the scene. They were supposed to look like they were having a grand old time, and luckily, Miriam Perez—who played Dahlia—was a comic actress with a ton of improv experience. Miriam kept Jasmine and Ashton grinning the whole time, doing things like feeding Ashton a taste of broth like he was a baby, airplane sounds and all. Ashton hoped that part made the final cut; Yadiel would get a kick out of it. And he had to admit he was having fun stretching his comedy muscles.

Ilba was all about making it as real as possible, so Ashton was tasked with keeping an eye on the broth and giving it the occasional stir. He was standing over the pot, inhaling the aroma that reminded him of home, when Jasmine appeared at his side.

Meeting his eyes, she dipped a fresh spoon into the broth. "If one has garlic, all must have garlic," she said.

Was she alluding to their upcoming kiss scene? He hoped so, because now it was all he could think about, and he didn't want to be the only one.

His gaze dropped as she brought the spoon to her mouth, her full lips enveloping the curved metal in a way that sent his heart racing. She swiped her tongue over her lower lip to catch an errant droplet of broth. Her lashes fluttered as she murmured a deep "mmm."

Ashton cleared his throat. "I have mouthwash in my dressing room."

Madre de Dios, he was the *fucking worst* at this.

"So do I. But still." Jasmine's smile was flirtatious as she dropped the spoon into her apron pocket and turned away. Ashton checked the urge to reach out for her. From the corner of his eye, he caught the camera tracking them. Only years of experience prevented him from making eye contact with the camera as he resumed stirring the broth.

Carajo. That was the realest moment they'd shared together as themselves, and it would likely end up in the final cut. Oh well. So be it. Their characters were supposed to be growing closer, right? Flirting and rekindling their abandoned romance. It fit the scene. No one else would think twice.

But Ashton had been acting opposite Jasmine for a few weeks now, and he knew the heat in her eyes, in her voice, had been real. She'd been flirting with him, and he wasn't sure how to feel about that.

Not true. He felt great about it. Too bad he was so out of practice he lacked the ability to flirt back.

It was for the best. The only romance he was here for was the one unfolding in front of the camera.

When the director gave them a break before filming the kiss, Ashton ran back to his dressing room to clean his mouth more thoroughly than he ever had in his life.

He imagined Jasmine in her own dressing room undergoing the same pre-kiss ritual, then gargled with mouthwash one more time.

Out of habit, he checked his phone before heading back to set, and frowned when he saw a voice mail from his father. Holding it to his ear, he listened to the message.

"Hola mijo," Ignacio began, his typical greeting. "No te preocupes, todo está bien."

Ashton's heart sank. Whenever his father started with, "Don't worry, everything's fine," things were not, in fact, fine.

"We're going to the ER," Ignacio went on in Spanish. "Yadi fell out of a tree and hurt his wrist. I think it's just a sprain, but we're getting X-rays. And your grandfather's cough still hasn't gone away, so he's going to get checked out too. Mi madre is coming along for the ride."

With a final "don't worry," Ignacio ended the message. Ashton squeezed his eyes shut for a second, then called back. It rang, and rang, then went to voice mail. Resisting the urge to call back repeatedly until his father picked up, Ashton sent a text instead, telling Ignacio that he was filming but wanted updates as soon as they were available. Short of running to the airport and hopping a flight to Puerto Rico, there was nothing else he could do.

This wasn't Yadiel's first trip to the ER. The kid never stopped climbing, which meant he fell a lot too. But each time, Ashton wished he could be there for the day-to-day bandaging of bumps and bruises. And his grandfather was eighty-three, so even a summer cold was a concern.

Someone knocked. "They're ready for you," a PA called out.

"Gracias," Ashton replied. Coño. While worrying about his family, he'd completely forgotten that he was about to film his first kiss with Jasmine. Out of habit, he reached up to run his hands through his hair, then quickly jerked them away. He didn't want to explain to the hair stylists why his hair was suddenly a mess.

What he needed to do was calm down, but with his father incommunicado and no time to wait around for a reply, that seemed unlikely to happen.

Nothing to do but show up on set and hope for the best.

Chapter 13

EPISODE 3

Scene: Carmen and Victor kiss.
INT: Serranos' kitchen—NIGHT

Ilba gave the cue, and Dahlia picked up the cell phone sitting on the kitchen island. She glanced at the screen. "It's Tía Jimena. Un momentito."

She walked to the back of the kitchen and took the stairs, leaving the set.

At the counter, Carmen huffed. "She'll be gone an hour."

Victor crossed his arms and slid his hip along the edge of the counter, bringing himself closer to Carmen, smoothly getting inside her personal space without towering over her. He flashed her a charming grin.

"Do you think I have a chance at winning?"

Carmen gazed up at him from where she leaned her elbows on the edge of the island, assessing. "I think so. *If* you remember every step of the recipe, execute it all perfectly, and finish on time."

He barked out a laugh. "No pressure."

And because she understood him and the tremendous standards he held himself to, she repeated his words, but softly, with no sarcasm. "No pressure."

Some of the tension left Victor's face as he gazed at her, then he uncrossed his arms, lifting a hand to her cheek. His strong fingers skimmed over her face, curling around her neck. She fought a shiver at his touch.

"You have something here," he murmured in a low, sweetly seductive voice that had made his first album go platinum. He stroked his thumb in achingly gentle passes over her cheekbone.

Carmen knew it for what it was. A line, an excuse to touch her. The distance between them was killing him, and he couldn't keep his hands to himself anymore. She knew, because she felt it too.

But she was still going to call him on his bullshit.

"No, I don't." Her voice came out confident, but the words vibrated with need.

His surprise showed on his face in the slight widening, then narrowing, of his dark eyes. Maybe she hadn't been so forward when they'd been together before.

"You're right," he said. "You don't. I just . . . wanted to . . ."

This was it.

His fingers didn't tighten on the side of her neck. He didn't pull her. It was important to show that she wanted this as much as he did, that they were on the same page, partners in what was to come.

Carmen rose from where she leaned on the counter, lifting her chin up toward him, reaching for him. He slid his other arm around her waist and used her own forward momentum to bring her closer. In a single smooth move, they were suddenly tangled up in each other, in the heat and closeness, with the comforting smells of home all around them.

For a split second, their eyes met, an unspoken confirmation. Yes, this was happening. Yes, they both wanted this. And then they were leaning in, their mouths meeting in the middle in a crush of lips.

Carmen sank her fingers into Victor's hair as he fisted his hand in the back of her dress. Lips pressed and nipped, chests heaved, mouths gasped as they shared a passionate kiss that seemed like it could go on forever.

The silence surrounding them was deafening, the only sounds their soft moans and breaths, picked up by the boom mic above them. Their attention was 100 percent focused on each other, except . . .

Except for a nagging feeling that *something was missing*.

And then:

"Cut! Going again!"

Chapter 14

As soon as Ilba released them, Ashton gave Jasmine a cursory high five and disappeared. Exhausted, Jasmine grabbed her sweater and phone from her actor chair. When she turned it on, the screen lit up with a series of texts from her cousins in their Primas of Power group chat.

Ava: Don't keep us in suspense! How was the kiss?

Michelle: I bet it was weird.

Ava: Probably, but I still want to know what it was like to kiss . . . EL LEÓN DORADO.

Michelle: And I'm sure EL DUQUE DE AMOR is GREAT at kissing.

Ava: Better than EL MATADOR, certainly.

It went on from there, with the two of them speculating about Ashton's kissing prowess while sharing emojis related to his many telenovela roles.

With a groan, Jasmine went in search of coffee while she read. Once she had another cup in her possession, she went to her dressing room to reply.

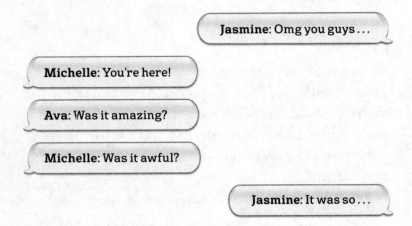

> **Jasmine:** Omg you guys . . .

> **Michelle:** You're here!

> **Ava:** Was it amazing?

> **Michelle:** Was it awful?

> **Jasmine:** It was so . . .

God, how could she even describe it?

> **Jasmine:** It was . . . fine.

After a short pause in which Jasmine imagined them howling in disbelief, Michelle's message popped up first.

> **Michelle:** FINE?

> **Ava:** Fine?????

> **Michelle:** WHAT DO YOU MEAN "FINE"?

Jasmine rubbed her forehead and took a deep chug of coffee before answering.

> **Jasmine**: Rehearsal went well, but then we didn't get to practice all the way through until it was time to film and then . . .

> **Michelle**: THEN WHAT

> **Jasmine**: And then the director made us shoot the take 17 FUCKING TIMES

She added a skull emoji to the end.

> **Ava**: OH MY GOD

Michelle sent a line of seventeen kiss emojis.

> **Ava**: That's so many times!

> **Jasmine**: Tell me about it!
> My face is sore!

> **Ava**: So what made it just "fine"?

This part was harder to put into words. Ilba hadn't been able to put her finger on it during filming either; she just knew it wasn't working. Ofelia had hovered around the edges, darting in occasionally to offer advice and suggestions. She must have asked if Jasmine felt "comfortable" at least fifty times—she'd clearly been prepped by Vera.

And Jasmine had been comfortable, at least for the first ten takes or so. As comfortable as one could be smashing faces with another human being in front of a room full of people. Ashton certainly wasn't the worst guy she'd ever had to kiss for a role. He smelled wonderful, and his lips were soft. And she'd be lying if she said she hadn't enjoyed being held in his arms. But still, there'd been something . . . missing . . . from the scene. Her mind kept drifting to Vera's instructions about the importance of communication.

Maybe it was just that simple. She and Ashton were missing the communication piece. True enough, they barely spoke to each other. She'd started to feel like he was warming up to her—she didn't think she'd imagined his reaction to her over the mofongo broth—but after that, he'd only looked at her when the script called for it.

Not to mention, their high fives were shameful. If they couldn't even get that right, how could they convince an audience that they were madly in lust?

And they had to. The show hinged on the rekindling of Carmen and Victor's romance. If they couldn't nail that, then what was the point? The show would flop. She'd be back to the dwindling world of soap operas, and it would be another mark against mainstream Latinx-led projects.

> **Jasmine:** I think we're just not communicating well.

Michelle: "Communicating." Is that what the kids call it these days?

Jasmine: You know what I mean. We never talk, so of course our characters are going to be weird around each other when it's time for THOSE scenes.

Ava: Is there one of THOSE scenes? Asking for a friend. Who is me.

Jasmine: I'm not 100% sure. We don't get the whole season of scripts in advance.

Michelle: What, are they scared they'll leak?

Jasmine: No, the writers are still working on later episodes as we film.

Ava: I don't think talking to him is a bad idea. You can get on the same page and agree to work together to make the show a success.

Michelle: LOL "on the same page." Nice one, Ava.

Ava added a winking emoji sticking out a tongue.

It seemed simple—just talk to him! But Ashton's behavior stirred up all her old fears of being rejected, and reaching out seemed like the most difficult task in the world. But if they weren't communicating well, sitting in separate dressing rooms between takes wasn't going to change that. He clearly wasn't going to bridge the gap between them, so that meant it was up to her.

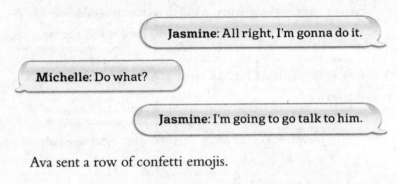

Jasmine: All right, I'm gonna do it.

Michelle: Do what?

Jasmine: I'm going to go talk to him.

Ava sent a row of confetti emojis.

Jasmine: Thanks, primas. What would
I do without you two?

Michelle replied with a winking kiss emoji.

Taking a deep breath, Jasmine freshened her lipstick, grabbed her script, and left the room.

WITH THE KITCHEN kiss complete, Ashton raced back to his dressing room to check his phone.

After finding a series of text updates—Abuelito Gus was given antibiotics and Yadiel's wrist was sprained but not broken—Ashton finally relaxed. Everyone was fine.

Except now he had time to think about what a disaster his performance today had been.

Seventeen takes? For a kiss that they'd rehearsed in detail? Ay Dios. He was losing his edge as a romantic male lead.

At thirty-eight, he worried about the gray hairs he'd started sporting in his beard and how much harder it had become to maintain his muscle tone. His skin care and workout routines were already ridiculous; he wasn't sure what else he could do in those areas, aside from finding a vampire to make him immortal. But if he did that, his grandmother would never speak to him again, so morning gym sessions and expensive lotions were all he had. But what if he was just a pretty face? He knew he had more to give as an actor, but now he was finally being given the chance to prove himself, and he was blowing it.

Jasmine had been amazing, immediately leaping into the emotions of the scene with each take and executing the kissing and heavy petting choreography perfectly. She had to have been getting tired of having his hands and mouth all over her, but she hadn't let any signs of exhaustion show. Ashton had taken strength from that. But he couldn't get out of his own head enough to let Victor take over 100 percent. And somehow, it had shown. Ilba, Ofelia, Marquita—none of them could place a finger on what was wrong with the scene, exactly. Just that something wasn't right.

Ashton couldn't argue with them. For one thing, he made a habit of not arguing with directors. But since he didn't know what was wrong, he didn't know how to fix it. So as much as it wasn't a hardship to be close to Jasmine—or her hot curves and lush mouth—he hadn't enjoyed it. It was *work*. And it sucked to feel like he wasn't doing well at his job.

Bypassing his new espresso machine for a sweeter option, Ashton popped a hazelnut pod into his dressing room's single cup coffee maker just as someone knocked on the door. It was so tentative, he wasn't sure it was a real knock, but he went to check anyway. On the other side, he found Jasmine staring up at him. Her dark eyes were hesitant, just like her knock.

"Hola," he said, then added, "Hello."

"Hi," she said, sounding shy. "Um, I was wondering if we could talk?"

God, she was gorgeous. *Esta es una mala idea.* But he stepped back to let her in, trying not to deeply inhale the sweet citrus scent trailing after her, a scent he'd been up close and personal with all day and which would be haunting his dreams all night. He poked his head into the hallway to make sure no one had seen her.

When he shut the door, her lips quirked into a small smile.

"What's wrong, scared to be seen with me?" she joked. Then her eyes widened and all traces of humor disappeared from her face. "Oh my god. You *are.* You're scared to be seen with me. *Shit.*" She squeezed her eyes shut and pressed a hand to her forehead. "I should've known. The McIntyre stuff. You've seen it. Of course you've seen it. How could you not?"

Ashton rushed in to try to soothe her, carefully placing his hands on her shoulders. It was more than he would have done with an acquaintance, but her distress was palpable. And really, after pretending to make out *seventeen times* in a row, touching her shoulders seemed pretty benign.

"Jasmine." Her name came out low, his voice more gravelly than he'd intended. "Yes, I did google you, but—"

"But what?" she interrupted. Her tone was brittle, but she didn't pull away from him. "Is that why you spilled coffee all over me? And why you're avoiding me? Are you a giant Mc-Intyre fan or something?"

He just stared at her, open-mouthed. A second later, they both burst into laughter.

Ashton stepped back and raised his hands in a shrug. "I don't even know who the guy is," he admitted. "But he seems like un pendejo, if you ask me."

"He *is*," Jasmine agreed vehemently. "The biggest pendejo."

"And I swear, the coffee was an accident."

Right then, the coffee maker sputtered, filling the room with a sweetly nutty scent, and they both turned to look at it.

"I'm just going to leave that alone," Ashton muttered, and Jasmine's lips pursed like she was holding back a smile.

"Probably for the best," she said, then gestured at the small sofa. "Can I sit?"

He nodded, but a sinking feeling dragged at his gut. He had some idea of what had brought her here. It wouldn't be the first time a female costar had proposed this, but it would be the first time in a long time he'd be tempted to say yes. Ever since Yadiel had been born, he had a strict policy against hooking up with costars. He'd tried dating with the intention of a relationship, but it had always gotten too complicated, and he'd finally given up. There was no room in his life for romance. Only the on-screen kind.

Although as Jasmine settled herself onto the sofa and crossed her long legs, he wished . . .

For something he couldn't have.

"Are you going to sit down?" she asked.

"Ah, sí." He perched on the rolling stool in front of the narrow counter.

"You disappeared pretty quickly," she remarked.

"I had to make a phone call."

She nodded, like she was waiting for him to offer more information, but when he didn't, she went on.

"There's something I wanted to propose—"

"Jasmine, I don't think it's such a good idea for us to—"

"You don't want to run lines together?" Her eyebrows dipped with hurt.

He blinked. "Run lines?"

"Yeah. You know, practice memorizing our lines?"

"Of course. I mean, yes, I know what—"

"Why, what did you think I was going to—"

Carajo, he'd really stepped in it now. The back of his neck burned with embarrassment. "I thought . . . never mind."

Her eyebrows arched. "Well, now you *have* to tell me."

It was going to sound horrible, but she pinned him with such a direct look, he couldn't think of a lie. "Ah, I thought you were going to . . . you know, suggest we . . ."

"What, *sleep together*?" she said, at the same time he said, "Practice kissing."

Jasmine shot to her feet, then froze. "Wait, what?"

Ashton rubbed the back of his neck and wished he really could disappear. "I thought you were going to say we should practice kissing since we did such a terrible job of it today."

She laughed. "No. I mean, yes, we did, but obviously that wasn't going to be my suggestion."

He gave a rueful smile. "Seventeen takes."

"*Exactly.* I mean, that's just embarrassing."

"I was thinking the same thing before you got here," he admitted. "It's totally embarrassing. I keep waiting for someone to bust in and revoke my Romantic Hero Card."

Her face broke into a grin. "Oh, stop."

"Verdad. That's who I thought was knocking."

She laughed full out, and he was struck again by her beauty, but also her openness. He was seeing the real Jasmine.

And he liked her.

No hay lugar en tu vida para ella, he reminded himself.

Still chuckling, Jasmine resumed her seat. "I'm sorry I accused you of accusing me of trying to proposition you. And I agree, we shouldn't practice kissing without Vera. But I do think she's on to something."

"Oh, yeah?" He couldn't help smiling. "Which part? Vera has a lot to say."

"The communication part." Jasmine worried her lower lip with her teeth and Ashton wished she'd stop. It was too enticing. "I just . . . I feel like we don't know each other. And you can't tell me you don't think it's affecting our performances."

"No. I can't." The words *well enough* echoed in his head.

Jasmine opened her shoulder bag and pulled out a script. "I brought episode four with me," she said. "We should talk about the scenes we're about to shoot, but I also think we need to debrief that terrible kiss."

"It was pretty bad," he agreed, then rushed to clarify. "Not you. But the whole thing . . ."

"We could've done better," she finished for him, then let out a breath. "Okay, communication time. I'll start by admitting that I was a little preoccupied."

"Preoccupied?" he prompted, eager to hear what she meant.

"Well." She shifted on the sofa like she was nervous, and her gaze darted away from his, ping-ponging around the room. "I can't help feeling . . . like you're mad at me."

His brow creased. She thought he was mad at her? "What would I have to be angry about?" he asked. "If anything, you're the one who should be mad at me for dumping an iced coffee on you."

She grimaced. "Yes, that was *very* cold. But you always run off after we're done filming, and never go out with the cast, so I . . . I thought it might be because of me."

She sounded so unsure and sad, he rushed to reassure her. "Jasmine, te lo prometo, no estoy enojado contigo."

When her brows drew together, he repeated the words in English. "I promise, I'm not mad at you."

She dropped her gaze. "You've probably guessed that I can't speak Spanish. Or at least, not fluently."

"That did occur to me," he said gently. "The audience won't be able to tell, though. You're doing great."

She rolled her eyes, and he was alarmed to see the sheen of moisture in them. "I feel like a fraud."

"Hey." He reached out to touch her then, scooting forward on the chair and circling her wrist with his fingers. Aiming to soothe, he stroked his thumb over the soft skin there. "They cast you for a reason. Carmen is fierce. She commands the space around her. I've seen clips of your other shows. You have that power."

She huffed out a humorless laugh. "I don't always feel like it."

Like a good scene partner, he matched her vulnerability with his own. "Jasmine, all I've ever wanted is to prove I'm more than just a telenovela hero. This is our chance to show everyone what we're made of. Me, with my accent that will never go away no matter how hard I try, and you, with your Nuyorican roots and toddler-level Spanglish."

She tried and failed to suppress a smile. "You're making fun of me."

"A little. It's not often I have the upper hand, language-wise." He grinned. "We'll help each other, okay?" He released her wrist and sat back in his chair. "We'll practice. We both have a lot riding on this."

She gave him a shrewd look. "I'm trying to shift the narrative away from my love life. What are you hoping to get out of this show?"

"I want to prove that I'm good enough for Hollywood," he said, then shrugged. "And yes, I want to make my last show regret killing my character off."

"So this is why you have a reputation for being conceited," she said with a smile.

"Conceited?" His eyes widened. "Who says that?"

"My cousins." She laughed at his dismissive eye roll.

"I'm not conceited," he scoffed. "I just want to be the best."

Jasmine's dark eyes sparkled with knowing, like she could see right through him. "I don't think that's it," she said, smooth as silk. "I think you already think you're the best, and you want everyone else to know it too."

His response came out low and flirtatious. "So, you've figured me out, Jasmine Lin."

Her eyes held his, and he could've sworn they were full of flames.

"Rodriguez," she whispered.

"¿Qué?"

She licked her lips. "Jasmine Lin Rodriguez. That's my full name."

Before he could talk himself out of it, he took a tremendous chance. "Ángel Luis."

At her quizzical look, he explained. "My name. It's not Ashton. It's Ángel Luis."

She repeated it, nailing the accent. The sound of his name— his real name—on her lips shot heat through him.

Then she said, "I did wonder where your parents had gotten a name like Ashton from."

And he laughed, breaking the tension. Tension he had no business encouraging. "They didn't," he admitted.

"Part of that big Hollywood goal?"

"Precisely."

She held up the script. "We'd better work on getting you there, then."

"Getting *us* there." He rolled to the end of the counter and picked up his own script. "Where should we begin?"

"You can begin by telling me why you were so preoccupied during the last shoot," she said, nailing him with a direct look. "I told you my reason."

He busied himself flipping through the pages and told a half-truth. "My grandfather went to the ER today. I was waiting for news."

Her face crumpled in concern. "Oh, I'm so sorry. Is everything okay? Is that why you went to Puerto Rico last weekend?"

Carajo, he'd forgotten he'd told her that when he'd run into her in the elevator. "Yes, that's why. And he's fine. Just a cough he let go unchecked for too long. They gave him stronger medicine."

"You must have been so worried," she murmured, and to his surprise, her genuine distress hit him right in the chest. He couldn't reply, so he just nodded.

"My grandparents mean the world to me," she went on. "They're getting older and I just . . . anyway, I get it. No wonder you were worried."

"Does that include your grandmother who adores me?" he asked, flashing a grin.

She groaned and covered her face with the script. "Oh my god, you remember that?"

"Of course. I'm full of myself, as you pointed out. I always remember compliments."

Laughing, she pretended to swat at him with the script. "Come on, let's practice our lines before they call us back."

Chapter 15

CARMEN IN CHARGE

EPISODE 4

Scene: Carmen and Victor have a heart-to-heart.
INT: Backstage tent at an outdoor concert—DAY

Carmen stormed into the tent with Victor close on her heels. As soon as the flap closed, she rounded on him, slapping a hand to his chest and squinting up at his face. She inhaled deeply, then stepped back, crossing her arms.

"I knew it." She sent him an accusing glare. "You're drunk."

"Cálmate, Carmencita—"

Her eyes flashed. "Don't tell me to calm down, and *don't* call me Carmencita."

"Fine, *Carmen*. But I'm not drunk. Just hungover."

"Oh, that's so much better." She let out a short, humorless laugh and jammed her hands onto her hips. And completely ignored the thrill she got when he rolled the *r* in Carmen.

He was doing it again, like he had throughout their marriage. Forcing her into the position of authority, making her act like his mother. She hated when he did this, and his immaturity had ultimately led to the downfall of their marriage.

Or at least, this was the context they'd determined in rehearsal with Vera and Marquita.

"I'm okay to finish the set," Victor said, but he was sweating, and his eyes were glassy.

Carmen didn't even bother to respond to that. "I should've known this would happen the second those idiotas showed up. Your little entourage has always been a bad influence on you. This is the whole reason why you're living in my parents' house, Victor. The whole reason why we're doing all of this." Her voice turned pleading. "Why are you letting them ruin your progress?"

At that, Victor slumped into a folding chair and dropped his head into his hands. After a long beat, he blew out a breath and lifted his head. His expression was bleak. "You're right."

Carmen stood very still. She didn't know how to handle a Victor who expressed emotions readily, much less one who agreed with her. It wasn't in Victor's nature, especially not where his friends were involved. When he lowered his face again, though, she stepped forward, her feet moving of their own volition.

"Oye." She took his face in her hands and gently raised his chin. "Mírame."

They held each other's gazes for a long, quiet moment, then Carmen leaned down and pressed a soft kiss to his forehead.

Victor exhaled, some of the tension draining out of his body. "I don't know how else to act around them," he said, and his voice held a note of confession.

"Around who?"

"Mi grupito, as you called them. The guys."

"What do you mean, you don't know how else to act?"

He shrugged, and she dropped a hand to his shoulder, massaging absently.

"They've been my friends since the beginning, my hype guys. But they expect me to act like the playboy, the star. Always cool, always down to party. But they're also my biggest fans. So I feel like I need to, I don't know, live up to that image, so they keep on supporting me."

"Oh, Victor." Carmen smiled, even though her heart was breaking a little. This man had always had the ability to hurt her, and yet, she'd loved him. Still loved him, in some ways. "*I* was your biggest fan."

As the truth of her words sank in, his expression cleared, and his eyes searched her face. She wished she knew what he was looking for.

"Lo siento, Carmen." His voice was soft as he caressed her cheek. She couldn't help leaning into his touch. "I have so many . . . regrets. Especially where you're concerned. I shouldn't have let my friends come between us."

"We both made mistakes," she admitted. "I was hurt. I could've reacted differently."

"You shut me out," he reminded her, but there was no censure in his tone. Only memory.

"I know." Her own voice sounded wistful, sad. He wasn't the only one with regrets. "But you were doing so much better. What happened last night?"

He sighed. "One of them saw pictures of us on the red carpet. His sister still follows my career, and she showed him. So they made a plan to get together last night, hit me up on our old group text, and—"

"And you snuck out of my parents' house like a teenager to go hang out with your friends?" She smiled to show she was teasing.

He huffed out a short laugh. "Yeah, basically."

"But why, Victor?" This was the part she couldn't understand. "You agreed to avoid this kind of temptation. You knew the concert was today. Why jeopardize everything for a night out drinking?"

His gaze fell, like he couldn't meet her eyes. Silence stretched between them before he answered. "I'm afraid."

Sensing they were on a precipice here, Carmen kept her voice barely above a whisper. "Of what?"

He swallowed. "I'm afraid that if I don't live up to the image, or do what everyone expects of me, that they'll all find out the truth."

Heart in her throat, Carmen brushed his hair back with her fingers. "What truth?"

His eyes shot to hers, and they blazed with emotion. "That I'm nothing."

It would be a perfect commercial break moment, but they didn't have that. There was nothing to alleviate the tension stretching taut between them. Carmen's breath trembled out. Her heart ached for him. "How can you—"

"It's all just an illusion, a spectacle, hinged on a pretty voice and some talented music producers." His voice was harsh now, and he got to his feet to pace the small area inside the tent. "If I don't keep playing the part, like a goddamned trained monkey, they'll all find out there's nothing but smoke and mirrors, and I'll lose everything."

"Who?" Carmen demanded. "If who finds out?"

"Everyone." He slashed a hand through the air, getting really worked up now. "The fans. The media. *You*."

"Me?" She stared, taken aback. "I know you better than anyone. I was your *wife*."

He came back to her then and took her face in his hands. "I was worried about you most of all. Don't you see? If I'd really let you in, if I'd really let you see me, you'd know."

Her breathing came fast. She gripped his wrists but didn't pull him off her. "Know what?"

His expression was bleak. "That you deserved better than me."

Her breath seized in her throat, wringing out the truth. "But I wanted *you*."

There was pain in his eyes as he asked, "Do you still?"

Her reply was faint, but clear as a bell. "Yes."

Victor brought his mouth down on hers in a searing kiss.

Carmen kissed him back fiercely, then broke away to meet his eyes. "Victor. Listen to me. You're not nothing."

"I am. I am." The words came out like a moan as he trailed his mouth down her neck, leaving a path of hot kisses. "I've proven it to you so many times over. Why don't you believe it yet?"

"Because I believe in *you*, estúpido. And I'm never wrong."

His laugh was cut off when she dragged his face back to hers and fused their mouths together. When he came up for air, he was breathless, but smiling. "I hate how bossy you are."

She scoffed and reached down to place a hand over the front of his pants. "You love it."

He groaned. "You're right. I love it."

Then he lifted her up. She clamped her thighs around his hips. The move shoved her skirt up, and he grasped her bare legs with his strong hands. The heat from his fingers seared into her thighs, sending a bolt of genuine arousal through her as his lips moved hungrily against hers.

He broke the kiss to look for a surface to set her on. But the second he spotted the rickety folding table at one end of the tent, the walkie on Carmen's waistband squawked.

"Carmen?" a tinny voice called out. "We need Victor on stage in five."

Breathing hard, Victor looked to Carmen, their noses inches apart. "Think we can do this in five minutes?"

Her bland stare was unamused. "Victor, put me down."

With a disappointed sigh, he set her on her feet, then helped her straighten her hair and her clothes.

"Well, at least you look more alert now," she remarked, reaching up to fix his hair.

"Oh, I am." His voice was thick with innuendo.

She glanced down at his pants, then gave him a stern look. "You better get that under control before you give the audience the wrong kind of show."

"Keep bossing me around and it's not going anywhere. I told you, I love it."

That made her laugh. She gave him a small peck on the lips, glad that he was in better spirits.

"You're not nothing," she said fiercely. "And everyone knows it. I think that's what really worries you."

His brows creased. "What?"

"If everyone knows you're extraordinary"—she jabbed a finger in his chest—"then you have to know it too. And it means you can't get away with acting like a scared little boy anymore. But we'll deal with that later. Come on."

She took his hand and led him out of the tent.

"Cut!"

Chapter 16

Outside the tent set, Jasmine turned to Ashton, adrenaline coursing through her. With a big smile on his handsome face, he raised his hand. She smacked it with her own. The sound rang out and the slap reverberated through her palm. Now *that* was a satisfying high five.

"We *did that*," she said.

"Hell yeah, we did," he agreed.

On the sideline, Ofelia, the first AD, was positively beaming. "Whatever you're doing, keep it up," she said.

The episode four director came over too. "Playback looks good. Let's go from wide to medium."

Ashton shot Jasmine a thumbs-up, and she grinned back, but deep down, she knew she was a *liar, liar, pants on fire*. In Ashton's dressing room, she'd acted all shocked and offended at the thought of them sleeping together. She deserved a damn Oscar for that performance, because there was nothing objectionable about the idea at all. Even now, her traitorous mind couldn't stop replaying the sensation of his hands gripping her thighs.

Shit, she was experiencing the warning signs of a crush—the second point on the Jasmine Scale. That warm feeling in her solar plexus, as if they had a connection that was pulling her toward him. The desire to make him smile, asking questions and hanging on his every word when he answered, looking for hints that he might be crushing on her too.

It's all in your head, she told herself. *This isn't real.*

God, she was so predictable. Michelle was going to have a field day with this. Jasmine had developed a crush on nearly every cute guy she'd spoken to since the age of twelve, and she was terrible at hiding those feelings from her cousins.

But maybe she shouldn't hide them. Maybe her cousins' interference was exactly what she needed.

After they completed all the takes for the scene, Jasmine grabbed her phone from her chair and hurried back to her room. Once alone, she dashed off a text to Ava and Michelle.

> **Jasmine:** Quick. Remind me why having a fling with Ashton is a really bad idea.

Ava replied first.

> **Ava:** Because a Leading Lady is whole and happy on her own.

Her reply was so fast, Jasmine was sure Ava had copied Jasmine's list onto her own phone, just for this occasion. Michelle answered next.

> **Michelle:** And Leading Ladies don't piss where they eat.

Jasmine scowled at the screen.

> **Jasmine:** I don't think that was an
> official point on the list.

Michelle's reply was quick.

> **Michelle:** Two words: Seth Thomas.
> Two more words: Abuela's party.

Oh god, she was right. Jasmine had to get her growing attraction to Ashton under control before she did something stupid, like she had with Seth.

She'd been casually dating Seth Thomas, one of her costars on *Sunrise Vista*, a short-lived daytime soap about architects, before the writers decided to make their characters an item. Seth had interpreted this to mean he could take certain liberties with Jasmine on set. When she'd suggested they handle the scenes like professionals, he'd accused her of "running hot and cold"—among other things—and stormed off to his trailer.

Definitely not an experience she cared to repeat.

She also had to figure out a way to invite Ashton to the party. They were on better terms now, but she still didn't feel comfortable asking him yet. Especially after spilling how much her grandmother adored him. Ashton didn't say much, but she'd noticed that he kept to himself and avoided the press. What if he thought she was trying to use him? Or set him up? Maybe he didn't like fan attention. Would he think less of her grandma?

She'd have to kill him if he thought badly of her grandma, and that didn't bode well for a second season of *Carmen in Charge*.

Maybe private rehearsals weren't such a great idea after all. She couldn't deny that running lines with him had helped their performance in episode four, but it had the potential to wreak havoc on her Leading Lady Plan.

His sweet awkwardness was too endearing, especially when coupled with the face and body of a god and an outwardly aloof demeanor. Plus, he made her laugh, and he cared about his family. How could she not fall for him?

But she *couldn't*. Not this time. For once, she was going to cockblock her stupidly romantic heart.

Something else occurred to her, and she shot off another text to her cousins.

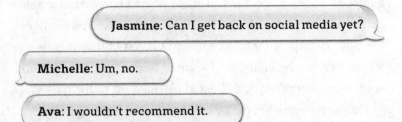

Jasmine: Can I get back on social media yet?

Michelle: Um, no.

Ava: I wouldn't recommend it.

Jasmine let out a sigh. She had Ava monitoring her accounts and Michelle keeping up with the Google alert. They were supposed to let her know when the gossip reporters had tired of speculating about her and McIntyre. In the meantime, she was staying off social media and the internet, and avoiding anywhere that sold entertainment magazines. It was easier while she was working on set, but it also meant she couldn't post any cute behind-the-scenes clips to drum up fan interest in *Carmen*.

If Ava and Michelle were suggesting she stay away, it meant the stories were still circulating. The last magazine she'd seen had claimed she was sending McIntyre late-night texts begging him to take her back. In reality, she'd blocked his number from her phone, but the lies still hurt.

Stupid McIntyre. She couldn't even kill time scrolling on Instagram because of him.

She didn't think she'd thrown herself at him, per se, as one particularly nasty "anonymous source" had claimed, but, with the clarity of hindsight, she knew that she'd done everything in her power to make him feel loved and appreciated. The way she wanted to feel.

Clingy. Obsessive. Desperate. Embarrassing.

Those were the kinds of words that showed up in the gossip pieces, but they weren't new to her. She'd been accused of being clingy ever since middle school, after Everett Giordano dumped her in sixth grade. She'd sprawled on her bedroom floor listening to her sister's Alanis Morissette CD for a week after that, because that's what she'd seen girls in movies do after a breakup. Everett had been the first to shatter her heart, but not the last. And eventually she'd gotten much better about breakups.

No, not breakups. Getting *dumped*. Just like the magazine cover on her grandmother's refrigerator door declared. Jasmine got dumped. Always. She never did the dumping because . . . well, because she was so afraid of being alone that she clung to guys she'd be better off kicking to the curb.

Guys like McIntyre. Like Seth Thomas. Like Everett Giordano.

How many more reasons did she need? Crushes were for suckers.

She opened the small fridge under the counter and pulled out a bottle of seltzer.

Her cousins said she was just picking the wrong guys, but sometimes, Jasmine wasn't so sure. After all, she was the common factor here.

A new text came through on her phone from a number she didn't recognize.

> **Unknown**: Since I'm leaving earlier today, do you want to meet me in the hotel gym tonight to go over the script for ep 5? —Ash

Warmth bubbled over her, bringing heat to her cheeks. Her lips spread in a small smile.

Without a second thought, she wrote back.

> **Jasmine**: Absolutely. 7pm?

> **Ashton**: Perfecto. See you there.

After adding his number into her phone under the name Ángel Luis, Jasmine switched back to the Primas of Power group text. Her thumb hovered over the empty message box. Then, instead of typing something, she shut the phone off, dropped it into her bag, and went back to set.

ASHTON HAD MADE a terrible mistake.

When he'd suggested Jasmine meet him in the hotel's fitness center, he figured it would be neutral ground. Less intimate than their dressing rooms or hotel suites, innocuous enough that no one would think anything of two costars reading from their scripts on separate machines. And with the scent of bleach and sweat in the air, not at all sexy.

But when Jasmine walked into the small workout space, Ashton caught sight of her in the mirrored wall and nearly fell off the treadmill.

Jasmine's face was clear of makeup and she wore her thick brown hair in a high ponytail, but in a hot pink sports bra and black yoga pants, she looked anything but plain. Spandex encased her curves enticingly, and she exuded strength and sensuality. She carried her script and a stainless steel water bottle in one arm, with a towel draped over her shoulder.

She greeted him with a sunny smile and a wave. He just gave her a nod, because he seemed to have swallowed his tongue.

Jasmine set her things in the treadmill's cup holders while Ashton tried not to stare at her ass. Why was women's workout gear so *tight*? His own tank top and shorts were loose. Wouldn't she have been more comfortable in a poncho or something?

Hell, she'd probably still find a way to make a poncho look sexy.

After setting her treadmill to a brisk walk, Jasmine flipped open the script.

"Let's start the way Vera does," she said. "What's the context?"

"Context?" He had no idea what she was talking about. He was trying to focus on running and not on the way her breasts bounced delightfully as she walked.

"Yeah. You know—what's happening in the episode?"

"This is the dancing one, right?"

"Right. Carmen tries to get Victor on that competition show where celebrities team up with professional dancers." She read the notes. "Do you know how to dance salsa?"

"Of course I do," he scoffed. "Do you?"

"Well, yeah," she said, laughing. "My mom taught me basic steps for salsa and tinikling."

"I don't think I've heard of that one," Ashton admitted.

"It's a traditional folk dance from the Philippines," she explained. "It's like doing double Dutch with long bamboo poles on the ground."

She demonstrated a few moves right there on the treadmill, rotating 360 degrees as she bounced her feet from the belt to the side rails and back.

Ashton gave a little clap. "I bet you were un petardito jumping rope. A little firecracker."

"Absolutely. All the other girls made me teach them how to do it too." She sent him a sidelong glance. "You like running, huh?"

"Clears my mind." The treadmill's incline setting changed and he dug in, relishing the burn. "I prefer running outside, but my producers in the past insisted I stay out of the sun."

When she gave him a curious look, he tapped the skin on his arm. "Can't be too dark in telenovelas, and I'm already pushing it."

She rolled her eyes. "Riiiight. Nice to see colorism is still alive and well in the Latinx community."

"It's gotten better now, but when I started acting, it was

really bad. If I tanned even a little bit, they'd get all bent out of shape." He shook his head, remembering the not-so-tactful comments he'd gotten before his career had taken off. "You know how hard it is to avoid the sun in Miami?"

"I get you." Jasmine upped the speed on her machine, her stride confident and energetic. "When I worked in commercials, I auditioned for all the 'racially ambiguous' roles. But even if there were a lot of people being hired, there was this whole *Highlander* 'there can be only one' mentality. They'd use me to check off the 'brown girl' box on their list and fill the rest of the commercial with white people."

He made a sound of disgust. "Lazy casting directors."

"Lazy agent too. This was before I signed with Riley, my current agent. She's biracial Chinese, so she understands me, but my first one would send me to casting calls for all kinds of ethnicities. In some cases, I'd show up at the audition and be totally mortified, especially since I was still using Rodriguez in my name. I finally put my foot down and refused to go to 'ethnic' casting calls unless they specifically listed South East Asian or Latina."

"What kind of commercials did you do?"

"Oh, lots." She squinted at the ceiling while she thought about it. "Shampoo, baby diapers, face wash, canned soup. Nothing super embarrassing."

"My first real role was playing a ranch hand," Ashton said. "I was twenty-three, living in Mexico, and I told them I could ride horses."

"Could you?"

He shrugged, feet pounding the treadmill belt in a steady,

metronomic rhythm he found so calming. "I'd sat in a saddle a few times, but I was not, by any means, a cowboy. Saying I could ride was a total exaggeration, and let me tell you, that horse knew it."

She laughed. "But you've played other roles that involved horses, right?"

"Well, yeah. After that, I figured I'd better learn to ride for real."

She gave him a sly look. "My cousin Michelle liked the show where you were a sheriff."

"*Las leyes del corazón y la insignia.*" He inclined his head. "That one is a fan favorite."

She tapped her chin. "I don't think I've worked with any horses. But my storyline on *The Glamour Squad* involved a poodle, and I had a recurring role on *The Young and the Restless* that required me to hold a hamster."

Ashton shook his head. "I can't imagine playing the same character for decades," he said, thinking about the English soap operas that ran for generations. He wanted to challenge himself, to improve his skills—but more than that, he wanted the recognition that went with it.

Jasmine shrugged. "It's good, steady work. Viewers get to watch the characters grow and develop over time. They become familiar." She shot him an exasperated glance. "Are you really going to keep running while we rehearse?"

"Ah, no." But he didn't stop. Running was the only thing keeping him from embarrassing them both. He'd managed not to sprout an erection while filming their make-out scenes together, but something about her bouncing around in spandex was really doing it for him. "What else happens in this episode?"

Jasmine skimmed through the pages as she walked. "There are some scenes where Victor struggles to record new music. Carmen has a heart-to-heart with her father about the family legacy, and Victor auditions for the dance show producers. But he doesn't get picked."

"Poor Victor. He'll be crushed." Ashton could relate. Even though it came with the territory of being an actor, it sucked not to get the part.

"It looks like the show's producers think he's too unreliable— thanks to canceling the tour—so they don't accept him."

"Luckily he has Carmen to comfort him."

"Yes, but she's Carmen, so you know she's going to make it a teachable moment." Jasmine reached over and tapped the rolled-up script he'd stuffed into the drink holder. "Ready to start?"

"Um, sure." Ashton lowered the speed on the treadmill and wiped his face with a towel. He had to get his desire for her in check. Thank god this episode required less touching.

When he lowered the towel, he caught sight of Jasmine's face and rushed to pause his treadmill.

Eyes wide, jaw slack, she stared at the wall-mounted TV in abject horror. Ashton reached over to shut off her machine before she tripped, then turned to see what she was looking at.

Puñeta. That pendejo McIntyre filled the screen, leaning in to talk to a very pretty, very young-looking entertainment reporter. The sound was off, but the closed-captioning appeared at the bottom: *So, McIntyre, tell us about your new girlfriend. A* second later, Jasmine's face appeared in a box in the corner, next to a photo of another woman who shared an uncanny resemblance.

Before Ashton could say a word, Jasmine scrambled off the treadmill and dashed over to the TV. With desperate movements, she ran her fingers over the edges, probably looking for an off button. When she didn't find it, she reached behind the TV and yanked the plug. The screen went black.

Breathing hard, she kept her back to him, but Ashton could see her stricken expression in the mirrors.

"I'm sorry," she said, her voice hoarse. "But that—"

"I know." Ashton got off his treadmill and went to stand next to her.

When she didn't move, Ashton placed a hand on her shoulder and gently led her to the weight bench to sit. Then he retrieved her water bottle and brought it to her. He sat next to her while she took a long drink.

When she finally lowered the bottle, her expression was bleak.

"Can I tell you the worst part?" she whispered.

He would have given her anything she asked for in that moment. "Dime. I mean, tell me."

She swallowed hard and hunched her shoulders. "I don't even think I liked him that much. I just . . . wanted to be liked. And I thought he did."

Ashton's heart broke for her. What could he say to that? More than anything, he wanted to take her in his arms, to comfort her. But they weren't close like that. Victor and Carmen were, but Ashton and Jasmine weren't.

Still, she'd just revealed something big, and he needed to respond. *I like you* was on the tip of his tongue, but instead, he took her hand and just held it. When her fingers tightened, he stroked her knuckles with his thumb.

She gave herself a little shake. "My cousins want me to move back to New York. Because of all . . . that." She gestured at the blank TV screen with her free hand.

"You grew up here, right?"

She nodded. "Most of my immediate family is here. My grandparents on my mother's side live in San Diego, but the Rodriguez side? They're here. New York is home."

"But you live in Los Angeles now."

"It's where the soaps film, but I dread going back." She gave a sad little shrug. "The traffic, the stress, the fake friends . . . I don't even know which of my so-called friends took money in exchange for giving anonymous statements to the tabloids—multiple people, I suspect, probably even some of my castmates on *The Glamour Squad*. How do you know who to trust after something like that?"

"No sé," he said. "Yo sólo confío en mi familia."

Her forehead scrunched, like she was trying to translate in her head. "I only . . . something . . . in my family. Sorry, I don't know that word. Confío."

He gave her hand a squeeze, then let go. "Trust," he said. "Confiar means to trust."

She nodded, and the hand he'd just released clenched into a fist.

"I hate LA," Ashton said, trying to lighten the mood. He stretched out his legs and crossed them at the ankles. "Do I want to work in Hollywood? Absolutely. But I don't think I could ever live there full time."

He didn't mention that he didn't want his son growing up there. Or that California was too far from Puerto Rico.

He didn't say any of that, which wasn't unusual. What was unusual was that he *wanted* to. He wanted to open up and confide in Jasmine. He suspected she'd be a good listener. But then she'd look at him with compassion in those stunning eyes of hers, and he'd be lost. And he couldn't afford to lose himself when his whole family relied on him to stay strong.

Instead, he just said, "Let's rehearse. And you can show all of them how wrong they are about you."

"Thank you." Her smile was sweet, but sad. "I mean that."

As they returned to the treadmills and picked up their scripts, Ashton wondered what it would be like if they were two different people in a different situation. If he were just a single dad who didn't have to worry about keeping his son's existence a secret, and if Jasmine were just a woman who didn't have national media attention focused on her.

What would she think if she knew about Yadiel?

But she couldn't know. And that was that.

Chapter 17

After a few days, Jasmine worked up the nerve to ask Ashton to help her practice Spanish. She'd worked on it a little with Miriam and Peter, but asking Ashton for help seemed like a bigger deal. Not that she thought he'd say no—their rapport had improved substantially, especially after their talk at the gym—but because she still felt self-conscious about her command of the language.

She thought they'd practice in one of their dressing rooms, so she was surprised when he suggested they go to the grocery store near the hotel one evening after filming.

It was one of those Manhattan supermarkets with high shelves, narrow aisles, and fancy food. Ashton claimed he actually needed to buy groceries, but Jasmine didn't fully believe he needed the ginger ale and peanut butter in his basket.

They were incognito, Ashton in another guayabera shirt, cargo shorts, and leather sandals, plus a Yankees hat and a pair of sunglasses he removed once they were inside. Jasmine wore yoga pants, a plain white T-shirt, and sneakers, with her hair in a messy bun. She imagined they looked like a good-looking upper-class Latinx couple, shopping for a dinner they'd cook together in their Upper East Side apartment. He was a doctor maybe, and she . . . a Pilates instructor?

Whoa, wait a second. Why couldn't she be the doctor? And Ashton a . . . personal trainer, maybe. It was easy—and delightful—to picture him demonstrating proper exercise form.

As they strolled up and down the aisles, Jasmine tried to stop sneaking appreciative glances at him and imagining them as different characters. He was here to help her out—nothing more. Well, maybe to buy some peanut butter.

But he was just so handsome, even in his Rich Latino Dad disguise.

She shouldn't have gone to meet him at the gym. And she definitely shouldn't have worn her best sports bra, the one that gave lift and separation instead of uni-boob. She knew it wasn't playing fair, but Ashton's reaction had been worth it.

On a personal level. On a professional level, she was annoyed with herself. She wasn't supposed to be making herself attractive for him.

But then, there'd been nothing attractive about her reaction to seeing McIntyre on TV. She'd been scared to return to the Hutton Court's fitness room, in case she'd broken it. And when she thought about how much she'd opened up to Ashton, she got a flush of embarrassment. He was a good listener, easy to talk to. So different from the character he played—Ashton was quieter and far more reserved than Victor—but there must have been some part of him that connected with Victor, because he was able to turn the sexy on like a light switch.

And he had looked so freaking hot, running hard in those

clingy shorts, with his bare, muscled arms pumping. Thanks to their scenes as Carmen and Victor, she'd known he was hiding some serious muscles under his costumes, but seeing him revealed had been worth the wait.

"¿Y esto?" Ashton held up a box of saltines.

Jasmine sighed and stopped eyeing Ashton's ass. "Galletas. I told you, I already know words for food."

He shook the box at her and said in a patient tone, "Usa la palabra en una oración completa."

A complete sentence. Fine. "Um . . . me gusta comer galletas con . . . queso?"

He replaced the crackers on the shelf. "Adequate, but maybe come up with a different sentence starter than 'I like.' So far you've said you like bread, wine, and now crackers with cheese."

"I do like bread, wine, and crackers with cheese," she grumbled, then took the box back off the shelf and put it in her basket. "Speaking of, let's go get some cheese."

"En español," he reminded her in a singsong voice.

She rolled her eyes, but grinned. "Vamos a buscar el queso. Happy?"

"Claro que sí." From under the brim of his fitted cap, he sent her a warm smile that made her toes curl in her Adidas.

On the way to the dairy section, "I Wanna Dance with Somebody" came on over the grocery store's speakers.

"Hold up. I love this song." Jasmine stopped in the middle of the aisle and did a few dance moves as she sang along softly with Whitney Houston.

Ashton raised his eyebrows and repeated the words in Spanish, but he turned it into a question. "¿Quieres bailar con alguien?"

She sent him a cheeky grin and said, "Sí," as if he'd actually meant to ask her to dance with him.

To her surprise, he inclined his head and said, "Bueno." Before she knew what was happening, he took her hand, spinning her under his arm before twirling her out, then back in toward his body, where he caught her in a dance hold.

Jasmine spun to a stop, breathing hard from surprise and from being so close to him. His body was warm and hard, and he smelled delicious. His hand held hers in a solid grip, different from the way he'd gently stroked her fingers while comforting her at the gym. She wanted to keep dancing. Or undress him with her teeth. Either one would be fine.

But they were in a grocery store, so instead, she changed the subject. "You have your dance scene tomorrow, right?"

"Sí."

"Are you nervous?" At his pointed look, she repeated the question in Spanish. "¿Estás nervioso?"

He shook his head, then looked past her, toward the end of the aisle. "No, I . . ."

When he trailed off, Jasmine followed his gaze. By the freezer section, a woman wearing an apron with the store's name on it looked down at her phone screen, but she held it at an awkward angle, almost as if . . .

As if she were taking their picture.

Jasmine's stomach dropped to her feet. This was truly the worst part of fame—the loss of privacy, of anonymity. She felt raw, exposed, and . . . bitter. She couldn't even act silly in an overpriced supermarket without worrying about someone watching her.

Ashton's jaw tightened. He released Jasmine abruptly and slipped his sunglasses back on. "We should be more careful."

Jasmine nodded. "You're right."

Leading Ladies only end up on magazine covers with good reason.

Galletas con queso and "I Wanna Dance with Somebody" were *not* good reasons.

"Let's go." Ashton turned his back to the woman and left the aisle in the opposite direction. They paid for their items in silence and exited the store.

Back at the hotel, they didn't speak much except to say good night, and Jasmine returned to her room alone. In the suite's tiny kitchen, she put away her items—she'd gotten the crackers, but no cheese to go with them—and wondered what might have happened if the woman with the phone hadn't interrupted them.

JASMINE'S NERVES ABOUT the grocery store didn't last. As she was getting ready for bed, she received an email alerting her to some changes. Everyone had been so happy with how she and Ashton were performing together that they'd written her into the dance scenes.

She'd rushed through her moisturizing routine—every time she was tempted to skip a step, she heard her grandmother's voice in her head warning her about wrinkles—and flung herself into bed with her tablet. She opened the script file and flipped through at warp speed.

Some actors got better with reading and memorizing lines as they progressed. Some always struggled with it. Jasmine was in the third camp, and it was what had made her excellent at soaps—she could speed-read like nobody's business, and had an excellent memory for things like song lyrics, poems, and, most importantly, scripts.

She found the scene where Victor was supposed to practice for his meeting with the producers. She and Ashton had already rehearsed it, with Jasmine reading the part of the producers. Originally, the intention was to show Victor on his own, without Carmen. But now . . . Jasmine kept skimming. In the updated version, Victor insisted Carmen be his dance partner for the rehearsal and audition.

Jasmine checked the call sheet. Apparently production was bringing in two pro dancers to help them practice for the scenes. Which meant . . .

She was going to get to dance with Ashton.

Since she was alone, Jasmine punched her fist into the air and yelled, "Yes!"

Then she gathered the tablet to her chest and let herself picture it. The few steps they'd danced together in the grocery store had left her craving more. His body was so strong and steady, and as she'd observed from watching him run on the treadmill, he moved with fluid grace. The thought of dancing in his arms, generating heat for the camera, and giving Carmen the chance to really let loose thrilled her. She couldn't *wait*.

In the midst of fantasizing, Jasmine also experienced a spark of pride for the show's writers. The change was very much in character for Victor, especially after he'd insisted Carmen be his red-carpet date in the second episode, and it allowed for more up close and personal on-screen interaction between Carmen and Victor, which the viewers would love.

The only downside was that Jasmine now had new lines to learn, *and* a dance routine. But she was excited. She went to sleep that night with a smile on her face.

When she arrived at the dance studio the next day, worry gnawed at her. Would Ashton pull away from her again after possibly being photographed in the grocery store? But her fear was surpassed by her anticipation at getting to dance with him. She swung by craft services for a protein bar and coffee, then hurried inside the real dance studio where they would rehearse.

A PA directed her to a spacious room, complete with floor-to-ceiling mirrors, a ballet barre, sound system, and shiny light wood floor. Narrow windows overlooked Forty-Fifth Street.

Jess and Nik, the dancers who'd been hired to choreograph Carmen and Victor's salsa, were beautiful, professional, and—Jasmine could tell just from the way they looked at each other—100 percent in love with each other. Jess was petite, with creamy brown skin and gorgeous curls. Nik had a quick smile and a thick Brooklyn accent, and he moved like a leopard.

The first thing the dancers asked, after introductions, was whether Jasmine and Ashton had any experience dancing salsa. When they both nodded, Jess clapped her hands in delight.

"Well, that just makes things so much easier, doesn't it?"

Nik turned on a Gloria Estefan song. "Why don't you two show us a little of what you can do?"

Jasmine's breath caught in her throat. This was the opposite of what they'd done with Vera, who outlined and directed every move before they made it. While it had initially been weird, it also took away the awkwardness of just jumping into an intimate encounter with the other actor—which, she supposed, was the whole point of having an intimacy coordinator attached to the production. Today, they were on their own.

Ashton held out his hand and Jasmine met his eyes. She'd have killed to know what he was thinking right then. Was he excited to dance with her? Annoyed? She couldn't tell. But she took his hand, and just like that, they were dancing.

Years of ingrained muscle memory took over. Jasmine had learned these moves at a very young age, and had danced them with her abuelos and tíos at every wedding, birthday, and christening she'd ever attended. Her spine arched into the proper pose as her feet picked up the beat and her hips connected to the rhythm. Salsa music was in her blood, the combination of congas, trumpets, and smoky vocals flowing through her and begging her to move with them.

And Ashton . . .

Ashton knew how to lead.

He took her through spins and twirls, giving her slight cues through his hand on her back, or a tug on her fingers. She moved to the music, following his guidance, all of her attention glued to him. There was a light in his eyes she'd never seen before, and his lips curved in a confident smile that had her melting inside.

Now she knew why he'd said he wasn't nervous about dancing. He was *amazing* at this.

Their dance only lasted a few seconds before Nik turned the music off, and Jasmine's heart cried out for more. She was breathing fast when she turned to face the others, but it wasn't from exertion.

Ashton had left her breathless.

And he was still holding her hand.

He gave her fingers the slightest squeeze, then released her. And Jasmine's treasonous heart soaked it up like it was a declaration of love.

"You two clearly have moves," Nik said, coming over to join them.

"And chemistry," Jess added, beaming. "This makes our job a lot easier, as we can focus on form and choreography. Sound good?"

They got to work, and it was the most fun Jasmine could remember having on set in a long time. No offense to Vera.

When the day was over, Jasmine was tired, but exhilarated. For the first time, she let herself imagine the audience response to *Carmen*. It was something she shut off while filming, because if she acted with the audience reaction in mind, it would trap her in her own head and damage the performance. But with the way the last few episodes had gone, she was sure people would love it.

She just hoped enough of them watched to warrant a second season. She was growing to adore Carmen and Victor, and she was curious to see what the writers would do with more episodes.

Riding high, Jasmine stopped Ashton on his way to their double-banger trailer and made the offer before her common sense could catch up.

"Want to practice tonight?" she asked, her voice nonchalant. "You can swing by my room."

He looked at her for a moment that seemed to last forever while she waited for his answer.

In the back of her mind, common sense finally piped up like a warning alarm.

Bad idea bad idea bad id—

"Sure," he said, and she couldn't stop the flash of pleasure she felt at his agreement.

The voice of common sense nagged at her as she entered her side of the trailer, through changing and removing her makeup, and into the black SUV that would drive her back to the Hutton Court. Finally, she couldn't ignore it anymore and reached out to the Primas of Power.

Jasmine: Help. I've done something incredibly stupid.

Chapter 18

Ashton didn't know what had possessed him to accept Jasmine's invitation.

Well, he *did*—it was pure, ill-advised lust, currently on overdrive after dancing with her all day—but he still should have turned her down. There were so many reasons to be careful about meeting with fellow actors in private places.

Not that he thought she had ulterior motives. He believed her when she said she wanted to rehearse. Their performances had clearly improved since they'd started hanging out together, but he was still wary of anyone finding out what they were up to. The grocery store was bad enough. Going to her hotel room after hours was amateur shit, just begging to be caught.

And yet here he was, outside her door.

He could tell himself it was because he wanted to bring out the best performances in both of them, and on some level, it was true.

But on another level, he just wanted to spend time with her.

No point standing around in the hallway where he could be spotted more easily. He lifted his fist and knocked.

A second later, the door swung inward, revealing Jasmine's smiling face. "Hi," she said brightly. "Come on in."

He followed her into the hotel suite, which was laid out just like his—a small kitchen on the right, leading into a living room with a separate bedroom off to the side. It wasn't trendy, but functional and spacious enough for a few months' stay.

The room was quiet, and he was hyperaware of the fact that it was just the two of them. Most of their interactions took place with an audience present, or the potential for someone to interrupt them. But now, they were alone.

And there was a bed just behind that door . . .

Don't think about the bed, cabrón. That's not why you're here.

"I figured you hadn't eaten dinner yet either, so I ordered an antipasto plate." Jasmine gestured toward the platter of sliced meat, cubed cheese, and olives set on the round dining table in the corner. A bottle of San Pellegrino sat in an ice bucket.

"I didn't get any wine," she added hastily when she saw him looking. "Because—"

"You were worried I'd spill it on you?" he joked to cut the tension building between them.

It worked. She laughed and shook her head. "I'm convinced that was an accident. No, I didn't get wine because . . . um, we have an early day tomorrow."

Ashton didn't think that was why, but he didn't press. Instead, he passed her a small gift bag.

"What's this?" She peeked inside, then let out a surprised laugh. "Are you kidding me?"

He grinned as she withdrew a Café Bustelo coffee pod from the bag.

"To make up for the coffee I spilled," he said. "I figured it was about time."

Jasmine dropped the pod back into the bag with the others and sent him a sunny smile. "Unnecessary, but appreciated all the same. I'll put them in the kitchen."

While she was gone, Ashton took a seat at the table and poured them each a glass of seltzer. Jasmine came back and took the seat across from him.

After placing some prosciutto and goat cheese on his plate, Ashton opened his script. "All right, let's get the context part over with."

"This is the episode where Carmen pulls out the big guns— so to speak—to boost Victor's public image," she said, popping an olive in her mouth.

Ashton skimmed the scene notes. "We've got cute animals up for adoption and a visit to a children's hospital."

Jasmine held up the script to show him a page number. "Then Carmen and Victor have a heavy conversation about the future they never had together."

"We should probably practice that part," Ashton suggested. "Some of it is in Spanish too."

"And we know I need a lot of practice with that," Jasmine muttered, making a note in the margins of the script.

"Oye." He waited until she looked up at him. "You're being too hard on yourself. I know what it's like to act in your second language, and you're doing great."

Her expression softened, making her look younger, lighter, and so damn sweet. "Thank you. But now I feel bad for complaining."

"No offense, but I think my English is way better than your Spanish." He grinned to show he was just teasing, and she laughed and covered her face with her hands.

"You're right." She pursed her lips in thought. "It's weird how some of my cousins picked up more Spanish than others. For instance, my brother doesn't speak it at all, but my cousin Ava is near fluent."

"You said your grandparents were born in Puerto Rico?" he asked.

"My father's parents were—he was born in New York, but Spanish was his first language. My mother's parents were born in Hawaii, although my grandfather is Puerto Rican and my grandmother's family was from the Philippines. Mom only speaks English, so all the Spanish I picked up was from being around my grandparents here in New York."

He nodded, thinking about Yadiel, who spoke Spanish at home and English in school. "You have the diaspora experience on both sides."

"It's one of the things that drew me to Carmen," she admitted, tapping the script. "She's Nuyorican."

"Y Victor es borinqueño." Ashton smiled. "It's rare to find ourselves so well-represented in pop culture."

"Especially with such obvious parallels," she muttered.

"What do you mean?"

Her lips curved in amusement. "Don't tell me you haven't noticed? Our roles are reversed. I've got paparazzi hounding me, like Victor does. And you—"

"I avoid the media, which is more like Carmen." He nodded slowly. "I see what you're saying."

She shrugged. "Except I also dated an internationally known singer, so I guess I do have something in common with Carmen after all."

"You have more in common with her than you realize," Ashton said in a quiet voice, wishing she could see herself the way he saw her. Strong, sexy, with a good heart.

Before he did something really stupid, like *tell her* how highly he thought of her, he picked up his seltzer and drank deep, hoping it would cool him down.

"It's so interesting how the telenovela industry is growing while soaps are shrinking," Jasmine mused. "We work *so hard*, but soaps still have a bad rep."

"So do telenovelas," Ashton pointed out. "Everyone thinks they're low budget and ridiculous, but it's a huge industry. So much of the culture comes out through the stories and characters. There's romance and angst, imagination and emotion. They've come a long way, but when people think of telenovelas, they only think of the wild storylines of *María la del barrio* and *Marimar*, even though those shows achieved global popularity and Thalía's now a Latin Pop icon."

"Oh, yes, I remember those shows," Jasmine said with a grin. "My aunt watched them when I was very little."

He covered his eyes. "No me digas, you're making me feel old. But that's what I mean—telenovelas have something for everyone, and people watch as a family. I grew up watching with my mother and grandmother."

"They must have been so proud when you started acting," Jasmine said, her smile genuine.

"They were. My parents . . . they did everything they could

to help me pursue this goal." He cut himself off, because thinking about it made him think of his mother, which made him miss her.

His mother had always believed in him. She was his first and biggest fan, even when he was just doing children's theater in elementary school. When he didn't get the part he wanted or messed up his lines, she still praised him for trying, and always told him she was proud of him. At the time, he'd found her constant support almost suffocating. She said he was great when he knew he wasn't, looked on the bright side when he wanted to wallow over rejection.

Now, he would have given anything to have one more second with her, so he could introduce her to Yadiel. His biggest triumph. It was cliché, but Yadi was his pride and his joy, and he mourned every day that his mother had never seen his son, and that Yadiel would never know her love. In those moments of darkest grief, he wished Yadiel had a mother who loved him as much as Ashton's had. But he couldn't change how things had turned out, and he wouldn't anyway. Everything that had happened led to him being Yadiel's father, and he wouldn't give that up for anything.

Guilt pricked him, sharp and swift. Wasn't he giving that up in pursuit of his career? Shoving off the responsibility onto his father and his aging grandparents?

Jasmine, oblivious to the direction of his thoughts, carried on, and he latched onto her words to pull him out of the dark.

"My abuela is a huge telenovela fan, but my other grandmother watches American soaps," she said, adding more olives and meat to her plate. "I started watching *The Young and the*

Restless and *The Bold and the Beautiful* while visiting my mom's parents' on summer vacation. But my absolute favorite, which I will deny if you ever tell anyone, was *Passions*."

"*Passions?*" His eyebrows shot up. "The one with the—"

"Yes," she said with a laugh. "The one with the *everything*. It was so over the top, I couldn't get enough. But keep in mind, I was probably eight when it started, so not exactly the most discriminating viewer."

"Eight?" He groaned. "You're making me feel old again. I think I was in high school then."

"All right, *viejo*, what was your favorite? I told you mine."

He didn't love that she'd called him an old man, but that she'd said it in Spanish, and as a term of endearment, pleased him. "*Café, con aroma de mujer* because . . . well, because it was about coffee."

Jasmine snickered. "How very on brand for you."

Ashton piled more food on his plate, surprised he'd already finished the first serving. He was enjoying talking to her. This was way better than fitting in a second workout or channel surfing alone in his suite. "How did you get into soaps?"

"I was doing commercials and my agent booked me an under-five role on *General Hospital*. I was living the dream! That led to a stint on *Days*, and then a slightly bigger role on *Y&R*, and then I did *Sunrise Vista*. It didn't last long, but it got me on *The Glamour Squad*—"

"And then you got a Daytime Emmy nomination." He clapped. "You should be proud."

She shrugged. "I am, but I'm not doing it for the accolades; I just want to be a working actor with consistent gigs. I don't want to struggle. And both of my grandmothers are over the moon about it, even if the rest of my family acts like I don't have a quote-unquote *real job*."

"I feel the opposite about telenovelas," he admitted. "I'm proud of the work I've done and the awards I've received, but they mean nothing if I can't break out."

"Nothing?" She raised an eyebrow. "Now you sound like Victor."

He laughed. "God forbid. And don't get me wrong. This work is important. We're normalizing people who look and sound like us being happy and successful."

"But you want to be in Hollywood movies?"

He took a long drink of seltzer, wishing it were something stronger. "I do."

"Why keep working in TV if you hate it so much?" she asked, a slight frown on her face.

The question made him fidget, and he wasn't sure why. "I don't hate TV, but I'm tired. Telenovelas were supposed to be a stepping stone to the next level. I just didn't expect to get stuck there for so long. My hope is that *Carmen* will be the project that bridges the gap."

Jasmine stared at him over the antipasto platter with a dazzling, intense gaze. "I think you secretly love it," she said in a low voice. "Eliciting an emotional reaction from the audience? It's like the best drug there is. Soaps and telenovelas—we're experts at it. Love. Hate. *Passion*. You live for the viewer reactions. You *crave* them."

Lulled into a spell by her words and the silky tone of her voice, he lowered his own as well. They were getting into dangerous ground, and he didn't care. "And what reaction do I elicit from you?"

She shrugged, feigning nonchalance. "Nada."

Heat bloomed in his belly and spread. "Ay, linda. Estás mintiendo."

You're lying.

Jasmine opened her mouth to reply—and was interrupted by a brusque knock on the door. A chorus of voices called out, "Jaaaaaasmine, we're heeeeere!"

His eyes shot to hers. He yearned to know what she would've said, but the impulse was tempered by a growing sense of horror and betrayal.

She'd told someone.

Was it the press? Their coworkers?

Jasmine sucked in a breath. "It's my cousins."

Ay, Dios. Even worse.

Chapter 19

Jasmine opened the door to find Michelle and Ava standing in the hallway. Michelle held up a tote bag that clanked. "We come bearing wine."

"And pizza!" Ava bustled past Jasmine into the kitchen, carrying a large cardboard box that brought heavenly smells into the suite.

Michelle glanced over at Ashton like she was just noticing him. "Oh, do you have company?"

She knew damn well Ashton was there, since Jasmine had texted them on the way home admitting she'd invited him over. They'd reminded her about her Leading Lady Plan and then gone silent. Jasmine should've guessed they were up to something, but she'd been preoccupied with ordering food and freshening up before Ashton arrived.

"What are you doing here?" Jasmine whispered while Ava introduced herself to Ashton.

Michelle gave her a pointed look. "Saving you from yourself." Then she strolled over to Ashton and said, "Well, well, if it isn't el león dorado."

Jasmine completed the introductions, everyone kissed hello on the cheek, and soon they were all seated at the round dining table, digging into the pizza.

"Ooh, toppings!" Michelle grabbed olives and roasted red peppers from the antipasto plate and piled them onto her pizza slice. "So what were you two up to?"

Ashton passed around napkins. "Rehearsing lines."

This was a slight exaggeration, considering they had yet to open their scripts, but it was better than admitting they'd been flirting over olives and telenovelas.

"Excellent," Michelle said. "We'll help you. Jasmine's the pro, but Ava and I also took drama classes in school."

"What do you do now?" Ashton asked politely.

"Freelance graphic designer."

Michelle did so much more than that, but Jasmine didn't contradict. Starting the freelance business had been Michelle's way of recovering from her high-level—and extremely stressful—corporate job.

"And you?" Ashton asked, turning to Ava.

"Middle school teacher." Ava yanked the cork out of the wine bottle. "But I'm on summer break now."

"And how about you?" Michelle asked Ashton, as if she didn't know. Jasmine rolled her eyes as Ava filled her wineglass.

Ashton replied with a rueful grin. "Well, I've been a gold miner, sheriff, CEO, duke, and now I'm a singer."

Michelle nodded. "A man of many talents. Wine?"

Jasmine hid her smile in her glass. Michelle was like that. She could charm anyone with her particular blend of dark wit and smooth delivery. Jasmine knew what she was doing, though. Michelle was taking Ashton's measure, gauging if he could hang.

And so far, Ashton—the same guy who hid from everyone else on the cast—was holding his own. He joked and bantered back and forth with Michelle, talked movies with Ava, and chowed down on pizza.

"Who's in this scene?" Michelle asked, picking up Jasmine's script.

"Carmen's family," Ashton replied.

Ava gestured at Jasmine. "You obviously have to play Carmen. I'll read her mother's lines."

"I'll be the dad," Michelle said, then sent Ashton a sunny smile. "That leaves you as Carmen's sister, Helen."

Jasmine expected him to protest, or insist on reading Ernesto's lines. Instead, Ashton leaned back in his chair, like he was lounging. He gave a little shoulder shake and a head toss, to mime throwing back a long mane of hair.

Jasmine let out a giggle. The posturing was a perfect imitation of the way Lily played Helen. And when Ashton spoke, it was with Helen's attitude and Lily's intonation.

"I'm ready," he said with another head toss, and Jasmine laughed because Lily really did throw her hair around a lot.

"You *are* a good actor," she teased.

He chuckled and sent her a wink. "Just don't tell Lily. She'll think I'm after her job."

They drank wine and read parts of the script out loud, getting sillier as the night wore on. Finally, Ashton begged off—they had an early call time, and he always hit the gym first thing in the morning.

As he gathered the plates and loaded them in the dishwasher—something that had hearts forming in Ava's eyes—Michelle elbowed Jasmine in the ribs.

"Ow! What?" Jasmine scowled and rubbed her side.

"Ask him," Michelle hissed.

"I don't want to ask him," Jasmine shot back in a whisper.

"Abuela would *love* it if he came to her party," Ava added in a low voice. "And it would totally put you over Jillian in the Ranking."

Jasmine narrowed her eyes. "Low blow, Ava."

The Ranking was a list they'd come up with in middle school, putting all the cousins in order from their grandmother's most favorite to least favorite. It had been updated many times over the years as all the cousins grew up and became either more or less favorable in their abuela's eyes. They hypothesized that Ava was always near the top—she spoke the most Spanish, helped Esperanza clean the house before parties, and went over a few evenings a week to help cook and watch telenovelas with her. Michelle, being "the mouthy one," as she called herself, figured she was near the bottom. Jasmine was convinced that her older sister, Jillian, with her beautiful children and "regular job" on Wall Street, must be high up in the Ranking too. Higher than Jasmine was, anyway.

Bringing Ashton to the party would almost certainly skyrocket Jasmine to the top.

And it would make Esperanza really, really happy.

"Fine, I'll ask him," she grumbled. "Don't interfere."

Michelle gave her an innocent grin. "Wouldn't dream of it."

Jasmine caught up to Ashton as he was leaving the tiny kitchen.

"Hey, um, I have a question for you," she said, then groaned inwardly. *Real smooth.*

His expressive eyebrows rose, inviting her to speak.

"My grandmother's eightieth birthday party is coming up right after we wrap the season."

The corners of his mouth turned up. "The grandmother who adores me?"

Now Jasmine groaned out loud. "Yes, that one. Anyway, we're having a huge party for her, and if you wanted to—I mean, it would just really make her day if—"

"Jasmine." He said her name in a low voice that set off all kinds of pleasant vibrations in her body.

"Mm-hmm?" What else could she say when consumed with pure lust?

"Are you inviting me to your abuela's birthday party?"

"Um . . . yeah. I am. Which sounds kind of dull, but I promise, it'll be a lot of fun. The Rodriguez fam knows how to throw a party."

He stared at her for what felt like a long time, his expression inscrutable. Just when she was sure he was about to say no, he spoke. "I don't have my return flight booked yet, and it will depend on the needs of my own grandparents, but if I'm in New York, I'll attend."

She blinked. "Really?"

His lips curved in a small smile. "Yes, really."

"Great. Thank you."

Their eyes held, and Jasmine's body grew warm all over. Her gaze dropped to his mouth, and when he leaned in to drop a farewell kiss to her cheek, she inhaled sharply and fought a full body shiver. She *had* to find out what cologne he wore.

"Goodnight, Jasmine."

The low rumble thudded through her. "Good night," she echoed, voice hoarse with desire.

Then he raised his voice and called out, "Nice meeting you both." Ava and Michelle yelled their goodbyes in harmony, something the three of them had done since they were kids, and then Ashton slipped out the door, leaving Jasmine trying to catch her breath.

Whew.

That was . . .

Whew. Later on, she was going to have to think about why she found his hellos and goodbyes so arousing.

Crisis averted, Michelle and Ava left shortly after Ashton did. Michelle's parting words were, "You're welcome," paired with a meaningful glance. Ava had mouthed, "We'll discuss later." And then they were gone, too, leaving Jasmine alone with one single thought.

Ashton had been flirting with her.

Why else would he ask about her reaction to him? And he'd called her pretty, albeit in an offhand, term of endearment kind of way.

But then he'd called her a liar when she claimed not to have an emotional reaction to him. And the way he'd said "good night" just now was probably illegal in twelve states.

He was right. She was lying. The truth was, she had all sorts of emotional reactions to him. But she wouldn't—couldn't—let him know the effect he had on her.

Her traitorous little heart converted pants feelings into emotions far too readily. It was rather efficient that way.

But now wasn't the time or place. Her feelings for him had to stay firmly within lust territory. The Leading Lady Plan was in action, and this opportunity was too big to screw up.

And besides. No rebounds. She'd promised herself and her cousins.

If she went back on it now, Ava and Michelle would never let her live it down.

Crushes were fleeting. Family teasing was forever.

Chapter 20

EPISODE 6

Scene: Victor attends a charity event for an animal
    shelter.
INT: Elementary school gymnasium—DAY

"You did well with the kids," Carmen said.

"You don't have to sound so surprised," Victor replied, feeling a little wounded. "I'm not a monster."

"It's not that." She straightened a stack of pamphlets for the animal shelter. "I just . . . didn't think you liked kids."

"I do." He got the sense she wasn't talking about the kids at the children's hospital they'd visited earlier in the episode. He could pretend not to know what she meant, or he could cut to the chase. They'd done enough pretending while they were married. "You're wondering why we didn't have kids."

She crossed her arms, hugging herself, and turned away

from him so he couldn't see her face. "We never even talked about it."

"I . . ." It was time for honesty. "I didn't think you wanted them."

She spun back to him then, and there was a wealth of emotion in her dark eyes. "Why would you think that?"

He shrugged as old hurts rose from where he'd buried them long ago. "You made it clear that your career came first. Serrano PR was your family legacy."

"But you didn't ask."

He sighed. "No. I didn't. But neither did you." He said it gently, without censure. They'd both made mistakes.

"This feels years too late, but . . . did you want children, Victor?"

He looked over at the animals penned in their play areas. "Sí, Carmencita. I wanted children with you. Eventually. But we didn't get there."

When she didn't yell at him for using the diminutive of her name, he took it as a sign of progress.

"We didn't get to a lot of places," she said softly, then checked her watch. "They're about to open the doors. Are you ready?"

Victor steeled himself, ignoring the barks and meows coming from behind him. "As I'll ever be."

The doors opened and a crowd rushed into the gymnasium, shoes squeaking on the waxed floors and murmurs echoing around the space.

From his spot in front of the photo backdrop emblazoned with the animal shelter's logo, Victor smiled and signed autographs and posed for pictures as Carmen handed him one puppy or kitten after another.

His fingers were nipped by needle-pointed puppy teeth, his jacket was scratched by razor-sharp kitten claws, and he was nearly peed on—twice. But he suffered through it, charming the people who were there to help him improve his public image.

Even as his allergies started to kick in.

He tried not to sniffle too loudly as Carmen gave him three kittens to hold up near his face, but he was fighting a losing battle, despite the meds he'd downed that morning.

And then they brought out Luther.

Luther was a five-foot-long female ball python whose name was actually Lucy.

The script didn't say that Victor was afraid of snakes. And if you asked him, he wouldn't have said he was.

But he wasn't overly fond of them either. And he had never in his life wanted to hold one.

"Here comes Luther," Carmen called in a singsong voice. The children assembled around Victor cheered. The parents oohed and ahhed.

And Victor was very nearly about to break character.

Cálmate, cabrón, he told himself. *You're an international superstar. You've played sold-out shows all over the world, in the biggest venues. This is just one harmless snake!*

The snake, still in its handler's arms, eyed him impassively.

Victor's armpits began to sweat.

The snake came closer.

Swallowing hard, Victor raised his arms, tensed all his muscles, and let them hand him the python.

The kids crowded around him. He smiled for the camera.

The snake shifted its weight. Victor's arms trembled from the stress. And then . . .

His nose started to tickle.

"Three . . ." the photographer counted down. "Two . . ."

On "one," Victor sneezed, nearly dropping Luther. Reflexively, his arms clenched, gathering the snake close to his chest. Luther—Lucy—whatever—slithered its head over his shoulder and around the back of his neck.

Victor froze. *Fuck. This.*

"Somebody take this snake!" he shouted.

"Cut!"

Chapter 21

Ashton's eyes itched, his nose ran, and if he never heard "Somebody take this snake!" again in his life, it would be too soon. Worse, the director had *loved* it and decided to keep it for the final cut.

Between the children and the animals, Ashton's sneezing, and everyone breaking character left and right, the animal charity event required the most takes of any scene they'd filmed yet. By the end, people were already talking about the blooper reel, and Ashton's allergies were in full swing, but he had to admit, he was having fun. So when Jasmine told him the cast was going out for karaoke that night, he surprised them all by saying yes.

"I'm not sure how good my singing will be," he warned, sniffling. "You might have noticed I'm having an allergy attack."

Jasmine handed him a pack of tissues. "Was it the cats or the dogs?"

"The kittens," he admitted. "Cute little things, but I'm severely allergic to them. Ya—you know what I mean?"

She simply nodded, not catching his slip, but his insides

turned to ice. He'd almost said Yadiel's name—his son was always begging for a pet. Ashton's cat allergies and Abuelita Bibi's aversion to dogs made that impossible, but didn't stop Yadiel from making pointed comments about the cuteness of every dog and cat he encountered.

Ashton was the last to arrive at the karaoke place in Midtown where Jasmine had booked a private room. Three bottles of wine and two pitchers of beer sat on the low table in the center of the room, and Miriam was in the middle of belting out a Selena song.

Jasmine sidled up and nudged him with her shoulder. "I didn't think you were going to show."

"I said I would." It sounded curt, but he hadn't meant it to. It was just that his mouth had gone bone-dry at the sight of her. She wore some lacy scrap of a shirt that left her shoulders and midriff bare and revealed an enticing curve of cleavage. He'd seen her in sexy outfits—Carmen went through a lot of wardrobe changes—but knowing Jasmine had picked this out herself made a difference. It was whimsical and sexy all at once. Just like her.

"Besides," he added, trying to lighten his tone. "How could I miss this?"

At the moment, Miriam was bidi-bidi-bom-bomming her way across the room to whoops and wepas from the other *Carmen in Charge* actors.

Ashton clapped as the song came to an end, and in the silence before the next one began, he let loose a tremendous sneeze.

"¡Salud!" the group chorused.

Ashton's face heated, but he raised his voice and said, "Gracias." A second later, a Thalía song came on, and everyone turned back to the screen.

Jasmine patted his arm. "I have extra tissues for you in my purse."

Despite this being Ashton's first time socializing with the cast outside of work, everyone seemed happy to see him. He accepted a glass of wine from Lily and got into a deep discussion with Peter and Nino about the Yankees.

While he waited for his song to start, Ashton reflected on the diverse makeup of the cast. He was puertorriqueño, born on the island. Jasmine was second generation Puerto Rican and Filipina. Nino was first gen Dominican and Haitian. Lily was Mexican American. Peter was Dominican, but had lived in New York most of his life. And Miriam was Cuban American from Miami.

They were a mix of immigrants, first generation, and those whose heritage went further back. Lily's family had lived in Arizona for multiple generations. And the rest of the cast and crew hailed from many other Latin American countries: Colombia, Panama, Brazil, Ecuador, and more.

On a bulletin board outside the showrunner's office, Marquita had posted a sign that said QUÉ BONITAS BANDERAS and invited everyone to tack up their respective flags to show the range of nationalities in the production, but also that the strength of the Latinx comunidad was in its diversity. Marquita had also made a point to include a rainbow pride flag and the pink, white, and light blue trans flag. Nino had gone still as a statue when he'd seen it, then hugged Marquita tight.

Ashton had been on many sets that were majority Latinx,

but there was something different about this one. Maybe because it was for a mainstream streaming service, but there was a fierce pride in what they were doing here, a shared determination to make *Carmen in Charge* the very best it could be. And now, it showed in the way they let loose.

The thing about doing karaoke with actors was that they didn't just sit around singing. They *performed*. Lily and Nino knew all the dance moves to *NSYNC's "Bye Bye Bye." Peter treated them to a rendition of "My Way" that would've made Sinatra proud. And when Jasmine's song choice finally came up, she took the mic and said, "Yes, I am that basic karaoke bitch," as the first strains of "Everlasting Love" rang out.

And then she turned and held out the other mic. "Sing with me, Ashton."

He couldn't refuse.

By tacit agreement, they alternated lyrics and harmonized on the chorus, like in the Rex Smith version of the song. It could have been sexy. It could have been emotional. But they did sexy and emotional every day for work. Instead, they made it as silly as fucking possible.

Ashton couldn't remember the last time he'd had more fun.

When they took their seats again, it was to a round of applause and hollers. Then a Marc Anthony ballad came on and Nino took the mic.

Ashton flopped down on the purple vinyl couch. It had been years since he'd done karaoke, and he'd forgotten how much he enjoyed it. Still, thanks to kitten-induced congestion, he was worn out. He stretched his arms across the back of the sofa and fought to catch his breath.

"Well, that was fun." Jasmine took the seat next to him and cozied up to his side. "I knew you'd be a good singer."

"Nah, I just play one on TV," he said, and she giggled.

Damn, he loved making her laugh. The joyful sound, the way her cheeks scrunched up, the way her warm body shook against him. He wanted to put his arm around her, to hold her close. To look deeply in her eyes and then—

But they weren't alone. And he wasn't supposed to want that, although he was starting to forget why. Instead, he just played with the ends of her hair, styled into a mass of defined curls by the hair team at *Carmen*. When she tilted her head closer, he let the backs of his fingers lightly brush her bare shoulders and pretended her shirt wasn't setting him on fire.

Movement out of the corner of his eye made him turn. Lily Benitez crawled across the long sofa to Jasmine's side. "Oh my god, you guys," she said, slurring her words a little. "You two are *so cute* together. Is there, like, something going on?"

Ashton snatched his hand away from Jasmine's shoulder like it was a hot stove. His throat locked and his heart rate rocketed.

Coño. This was how rumors started. How could he have been so stupid? He should have known better than to—

Jasmine just gave Lily an unconcerned smile. "Nah. Why do you ask?"

At that, Lily shrugged and slumped against Jasmine's shoulder. "Just curious. It happens on a lot of sets, you know."

Jasmine laughed. "Oh, I know."

"Cool." And then Lily flipped her hair and went back to nursing a cup of water at the other end of the room.

While Ashton struggled to get his pulse under control,

Jasmine looked up at him from under her lashes. Her eyes were dark and unreadable, reflecting the light from the screen flashing lyrics for "You Sang to Me."

Then she poked him in the side and muttered, "Don't get bent out of shape."

"You handled that well," Ashton told her, impressed by how easily she managed awkward interactions. He would have stammered and rambled, then run away.

Her gaze held his for a long moment before she looked away. "Nothing to tell."

Her tone was cool, but there were many things unsaid in those words, and they were at odds with the heat in her eyes. Ashton felt like he did when they were on set together, when Carmen and Victor spoke without speaking, conveying so much connection in a single look or touch. Right then, he felt it. Like he knew her deeply, as if all their time on set pretending to be other people had also brought them closer together.

The powerful impulse to know her even more deeply rose up inside him.

But as much as he wanted to kiss her right now, as *himself*, they were in a room full of their coworkers. And this was a line he'd sworn he wouldn't cross ever again.

A shout went up as the others recognized the opening bars of "Livin' La Vida Loca."

"That's my song," he whispered to Jasmine alone.

Her teeth bared in a fierce smile and her eyes gleamed. She handed him the extra mic and said, "Kill it."

He did. Allergies be damned. He gave the song his all, copying Ricky Martin's mannerisms and revving his voice. The others danced and sang along, urging on his theatrics. Through it all, he kept finding Jasmine's eyes shining at him from across the room.

It was all for her. He wanted Jasmine to see him, the real him. Ángel Luis, the boy who'd grown up dreaming of being a big movie star. And Ashton, the man who ran around with his son playing superheroes.

He wanted to tell her everything, but he couldn't. Instead, he let her see a glimpse of who he felt himself to be inside . . . through the words and moves of the great Ricky Martin.

When it was over, the crowd, as they say, went wild. Jasmine found him and slipped a hand around his waist when no one was looking.

"You're amazing." Genuine admiration glowed on her face, lighting him up from within. Then she winked and grabbed the mic from him as "Jenny from the Block" flashed across the screen in garish pink. "But let me show you how it's done."

Jasmine raised the mic to her mouth. "Gotta remember your roots," she said, then proceeded to serenade the room with a powerful rendition of JLo's early hit about growing up in the Bronx.

Ashton couldn't take his eyes off her. She shone like the brightest star in the sky, commanding the heart and imagination. Everything else paled in comparison to her radiance.

He should leave. Watch some TV, go to sleep, wake up tomorrow with new resolve to keep his distance. His life was complicated enough without developing feelings for his costar.

Instead, Ashton drank more. He sang more. He chatted with the others and shared a basket of french fries—his weakness—

with Nino. And somehow, he never lost track of Jasmine. She appeared at his side periodically, checking in on him, handing him wine, water, tissues. Touching his waist, his back, his arm. Driving him wild with her smiles and small touches.

And despite his reservations, he touched her too. With as close as they got on set, it seemed normal to rest his hand on her hip when she reached past him to steal a fry, or to trail his fingers down her arm while she whispered anecdotes to him about the songs, her lips achingly close to his ear, sending tingles across his scalp.

He already knew the feel of her mouth under his. But those kisses had been choreographed, controlled, and scrutinized by others. He wanted to know how she *tasted*.

As Lily treated them all to a wild interpretation of a Shakira song, Jasmine found her way to his side once again.

"I'm going to go back to the hotel," she told him, pitching her voice low.

"I'll go with you." The words came without forethought. He knew how it would look if they left together, but he didn't give a shit. As much fun as he was having with the rest of the cast, he didn't want to be there without her.

"Okay," she said softly.

They made their farewells, delivering the expected goodbye kiss on every cheek. When Peter exclaimed, "Leaving so soon?" Ashton blamed it on his allergies, even though his nose had stopped running sometime during the night.

Outside, he and Jasmine caught a taxi back to the hotel. They rode in silence, walked through the lobby in silence, and when they stepped into the elevator, Jasmine pushed the button for her floor and turned to him, blocking the control panel. The doors whooshed shut.

In a quiet voice, she asked, "Do you want to come to my room?"

Ashton searched her face, her eyes, the way she held herself. He knew this woman's mannerisms, her body language and nonverbal cues. He knew exactly what she was asking.

And he wanted it too.

"Yes," he said.

The elevator doors pinged open on her floor.

Chapter 22

Jasmine's fingers trembled as she removed the key card from her purse and unlocked her hotel room door. She didn't turn to look at Ashton as she opened it and entered the room, trusting—hoping—that he would follow her.

He did.

The second the door clicked shut behind them, he pressed her up against the wall and brought his mouth down on hers.

Jasmine dropped everything. Her arms banded around his neck, and she arched her body flush against his. His body was a revelation, all hard muscles and the thick, solid length of his cock pressing into her abdomen.

She knew his touch, his scent, the feel of his lips against hers. But this was different. This time was for real.

When his tongue slid against her lips, she opened for him with a moan. *Finally* they would do this right.

Their tongues touched, tasted, caressed. His kiss was stronger, more audacious, than when he was Victor. And she relished in it.

As many times as they had done this before, this was all

new. They weren't Carmen and Victor now. They were just Jasmine and—

"Ashton," she whispered against his mouth.

He pressed his lips to the curve of her neck and made a questioning noise in the back of his throat.

"Touch me. Please."

He did.

His hands slid down her back in an unerring path, molding over her sides, her hips, stopping at her butt to give it a squeeze, then traveling down to the backs of her thighs. He lifted her like he had when they'd filmed episode four. The move had thrilled her then and it thrilled her now. Still kissing, he carried her to the table where they had once shared wine and pizza and set her down on top. Then he pressed his pelvis to hers and the feel of him against her made her desperate to touch him.

"Off," she pleaded, tugging at his T-shirt. "Take this off."

He released her for just a moment to reach back, fisting his hand in the material and yanking the whole thing over his head. In the dreamy ambient light of New York City filtering in through the windows—they hadn't even thought to turn on the lamp—she trailed her gaze and her fingers over the angles and planes of his muscled form. When she'd seen him on the treadmill in the fitness center, she'd wanted to touch him. And now she could.

But Ashton wasn't content to just sit back and be touched. He leaned into her, capturing her mouth again with fervor.

Then he surprised her by murmuring against her lips, "This is not kissing practice."

"No," she agreed, tangling her tongue with his, just to prove it to herself. Full-on tongue kissing was a line they'd never crossed at work. "Besides, you clearly don't need any practice."

He chuckled, then his mouth left hers to trace a line down her neck and over her bare shoulder.

"This shirt," he muttered, his fingers crawling under the band. "Did you wear it to drive me wild?"

"Maybe." She'd picked the lacy white crop top because it was cute, but she'd worn her most effective strapless bra underneath because she'd known he would be there tonight. "Okay, yes. I wore it for you"

"Sinvergüenza," he scolded, then peeled the shirt from her body.

He'd called her shameless, and when he unhooked her bra and cupped her bare breasts in his hands, all she could do was sigh and say, "You know it."

Then he dipped his head and pressed his open mouth to her nipple, and she was beyond words.

She locked her legs around his hips and pulled him against her, grinding on him through their pants as he sucked and tugged at her nipples with his mouth and fingers. Bolts of electric desire streaked through her body at his touch, building a roiling sense of pure need deep within her.

She pulled at his hair, whimpered his name, and rocked her pelvis against his until finally, he said the best word in the world: "Bed."

Jasmine slid off the table, grabbing his hand and pulling him into the bedroom after her. They fell onto the bed together and he made quick work of her pants. Her sandals had already been lost by the door. Ashton peeled her jeans and simple black panties down her legs, then he stood and just gazed at her. His expression showed hunger, yes, and appreciation, but also something like affection. Right then, Jasmine felt like the most beautiful, most loved, most desired woman in the world.

"Come here," she said, and while she meant it to sound seductive and alluring, it just sounded desperate. But she didn't care.

At her breathless command, a new urgency overtook him. He kicked off his shoes and shoved down his jeans. She sucked in a breath and bit her lower lip at the sight of his rigid cock, outlined beautifully by tight dark blue briefs. The head peeked out over the waistband. She couldn't fucking wait to get her hands on him.

With something like a growl, he slid next to her and gathered her close, kissing her like their lives depended on it.

This was a side of Ashton she hadn't seen before. She'd caught glimpses of it when he played Victor, a sexy intensity that came out when he acted. But this was more—more passionate, more overwhelming—and she loved it. All she ever wanted was to be the single-minded focus of someone's attention. And his was 100 percent entirely focused on her.

His mouth moved over hers like all the stage kisses they'd shared had been foreplay, a prelude to what he was truly capable of and what he'd wanted to do. Now, finally, he was kissing her for real. No pretense, no direction from others. This was pure, unfiltered Ashton. No holding back.

Jasmine took everything he offered and gave him every-thing she could. Their hands roamed, learning each other's bodies more intimately and more ardently than they ever had on set. Jasmine grasped the waistband of his underwear and shoved them down over his taut ass before taking his cock in hand.

It was thick and fully rigid, his skin hot against her palm. She gave him a few experimental pumps and he groaned against her mouth.

"Jasmine, what are we doing?" His voice was hoarse, rough with need. He sucked in a breath when she wrapped her fingers around his shaft and gave him a gentle squeeze.

"I don't know," she whispered, meeting his eyes. "But I don't want to stop."

"Yo tampoco." The words held a note of confession. He cupped her cheek and kissed her, then shifted out of reach. She almost whimpered in dismay when the move pulled his cock from her grasp, but then his mouth found her breasts again and one of his hands slid up her inner thigh. With a satisfied hum, she decided that, on second thought, she was totally okay with these new positions.

ALL THOUGHTS ABOUT what a bad idea this was had deserted Ashton's brain somewhere between walking through the door and Jasmine's ass hitting the table.

Now that they were naked and alone together in her bed, all he could think about was touching her more, tasting her more, and making her moan even more than she already was.

He sucked her tight little nipple deep into his mouth, rolling the bud with his tongue and nearly dying from pleasure at the breathy gasps and pants she made. Her response was genuine, and he hadn't realized how much he'd wanted that from her. Every other time he'd touched her, their reactions had been worked out in advance by committee.

But this? This was only between them.

She'd been right. He loved eliciting an emotional reaction from her. His hand slipped between her thighs to the warm, wet heart of her. Her fingers tangled in his hair, urging him on. Her legs parted, making room for him, inviting his touch.

Before he did, he moved up her body to bring his mouth back to hers. He wanted to be closer, to swallow her sounds of passion when he touched her for the first time. She clung to him, pressing closer and arching her hips.

But there was one thing he had to make clear first. Communication was key, right? That's what had gotten them here. Even though desire urged him to cast words aside, he had to make sure they were on the same page.

"Jasmine." His voice broke on her name.

"Hmm?" She shifted restlessly. The heat between her thighs called to him, but he had to get this out.

"I don't think—" He swallowed hard, wondering if he was just being stupid, then blurted it out. "We shouldn't have penetrative sex."

Don't ask why don't ask why don't—

She blinked like she was in a daze. "Okay?"

She sounded confused and he couldn't blame her. But she hadn't asked why, and she hadn't called a stop to this, so he dropped his voice to a purr and moved his hand so it covered her mound. "But don't worry, querida. I'm going to make you feel *so good*."

"Just touch me," she whined, arching impatiently against his hand.

He couldn't make either of them wait any longer. Slowly, he brought his middle finger down and slid it gently over her folds.

Jasmine threw her head back. "God, *yes*. Keep going."

He did it again, this time his fingertip slipping between and gathering her wetness. He parted her with two fingers and found her clit, rubbing it in small circles. She cried out against his lips, and he was lost. The taste of her, the smell of her, the feel of her so close against him, skin to skin. Time and space had no meaning anymore. There was only her.

"Lube," she whispered mid-kiss, so quick he almost missed it.

"¿Dónde?"

"Drawer."

He yanked open the bedside drawer, almost ripping it out of the nightstand in his haste, and removed a small zippered pouch. When he opened it, he found all sorts of interesting battery-operated things, but he only removed the small bottle of clear gel she'd asked for. After squirting some onto his hand, he reached between her legs again, groaning as his fingers sank right in.

She stretched her arms up over her head on the pillow. Eyes closed, she let out a throaty sigh every time he thrust into her, and a high moan when he slicked his fingertips over her clit. Unable to take it anymore, he kissed her hard, swallowing her sounds as her sheath, so tight and so hot, squeezed his fingers, killing him slowly. How good would she feel around his dick?

He wasn't going to find out, but that didn't mean he couldn't come with her.

"Jasmine." He ground himself against her hip, needing the friction. "Can I—"

"Yes." She nipped his lower lip to cut him off. "Anything you want."

With a groan, he grabbed the lube and applied a liberal amount to his cock. Pressing it between her hip and his belly, he worked them both. He teased her mouth with his lips, teeth, and tongue. Plied her hot, wet pussy with his fingers and hand. And rubbed his lubed-up dick against her soft, warm skin. When she went to touch him, he gently moved her hand away.

"I have this," he murmured. "Just feel."

The pressure built in him. It had been so long, and she was everything he'd dreamed of. Her gasps of pleasure, the way she held him close and kissed him like she'd never let go intoxicated his senses.

When her fingernails bit into his shoulders and she cried out his name, he knew she was close. He thrust a third finger inside her, filling her, and pressed her clit with renewed purpose.

A second later, the orgasm seized her. He held her through it, kissing her, rubbing her, barely holding it together as her cries filled the space around them.

Her body shook, ecstasy clear on her face and in the shivers running through her limbs. Her open response pushed him over the edge. He gripped her around the waist and thrust hard against her side. The orgasm shot through him in a rush, making his toes curl as all the tension he'd been carrying for weeks released with a guttural groan and a hot splash across her belly and hip.

Breathing hard, he set his head next to hers on the pillow and shut his eyes. Bliss washed through him in the wake of his climax, leaving him thoroughly sated and content for the first time in . . . he didn't know how long.

Jasmine was so quiet, he opened his eyes to check if she was still awake, and found her staring at him from just a few inches away on the pillow. His arms were still banded tightly around her. He didn't want to let go, but he was pretty sure she didn't want his cum to dry on her.

He cleared his throat, which felt rough from all the sex groans he'd been making. "Are you okay?"

Her lips curved a fraction. "Better than okay."

Well, that was a relief. He'd worried about how she'd respond to his directive that they not have penetrative sex, since it seemed like that's where they'd been headed, not sure if she'd be angry, disappointed, or insulted that he'd assume she'd ever consider it. He'd probably have to explain himself later, but now . . .

"I'll be right back." He pressed a kiss to her temple, then went to retrieve a wet towel. She lay still while he wiped the mess off her, then she slipped from the bed and went to the bathroom. When she was done, he took his turn, wondering what to say when he went back out. *Let's do it again* didn't seem appropriate. And now that his mind was clear, regrets were trying to push their way in.

Déjame, he told them. *Let me have this moment.*

He still hadn't figured out what to say by the time he left the bathroom. In the dark, he searched for his pants, when her voice stopped him.

"Please stay."

He looked up to see Jasmine sitting in the middle of the bed, holding the sheet over her lap and gorgeous breasts. Jasmine, who'd shown no qualms about revealing her body only moments earlier, was now covering herself. Her eyes, usually so expressive, were guarded. She bit the corner of her lip, her eyebrows creasing the barest fraction.

He shouldn't stay. This was a very, very bad idea, for so many reasons.

But he wanted to. And she wanted him to.

Wasn't that enough? Could it be enough? At least for one night.

Ashton dropped his pants back to the floor and slid onto the bed next to her, taking her in his arms. "Sí, me quedaré."

He realized a second too late that he'd said it in Spanish, but before he could repeat the words in English, her arms came around his neck. She snuggled her face into his shoulder, pressed her warm breasts against his chest, and tangled her legs with his.

It had been so long since he'd fallen asleep with a woman curled beside him like this. A warm, relaxed feeling spread over him, seeping into his bones. He pulled her closer, then drifted off into an easy, dreamless slumber.

Chapter 23

When Ashton's alarm went off at five in the morning, he shifted to shut it off—then noticed a warm, citrus-scented weight on his chest. *Jasmine.*

That's right. Last night, they'd—well, he hadn't been inside her, but there'd been an exchange of fluids and . . . god, he'd *come* on her, after humping her hip like . . . he didn't even know what. What had he been thinking? They'd had their first kiss—their first *real* kiss—and seconds later they'd been naked. Whatever this was between them, it was going too fast, getting too far out of control.

But it had also felt so damn *good*, he couldn't bring himself to regret it.

His phone alarm was still beeping insistently.

Jasmine made a cute little whimper and lifted her head to look at him in the dark. "What time is it?"

"Cinco de la—I mean, it's five."

Groaning, she dropped her head back to his chest and cuddled closer. "Why?"

A laugh rumbled deep inside him. "Why what?"

"Why . . . five," she answered sleepily. "And why . . . the alarm."

"It's my daily gym alarm."

"Ohhh." Her hands moved, slim fingers tracing his biceps. "Okay then."

He should get up. Now. He shouldn't have stayed in the first place. But he felt a tug in his gut as if an invisible anchor kept him rooted next to her.

He ignored it and slid out of the bed. He had commitments. Gym, yes, but he also had a call with Yadiel scheduled, and he'd be damned if he disappointed his kid because he was in bed with a woman.

Even if that woman was Jasmine. Even if all he wanted to do in that very moment was snuggle with her for ten more minutes.

Following the sound of the alarm, he found his phone in the pocket of the pants he'd left on the floor the night before. With the alarm silenced, he made a quick trip to the bathroom. When he came back out, her eyes were heavy-lidded with sleep, but alert. He felt her gaze following him around the room as he collected his various articles of clothing and got dressed.

And then there was nothing more to do but leave. He should say something meaningful, but he didn't know what. He certainly couldn't make any promises or plans. But he didn't have to be an asshole either, so before he left, he went back to the bed and sat beside her.

With gentle movements, he brushed her hair behind her ear and leaned down to press a kiss to her temple. When she lifted up on her elbows, he pulled her the rest of the way, gathering her warm, naked form in his lap and holding her tight. She clung to him, nuzzling her face in his neck. He held her until his alarm went off again.

"That's my cue," he said, reluctant to release her. "I'll . . . be back later." He shouldn't, but it was pointless to deny that he wanted to return.

She nodded and started to shift away. "We should go over our lines."

"We should," he agreed, as if it would be so easy to go back to their old dynamic after what they'd done in this bed. Since he couldn't resist, he cupped her chin and pressed a chaste kiss to her lips.

She kissed him back, so sweet, so soft. And although he felt the pull to stay, he left.

Back in his own room, he took off his clothes from the night before and decided on a quick shower before hitting the gym. His skin still carried the scent of her, which made him remember how he'd come on her the night before, and just like that, he was hard again.

Those pesky regrets were creeping closer. The last time he'd had sex with a costar, he'd gotten Yadiel, which was why he had a strict policy against it and hadn't wanted to have penetrative sex with Jasmine. Not that what they'd done was any less intimate. He'd had his hands all over her, his mouth—well, not on as much of her as he would have liked, but coño, he was trying to observe some boundaries.

Except now he was thinking of putting his mouth between her legs and licking her sweet pussy, of making her quake and cry out with pleasure. Of crawling up her body and sinking deep—

Fuck.

His dick wasn't going down as long as he kept thinking about Jasmine, and there was no way he was going to the fitness center with a raging hard-on. He turned the shower on hot and stepped in, lathering up his hands and body with shower gel. Then he braced one arm on the wall, wrapped his hand around his dick, and worked himself with quick, short strokes. Behind his closed eyelids, he saw Jasmine writhing naked on a bed, bathed in moonlight. Okay, so last night it hadn't been moonlight, but the city acting as a nightlight—whatever, it was close enough. The silvery gleam gilded her lush golden curves, her brown nipples peaking in the cool air. The white noise of the shower amplified the memory of her moans in his mind. He visualized her parting her legs for him, her pussy open and gleaming. He would kiss her there if she let him, lick her until she was mindless with need, as he'd been for her.

Groaning, he cupped his balls and gave them a quick squeeze. After adding more soap, he gripped the base of his dick and resumed stroking.

He wanted to touch her again, kiss her again. And damn it, he wanted to fuck her. To slide into her as far as he could go, to hold her close and hear those sexy little noises she made as he pumped inside her.

To kiss her good morning, to make her laugh, to hold her when she cried—

Whoa, where the fuck had that come from?

Didn't matter. He was on the edge. His muscles bunched, his balls tightened, and as he pictured Jasmine plumping her breasts together for him to spray his load on, he came.

A shudder racked his body, weakening his knees, and he pressed his forehead to the tile. Hot water washed over him, rinsing soap and his fluids down the drain.

This wasn't like him. He'd had more than his fair share of flings before Yadiel had been born. Since then, he'd focused only on career and family, and as he'd grown more cautious—or as his father said, *paranoid*—the less he'd let women get too close. A few dates here and there, including a couple of fake relationships for publicity purposes, some fooling around with non-coworkers, but nothing serious. He hadn't wanted anything serious. Until now.

Now, he wished they could be two different people, free to pursue what was clearly a mutual attraction and interest. What was between him and Jasmine was more than just a hookup between costars. He liked her. A lot.

And that made the whole thing all the more dangerous and complicated. Not only was he mixing business and pleasure, but he was doing it with the one person on the cast who could demolish his carefully constructed house of cards. The media paid far too much attention to her, and his family's safety relied on him flying under the radar, as far as his personal life was concerned. A relationship with Jasmine would be disastrous.

His familia was small, and they were all he had. Part of him envied Jasmine's big, sprawling family and the close relationship she had with her cousins. After Yadiel had been born, Ashton had pulled away from other people in an effort to keep his son a secret, but it wore on him. He could have confided in his father—of anyone, Ignacio would understand the most—but he felt too guilty to burden his father with these feelings, especially when Ignacio was handling all of the day-to-day tasks of raising the boy.

Ashton knew he should be grateful. His family had always supported his dreams and his acting career. When he was young, they'd scrimped and saved to send him to a private school with a good drama program, and attended every one of his performances. All he'd ever wanted was to work his way up as an actor, to achieve fame and recognition for his work, and to be able to support his family the way they'd done for him. But now it felt like he was half-assing both. He had absolutely no business starting something with Jasmine he couldn't finish.

But there was something about her that kept drawing him in. Her skill and instinct as a scene partner, her leadership among the cast, her innate sense for when they needed a fun break and bonding opportunity, even the way she laughed at his dad jokes.

Okay, especially the way she laughed at his dad jokes. He knew he was awkward with her sometimes, and she never made him feel bad about it.

All that, yet it was her vulnerability that seduced him the most. Like when she'd asked him to stay, or when she'd come to his dressing room worried that he was mad at her, or even when she talked about her past relationships and her family. She was beautiful, funny, and smart, but in her, he recognized a loneliness that resonated with his own. How could he resist her?

He finished showering and shut off the water. He didn't have answers. But he'd have to find them. He didn't want to be another man who left her hurting.

Although he feared he would be.

SHE'D ASKED HIM to stay. And he *had*.

As much as Jasmine wanted to bask in the afterglow of the night she'd shared with Ashton, family obligation won out. Still, she held that single, affirming thought—*he'd stayed*—close to her as she suffered through brunch with her immediate family at a crowded West Village bistro.

Saturday at noon was prime brunch time in New York City, when everyone recovered from Friday night partying with carbs, bottomless mimosas, and the knowledge that Monday morning was still a full day away.

If only Ava and Michelle could be there. But this was an immediate-family-only outing, and so here she sat with her parents—Lisa and Julio—and her siblings—Jillian and Jeremy. In *hell*.

"And here's Hunter at day camp," her mother said, holding out her phone to show Jasmine yet another photo of Jillian's youngest son.

Jasmine shoved a big bite of huevos rancheros into her mouth to keep from answering. "Mm-hmm."

"And here he is at swimming class." Lisa swiped, squinted at her phone screen, then held it back out across the table for Jasmine to see.

"Nice." Jasmine chugged half of her current mimosa and signaled for the harried-looking waitress to bring her another. She had one hour to drink as many as she could, and she planned to make the most of it.

"And here he is at karate!"

Jasmine narrowly resisted the urge to snatch her mother's phone and toss it into the pitcher of sangria on the next table.

She loved her nephews. Truly, she did. Jillian had two funny and rambunctious little boys, and Jeremy's son was sweet and inquisitive. But her mother's pointed comments about how wonderful they were only drove home what she *wasn't* saying—that Jasmine was a loser with no husband and no kids. Bad enough that she didn't have a *real* job, but no family? Worthless.

"I know you're not on Facebook, so you've probably missed a lot of pictures," Lisa added.

Ouch. Way to twist the knife, Mom. Lisa knew full well Jasmine wasn't on social media because of the shitstorm surrounding her breakup with McIntyre, something her parents liked to pretend didn't exist.

Instead of voicing her frustration, Jasmine sent her mom a sunny smile and kept her voice light. "Well, you know I've been super busy with the new show. Not much time to waste scrolling on my phone."

It was a slightly passive-aggressive dig, since her mom and sister were known in the family for posting an excessive number of memes on Facebook, and Jeremy was constantly on Instagram. Even now he was watching something on his phone and chuckling to himself.

"We're glad you could join us, Jas," her father said, reaching over to pat her hand. He'd likely picked up on her annoyance. "We know your schedule is very full."

"But you're going to abuela's party, right?" Jillian asked, somehow making it sound like a jab.

"Of course I am." Jasmine couldn't believe her sister would imply that she wasn't. "I've been on the phone with the venue every few days, making sure it's all going according to plan. I wouldn't miss it."

Without commenting, Jillian turned to Jeremy. "Did you hear Tony's engaged?"

"No way." Jeremy's eyes went wide as he looked up from his phone. "Didn't think he'd ever settle down."

Jasmine could have kicked Jillian under the table. But what would be the point? *Family first*, which meant the expansion of the family, through marriage and childbirth, outweighed every other accomplishment. She'd been nominated for a Daytime Emmy, for god's sake. But when the news had been announced, her parents had responded with the text message equivalent of "that's nice, dear."

They had always been this way. Even when Jasmine was younger, she'd more often than not been left to fend for herself. Her parents both worked full time, Lisa as a nurse and Julio as a professor. Jillian, always an overachiever, had been involved in a ton of extracurricular activities that consumed more time and attention from their parents. Jeremy, the youngest and the only boy in a Latinx family, was the proud recipient of perpetual babying. And Jasmine, a middle child and people pleaser to the core, had faded into the background at home, using performance as a way to earn positive attention. Her parents had praised her early musical theater exploits, which was why it had been so confusing when they didn't support her choice to pursue acting as a career.

"And my cousin Lupita's youngest daughter is pregnant," Lisa added, reminding Jasmine what was *truly* important in this family. "Remember her? She lives in Seattle now."

The waitress handed Jasmine another drink and Jasmine held up two fingers. With a faint smile, the other woman mouthed, "I got you," and headed for the bar.

"Jer, show Jas that video of Mason doing a somersault," her father said, and Jeremy passed Jasmine his phone as reluctantly as if she'd asked for one of his kidneys. Mason was almost three, and absolutely darling. But today, Jasmine couldn't take one more reminder of what she was missing in her life.

"I'll be right back," she said, grabbing her own phone and shoving her chair back. "My agent just called."

Riley had *not* called, but they didn't know that. Jasmine just needed a break.

The waitress intercepted her on the way, holding a champagne flute in each hand.

"They're light on the orange juice," she said, handing the drinks to Jasmine. "Figured you could use it."

Jasmine took them gratefully and made a mental note to leave an extra good tip. "You are a lifesaver."

The waitress bit her lip, stalling like she wanted to say something, and that was when Jasmine knew she'd been recognized. People always got that nervous look before they asked—

"Were you on that show? *Sunrise Vista*, I mean. Was that you?"

Jasmine nodded and smiled. No matter how she was feeling, she was *always* kind to fans. It took courage to approach someone considered to be a celebrity, and everyone remembered when those celebs let them down. "Yes, that was me."

The woman gave a little squeal and pulled out her phone. "I thought so! Oh my god, I loved that show. I used to watch it before my late-night bartending shifts, and was so sad when it ended. Can I take a picture with you?"

"Sure, just crop out the drinks," Jasmine said with a wink, then leaned in to take a selfie with her. "What's your name?"

"Bethany."

"Thanks for the drinks, Bethany."

"You're welcome. Also . . ." Bethany pointed to an empty stool at the bar. "There's a spot there if you need to have a moment alone."

Shit, how much had she overheard? With a grateful nod, Jasmine carried her drinks over to the bar and took a seat. Sipping slowly, she texted the Primas of Power for support.

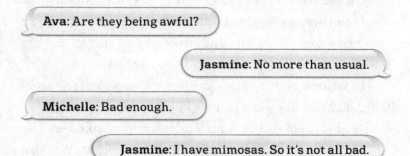

Jasmine: Help.

Ava: Are they being awful?

Jasmine: No more than usual.

Michelle: Bad enough.

Jasmine: I have mimosas. So it's not all bad.

She added some champagne glass emojis.

What she really wanted to do was tell them about Ashton and what she'd done with him last night. How he'd slept beside her and been so sweet this morning, holding her before he left.

And damn could he *kiss*. She didn't understand why he'd made a point of saying they shouldn't have intercourse, but it didn't bother her. He'd still made her feel cherished and wanted, and the orgasm had been amazing. Maybe he had an STI, and hadn't felt comfortable telling her in the moment? Or maybe he just wanted to take it slow, since this was technically their first *real* kiss? Either way, they could discuss it later.

She started to type a message to her cousins, but held back. The part of her brain that knew she was making stupid choices where a man was concerned had been flashing all sorts of warning signs. She just had years of practice ignoring them. If she told Ava and Michelle, she'd have to listen to that part of her mind, and then she'd have to listen as her cousins pointed out—rightly so—that she was not adhering to any of her goals. They'd remind her of the Leading Lady Plan and ask where she was on the Jasmine Scale. She'd blown so far past Crush that she didn't even want to think about when Infatuation had taken root.

Being with Ashton had been worth whatever second-guessing her common sense wanted to do. He'd made her feel special. And she hadn't only enjoyed their time in bed together—they'd had real fun during karaoke, and now that they were communicating, he was wonderful to act beside.

They'd have to "communicate" about this—about the way he'd touched her, stroked her, kissed her. Part of her really wanted to talk about it. But the other part knew they were better off sticking to the original plan of practicing their lines together, and no more.

She knew it. She just didn't care.

After finishing both drinks, she stood up, a little wobbly but with a nice enough buzz that she felt ready to face her family again. Determined to get through the rest of the meal without making any more passive-aggressive jabs—she'd be the better person, this time—she returned to the table . . . just in time for them to rehash all their old jokes about her vegan "phase," which had actually been an elimination diet to uncover food sensitivities.

Jasmine waved and got Bethany's attention again. "Just champagne," she said in a low voice. "Keep it coming."

Chapter 24

Ashton returned to Jasmine's room that evening with the script for episode seven and the best of intentions.

He'd spent two hours that morning sweating it out on the treadmill and with the weights, and then had an hour-long video call with his son that had reset his priorities. Yadiel was worried about the new school year because he'd heard from one of his friends that fourth grade was really hard, and he had a lot of thoughts about the latest Marvel movie. Afterward, Ashton had caught up with his father, who'd shared that Abuelito Gus's cough hadn't worsened, but neither had it gone away, and that Abuelita Bibi was experiencing knee pain but had refused to stop cooking at the restaurant.

Still, even with all that to think about, Ashton hadn't been able to put Jasmine out of his mind.

Bad idea, his brain told him as he knocked on the door. *You're going to end up hurting her.*

But he couldn't stay away.

Jasmine opened the door wearing a bright smile and the yellow floral romper she'd worn during their first rehearsal with Vera. Instantly, his anxiety eased.

"Hi," she said. "Come on in."

He followed her inside and was hit with the smell of hot pizza.

"Dinner?" he asked, spotting the box on the dining table. A half-eaten slice sat on a plate next to it. She picked it up and took a bite.

"I spent the day with my family and drank my weight in mimosas," she explained after she'd chewed. "All I want is pizza right now. Real New York City pizza with a soggy thin crust and too much cheese and oil."

"When in Rome, I guess." Ashton took a slice from the box. "Do you want to talk about it?"

"What, pizza?"

"No, your family."

She sighed dramatically and dropped into one of the chairs. "Not really? Maybe you can tell me about yours instead."

This was dangerous territory, but he sat and tried to answer without giving away too much. "My family owns a restaurant. My mother passed away ten years ago, but my father and grandparents still work there."

"They're in Puerto Rico, right?"

"Yes. I moved them to Miami after Maria, but they wanted to go back."

She took a fresh slice from the box. "They're okay with you being an actor?"

"Of course. They're my family. They've always supported my art."

Jasmine's eyebrows shot up and she gave him a look like, *Are you kidding me?* "What do you mean, *of course*? Don't take that for granted. I could win an Oscar and it wouldn't matter to my family."

Ashton shrugged as he chewed a bite of pizza. "My family has reacted to everything I've ever done like it's an Oscar win." That was why he wanted one so bad—so he could prove himself to everyone else.

Jasmine's expression turned wistful as she stared at the crust on her plate. "Must be nice. Mine only care if you're married and have kids. And yeah, I want those things, but I still have value as a person without them, you know?"

He blinked. She was right. He *was* lucky in how his parents supported his career. And also . . . she'd just revealed a lot about herself.

His heart ached for her, and he wanted to ask more, to hear the details of her day, of her family, of her childhood, but she flipped open her copy of the script and said blithely, "Episode seven. The penultimate episode. What happens?"

Ashton swallowed the food in his mouth. All right, she clearly didn't want to talk about her family, but he'd thought they'd at least discuss what they'd done last night on this very table. However, he recognized a subject change when he heard one, so he respected her wishes and answered. "Victor spills his guts on a bunch of talk shows."

"Oh, lots of *feelings*," she teased. "Marquita loves including those moments."

"From the top?" he asked.

"Sure, why not?" Jasmine kicked back in the chair and crossed her bare feet at the ankles. "Looks like it starts with a montage. I'll read the parts of the hosts."

They were halfway through the second scene, which featured a Kelly Ripa–like TV host, when Jasmine tossed a wadded-up paper napkin at him. It landed on his script.

He shot her a quizzical look, and she shook her head at him.

"What's up?" she asked. "You're distracted. You keep looking around the room."

"Oh." His face warmed. "I keep waiting for your cousins to barge through the door."

Her teasing expression smoothed and her gaze turned hot. "They don't know you're here."

"No? I thought you told them everything."

She shook her head slowly, her eyes never leaving his. "Not everything."

And there it was. An allusion to the previous night.

Suddenly, Ashton couldn't breathe. His chest tightened, his skin heated, and before he could talk himself out of it, he tossed his script on the floor and reached for her.

They came together, Jasmine all but leaping onto his lap to straddle his legs. He planted his hands on her round ass and squeezed as her mouth crushed down on his.

"You taste like pizza," she murmured against his lips.

"So do you."

Ashton pumped his hips up toward her heat, pressed so close to him. Slipping his fingers under the hem of her romper, he groaned when he found her bare. "No panties?"

"Nuh-uh." She grabbed his hands and pressed them to her chest. "No bra either."

"You're incredible." He breathed the words against her neck as his fingers flexed on her breasts, cupping them through the thin fabric. "How do you take this thing off?"

"Like this." She got off his lap, and when he would have protested, he swallowed his words instead, practically drooling as she yanked on the neckline and shimmied out of the garment. And then she was utterly, gloriously naked.

"Ven acá," he said with a growl, catching her wrist and pulling her over to him.

With a breathless giggle, she resumed her place on his lap and wrapped one arm around his shoulders. Her other hand snaked down between them to stroke him through the fabric of his pants. He gasped, his cock surging at her touch.

They were doing this. They were definitely doing this. Consequences be damned, he had to get inside her.

"Forget what I said yesterday." Desperation made his voice gravelly. "We should definitely have sex."

She met his eyes, her expression uncertain. "Are you sure?"

"I'm sure." He realized he was being presumptive and hastened to add, "If you are?"

She huffed out a laugh. "Oh, I am one hundred percent on board with having penetrative sex with you."

He groaned and pressed his face into her shoulder. "Did I really call it that?"

"You sure did." She touched his chin, gently urging him to look at her. "Do you want to tell me why?"

"I . . . don't cross that line with coworkers." It was as good a way to explain it as any.

She just nodded. "It's a smart policy. I get it."

"But I want to . . . with you." Total understatement.

Her smile was sweet, but that fire was back in her eyes. "Me too."

It seemed silly to sit around talking when he had a naked woman on his lap. And now that they were on the same page . . .

He gripped her thighs and stood, lifting her as he had the night before. "Condoms?"

She wrapped her arms and legs around him, arching to thrust her breasts in his face. "Bedroom."

He carried her in, but didn't set her by the bed. Instead, he put her on the dresser. "Quédate aquí," he ordered sternly, and she giggled.

He found the condoms in the drawer with the lube, so he grabbed that too. The assortment of pink and purple vibrating devices was interesting, but not for tonight. Tonight, he'd keep it simple.

That line of thinking implied they'd have more than just tonight, so he pushed the thought aside and returned to her with a deep, searching kiss.

She helped him undress, their movements frantic and fumbling. "Hurry," she kept saying, and he gloried in the knowledge that she was as anxious for this as he was. She already had a condom unwrapped by the time he'd shed his pants and underwear, so he held still—barely—while she unrolled it down his length with torturously slow movements. But when she reached for the bottle of lube, he shook his head and took it from her.

"Hop down," he said, helping her off the dresser. Then

he turned her around to face the rectangular mirror hanging over it.

Their eyes met in the reflection, and a slow, sensual smile spread over her lips.

Apparently she was on board with his idea, too, because she spread her feet and braced her hands on the edge of the dresser. Her willingness and enthusiasm were arousing all on their own, but damn, she was stunning too. He swallowed hard, admiring her long legs, the curve of her ass, the arch of her back—until she turned and raised her eyebrows at him.

"Are you going to take all day?"

"No, querida. I'm here."

And he was. He was here, all in, for whatever came next. For tonight, it was just them. Just this.

Tomorrow . . . well, they'd deal with tomorrow when it arrived.

QUERIDA. HE'D CALLED her *querida*.

Warmth spread over Jasmine's body at the term of endearment. The way it rolled off his tongue, the feeling of being dear to someone, made her want to get even closer to him. And tonight, they would.

She curled her toes into the carpet as she watched Ashton prepping behind her, the mirror affording her a front-row view. God, she loved the look of him naked. He was perfectly proportioned, with an easy strength and confidence in his own skin that was so damned attractive. And his cock was pretty great too.

He squirted some lube into his hand, then set the bottle aside. Stepping closer, he gripped her hip, then slipped the lubed-up hand between her legs.

At the first touch of his fingers on her pussy, she shut her eyes and let out a low moan. The way he caressed her there was so fucking lovely. Gentle, but sure. He smoothed the lube over her folds, coating her with the gel to make sure she was wet and open. His fingers teased her entrance and she sighed, her breath hitching when he found her clit and stroked.

"Please," she whispered, shaking her ass to hurry him along.

It worked. With a groan, he moved behind her and bent his knees. His thighs pressed against hers, and then the head of his cock prodded at her. Their eyes met in the mirror and she sucked in a breath. His handsome features were stark with the intensity of his concentration, and his dark gaze entranced her. This kind of single-minded focus—on her—was a turn-on like no other. Then he pushed forward, filling her, stretching her. Pleasure detonated her thoughts into stardust. The lube and her own readiness eased the way, but he still felt impossibly thick inside her.

And so fucking good.

He had to rock himself back and forth a bit to stretch her, but when he was fully sheathed, with his hips pressed against her ass, she dug her nails into the edge of the dresser and hissed out a breath.

Panting, he leaned over her back and braced his hands next to hers. "Okay?"

"Perfect." She thrust her butt back against him, and it was

like that one move broke his control. His arm snaked around her waist and he began to thrust, setting a fast, pounding pace that left her breathless. The power in those thighs, the passion in his gaze—he was consuming her from the inside out. And all she could do was hold on for the ride.

"Cójelo," he growled in her ear, and she just sobbed "yes" over and over in response.

Her entire world narrowed to his cock shuttling in and out of her, his skin slapping against hers, his harsh pants and growls, his lips hot against her ear whispering Spanish dirty talk. His hands moved up and down her body—rolling her tight nipples, squeezing her madly bouncing breasts, rubbing circles over her clit. She was a mass of throbbing sensation, originating from where he hammered into her. Just like before, her pleasure was his sole focus.

She loved it. She couldn't take it. She never wanted him to stop.

When her limbs threatened to give out, he gathered her close, letting her lean on him. He held her up with his hands on her breasts and between her legs, and with the force of his straining thighs and cock. Their sweat-dampened bodies slid together, generating heat and friction.

Through it all, they watched each other in the mirror. There were no barriers here, nothing but naked, hungry passion. She'd spent so long trying to get past his walls and now she was in. What she found there rocked her to the core. She hadn't been prepared, and now, with her emotional defenses demolished by the waves of arousal coursing through her, she was perilously close to the abyss at the end of the Jasmine Scale.

When her eyes tried to drift shut, powerless against the ecstasy he was building in her, he thrust harder and murmured, "Mírame."

Look at me.

Ashton's gaze was blazing hot, demanding that she feel everything he had to give and more. So she did.

Electric spirals of bliss flashed through her, and her cries took on an urgent pitch. She was close to her breaking point. This much sensation, this much emotion, couldn't sustain itself. It had to crest, or it would consume them.

She reached behind her and gripped his thigh with one hand, reveling in the unyielding muscles, in the strength behind his thrusts. And surrendered fully to the pleasure zinging through her.

"Querida," Ashton breathed in her ear. "*Come for me.*"

How could she do otherwise?

Her body tensed, all her muscles contracting. And then she exploded from within. She shook in his arms, racked by the waves of sensation flooding her senses and overloading her nerve endings. Euphoria cleared her mind and left her senseless to anything that wasn't the press of his skin on hers. She would have collapsed onto the carpet if it weren't for him.

His arm tightened around her waist. He braced himself against the dresser with his free hand. And with his eyes still on hers in the mirror, he pumped into her until, with a grimace and a groan, his body stiffened and he followed her over the edge.

The silence in the room was deafening without the sounds of their pants and moans. She couldn't have moved if she wanted to. Her mind was utterly blank, still focused on her body and taking stock of her limbs, her balance, and where they were still joined.

Then, a single thought came to her: Ashton Suarez had just fucked her brains out. And she'd *loved* it.

After a moment, Ashton slipped out of her. He kept his arm around her waist and shifted her to the bed. She sank onto it, boneless, as he stumbled drunkenly into the bathroom. Finally, she closed her eyes.

She thought she fell asleep, drifting in hazy bliss. Then Ashton stroked her arm. "Jasmine. Me voy."

"Hmm?" Wait, he was leaving?

She sat up and saw he was already fully dressed.

"If I stay, neither of us will get any sleep. And I can see that you're tired." He pulled the bedsheet over her legs, then bent and kissed her lips, long and sweet. "Tomorrow?"

"I have to go to the Bronx." Her thoughts were still a little scrambled and her voice was husky from the most amazing fucking orgasm she'd ever experienced in her entire life. "To see my grandparents. I'll text you when I get back?"

"Okay. We still have to go over our lines. We got a little . . . distracted tonight." His easy grin warmed her. It was on the tip of her tongue to ask him to stay again, but he did look tired, and she was ready to curl up and pass out.

She was also worried that she'd only be asking to see if he said yes again. And she didn't want to play those games with Ashton.

When she nodded, he cupped her face and kissed her again. "Dulces sueños, querida."

She heard him leave, then flopped back on the bed with a giddy smile on her face. Sweet dreams, indeed.

Chapter 25

For the next week, Ashton spent every nonworking minute he could with Jasmine. Not that there were many, since the seventh episode required long days and multiple on-location shoots, but they managed to steal time here and there.

He knew he was asking for trouble, sneaking around in a hotel where some of the other actors and higher-up crew members were also staying, but he couldn't stop.

They saw each other at work, of course, but it was different. They were careful not to do anything to arouse suspicion—no heated looks, no lingering glances—although Ofelia had remarked on their improved performances a few times, and Ashton worried the first AD was starting to suspect something was up.

However, they were most careful around Vera, who had an uncanny knack for tuning into their emotional states. Pretending that he wasn't falling locamente enamorado with Jasmine was the most difficult role he'd ever tried to pull off. Even harder than the time he'd played his own evil clone.

After being on location all week, it was nice to be back at the ScreenFlix Studios lot on Friday, which was gradually feeling more familiar to him. Ashton was in between filming Victor's daytime talk show performances when he ran into Jasmine chatting with Nino and Lily at craft services.

Nino waved him over. "Hey, Ash. You coming to the summit tonight?"

Ashton shot Jasmine a puzzled look. "What summit?"

"The Latinx in the Arts Summit," she told him. "It's a new group, and they're having their first big event tonight."

"The three of us are being honored together as part of their '30 Under 30' in the performing arts category," Lily explained.

"I'm technically already thirty," Jasmine admitted. "Do you think they'll drag me off the stage if they find out?"

"It's okay, vieja," Lily said with a grin. "If we average all three of our ages, we come out somewhere in our late twenties."

"Thanks to me," Nino scoffed. "So, Ash, you want to come with us? We have VIP tickets, which means open bar!"

Jasmine caught Ashton's eye. "You don't have to, if you don't want," she said quietly. "I know it's not really your thing."

It wasn't his thing at all, but supporting Jasmine had quickly *become* his thing. And in his view, you showed support by showing up, like his parents had done all those years for him.

"Sure, I'll go," he said.

"Really?" Jasmine's eyes went round.

"Awesome." Nino grinned. "I'm bringing my mom, and she can't wait to meet you. She loved *El duque de amor.*"

A sinking feeling dragged at Ashton's stomach, like a premonition, but it was just anxiety. Then he saw Jasmine's grateful smile, and knew he could endure the discomfort for her happiness.

The summit was held at an event space near Hudson Yards. After they were done shooting for the day, they all went back to the Hutton Court to change, and Ashton shared a taxi crosstown with Jasmine.

"I'm surprised you're not bringing anyone from your family," he said, lacing his fingers with hers on the seat between them and relishing in the private moment where he could touch her without worrying.

She shrugged and gazed out the window at the city passing by. "It was late notice. Ava's babysitting and Michelle is working on a big design project."

"What about your parents, or your brother or sister?"

She turned back to him with an incredulous laugh. "Are you kidding me? It would just stress me out to have any of them there."

He didn't say anything, but he hoped he got to meet her parents someday, so he could tell them how amazing their daughter was. They were missing out on knowing her.

"I appreciate that you're coming with me, especially since you don't like big events." She squeezed his hand. "I would have asked, you know. But I didn't want to put you on the spot."

Ashton brought their joined hands to his mouth and kissed her fingers. "You still could have asked."

The look in her eyes was so hopeful, it made his chest ache. "Now I know."

As the car pulled up near the event space, Ashton released her hand. They'd agreed to keep this—whatever it was—secret. Ashton didn't know how long they could keep it up, but he couldn't deny that he was feeling lighter and happier than he had in a long time. He entered the summit at Jasmine's side, riding a wave of optimism.

It took less than an hour to bring him back down to reality.

He *hated* events like this.

The crush of people was packed into an open space, hemmed in by a stage at one end and a bar at the other. The format was loose—more party than conference—and Ashton felt completely exposed and far too easily recognized. Everywhere he turned, someone saw his face and gasped, and then he had to make nice and pose for pictures until he could politely get away. Then someone else recognized him, and he had to do the whole thing all over.

He drank three gin and tonics during the first hour in an attempt to calm his nerves, but he was still ready to climb out a window. The party was on the ground floor, so it would probably work. Then he could hail a taxi, go back to the hotel, and—

Someone grabbed his elbow and he jumped, nearly spilling his fourth G&T. It was Tanya Onai, the ScreenFlix publicist assigned to *Carmen*. She was a pretty young woman, tall with dark brown skin and long box braids.

She was also the one with the power to make him do interviews, so he'd studiously avoided her thus far. But now she had him cornered.

He sipped his drink to clear his throat, then muttered a hello.

Tanya released his arm and gave him a bland smile. "You look like you're planning an escape."

"That obvious?"

She shook her head at him, sending her braids sliding over her shoulders. "I have a sense for when my actors are about to make a run for it. Also, you're getting drunk in a corner, staring longingly at the windows. Yes, it's obvious."

He set the drink aside, because she was right, and mumbled, "I don't like big crowds."

"They'll be on stage soon," she promised. "Stick it out a little longer. We'll clap, take some pictures, and then all of us can go home and start our weekends."

He nodded and accepted the carton of water she handed him. It was fine. He'd done this before, and he'd have to do it again. He was okay.

But that didn't stop him from looking over his shoulder or feeling better when his back was to the wall.

The best moment of the night was when Jasmine, Lily, and Nino were on stage. They were interviewed as a group by a Mexican American poet, who asked great questions about the ways personal identity and cultural history played into creative work.

Ashton nearly burst with pride every time Jasmine spoke. She captivated the audience in a way that had nothing to do with being an actor and everything to do with being *her*. Her smile, her humor, and her ability to share vulnerably had the room hanging on her every word.

Lily and Nino also shared moving stories about their own paths to becoming actors, about the struggles and triumphs, and Ashton felt honored to be working on *Carmen* with them too.

He clapped loudly at the end of their segment, but was interrupted by someone asking for a photo.

"Stop scowling," Tanya murmured when the person walked away. "Can't you at least act like you're enjoying yourself? You might as well get used to it. You have a press tour coming up. ScreenFlix wants to send you and Jasmine everywhere to drum up interest in the show."

Ashton attempted to relax his facial muscles. "Double-check my contract. I think you'll see there are limitations to the amount of press work I'm required to do."

Tanya's amused grin was as sharp as a blade. "We'll see about that."

Ominous. But Ashton didn't have a chance to dwell on it, since Jasmine, Nino, and Lily were leaving the stage and coming over to join them.

Jasmine took one look at his face and feigned a yawn. Ashton knew it was fake, because when she yawned for real, it was nowhere near as dainty.

"I'm super tired," she told the others. "I think I'll go back to the hotel."

Ashton narrowed his eyes and gave a barely perceptible shake of his head. He knew what she was doing, and he wouldn't let her leave early on his account.

Even though all he wanted to do was leave. And the thought of cuddling with her before heading back to his own room held a lot of appeal.

Still, this was her moment. She was being recognized for her contribution to Latinx representation in media. There was no reason for her to—

"I'll go too," Lily said. "My feet are killing me. Remind me to throw these shoes in la basura."

Well, that changed things.

Ashton pulled out his phone. "I'll get us a car."

Tanya shook her head. "Pictures first. Then you can all leave."

As she herded them over to the Latinx in the Arts photo backdrop, Jasmine sidled up next to Ashton and whispered, "I tried."

"I know. You didn't have to. But thank you."

Jasmine gave him a reassuring smile. "We'll leave soon, okay?"

It was almost another hour before Tanya released them, and by the time Ashton climbed into a car with Jasmine and Lily, he was practically vibrating with nerves. Jasmine shot him worried looks on the ride back to the Hutton Court, but Lily—who'd taken her heels off immediately upon getting in the taxi—kept up the conversation well enough that he didn't need to contribute much.

In the elevator, they all pressed the buttons for their floors. Lily—still barefoot—got off first, and when the elevator stopped on Jasmine's floor, Ashton got off with her. Once they were in her suite with the door firmly shut behind them, she caught him in a tight hug.

"I'm so sorry," she said into his chest. "You hated it. I knew you would hate it."

He wrapped his arms around her like he'd wanted to do all night, and breathed in the soothing citrus scent of her hair. "It's not your fault, querida. I'm an adult, and I agreed to go."

"I know, but—"

He cupped her face in his hands and kissed her deeply. "It means more to me than I can tell you that you tried to give me an out, twice. And while it's true that I don't enjoy events like that—"

"No kidding."

He smiled, and continued. "I was happy to be there to support you and the others."

"If you say so." She took his hand and led him to the sofa, where they sat and got comfortable—Jasmine kicking off her own high heels and Ashton shrugging out of his suit jacket.

"Do you want wine?" she asked. "I have a bottle of chardonnay in the fridge."

He shook his head. "I drank more than enough at the open bar."

She put a hand on his knee. "Do you want to talk about it?"

He covered her hand with his and looked down at the splay of their fingers. The truth was, he never wanted to talk about it, and he'd decided that if he didn't talk about it, it couldn't affect him. If no one else, aside from his family, knew what had happened, it couldn't haunt him.

That mindset didn't work. It still affected him. And he very much wanted to tell her. Now.

Before he could talk himself out of it, he said, "Around seven years ago, someone tried to break into my house."

She gasped, and the hand on his knee squeezed. "Oh, Ashton."

"I had a stalker. A fan. He'd been writing to me a lot. Letters, packages, that sort of thing. All of the mail got filtered through my agency, so it took a while for anyone to notice it had gotten excessive—and aggressive. And even when my agent's assistant realized it, I didn't want to believe it was a concern. I had enough to worry about without some overzealous fan, so I put it out of my head. Until . . ."

Jasmine shifted closer, her eyes shining with sympathy. "Until?"

He took a deep breath, let it out slowly. He had never talked about this with anyone who hadn't already known, and putting it into words was almost like reliving it. A reminder of the fear, of the destruction of his sense of safety in his own home.

It was why he wouldn't live in a house. He felt safer in apartments with doormen and security systems, high above the ground. No one could break his window when he was ten stories up.

She was waiting patiently. He wanted to kiss her, to forget about the Incident and lose himself in her touch, but it suddenly felt imperative that he get these words out. He swallowed hard and continued.

"Until he found out where I lived and tried to break in."

Saying the words out loud made him realize that this was the crux of his ongoing fear. Ashton had always thought that the scariest part of the whole thing was that the intruder had broken Yadiel's nursery window, endangering that which was most precious to him. But in telling Jasmine the story without mentioning Yadiel, Ashton realized . . . it was still pretty scary. The whole thing was scary.

And maybe . . . it was okay for him to have felt afraid. To *still* feel afraid.

Jasmine gently tugged on his hand, pulling him into her embrace. Ashton clung to her, letting her warmth anchor him. She held him for a long time, stroking his hair and his back, and he took the comfort she gave, soaking it in and letting it refill the well that had been empty for years.

Finally, she whispered, "Thank you for telling me."

He let out a shaky breath. "Thank you for listening. I think . . . I'll stay here, tonight, if that's okay."

He swore he could feel her smile against his hair. "Of course."

Ashton eased back first, because he got the feeling she'd hold on to him for as long as he needed it. And while he was starting to realize that he did need it, he knew she had to be tired.

They got ready for bed, taking turns in the bathroom, and then climbed under the covers together.

In the dark, all cozy under the covers with the soft whirr of the air-conditioning unit insulating them from the outside world, Ashton finally found the courage to ask her something he'd been wondering for a while. "Jasmine?"

"Yeah?"

"What happened with McIntyre?"

She let out a sigh and he felt her deflate next to him. "You want the whole story?"

"Not the whole thing. Just . . ."

"The end?"

He felt like a dick for asking. But he sensed that, like him, Jasmine also carried a burden. "Yeah."

She shifted, tangling her legs with his. "Well, he broke up with me. Via tabloid."

Ashton's eyes widened, though she couldn't see his reaction. "*No.*"

"Oh, yes." Her voice held a trace of amusement. "I thought he was traveling for a pop-up concert. It turned out he was in Mexico with my doppelgänger—you might remember seeing her picture before I broke the TV in the fitness center."

At the time, he'd wondered about that, but of course, hadn't wanted to ask.

"Anyway, he told a reporter—my nemesis, Kitty Sanchez— that we were over. It was supposedly an *exclusive interview* but was probably just some offhand comment while he was leaving the plane at LAX. The quote ran with the photos of him making out with this other actress, and I . . ." She shrugged. "I found out while I was buying paper towels at Target and saw my own face on the cover of *Buzz Weekly*."

He was stunned. "That must have been terrible."

"Yeah. I had to buy the damn magazine to find out that he'd broken up with me. They didn't even have the decency to put the pertinent info on the cover."

"Jasmine, please don't take this the wrong way . . ."

"I promise I won't."

"But that . . . that was it?"

She laughed. "Yup."

"I mean, he's clearly the most stupid man in the world to cheat on you. Especially with someone who looks just like you, but who I guarantee isn't as amazing as you are."

She squeezed him around the waist. "Thank you."

"But some pictures and a short quote . . . that's why they're hounding you at the studio every day?"

"Yup."

"And making up all those ridiculous stories and headlines?"

"I think my favorite was something like ROCK STAR RAKE REJECTS GIRLFRIEND IN RIVAL REBOUND. Totally false, since I'd never even heard of the other woman, but points for alliteration."

He cuddled her tighter. "I'm sorry you had to go through all that. Are *still* going through that. It's not fair. And you don't deserve it."

"Can I tell you something?" Her voice was soft and sleepy.

"Go ahead."

"I just . . . wanted to be in love. I wanted to love someone, and I wanted them to love me. And I thought he might. Instead, I got dragged by the press for daring to believe a man more famous than I am might possibly love me."

She let out a huge yawn, then snuggled closer to his chest.

Ashton tightened his hold on her, but inside, he'd gone cold.

It wasn't her confession that scared him. She was a beautiful person inside and out, and she deserved to love and be loved. He hated that this McIntyre pendejo had treated her so poorly, and that the tabloid machine had made it worse. Except her words made him realize something he should have thought of on his own.

All this time, he'd worried what would happen to *him* if someone started rumors about the two of them. He was such a fool. The whole time, he should have been more worried about what would happen to *her*.

Because yes, while his feelings for her were real, and growing stronger every day, there could be no future for them. Nothing long-term, anyway. He was a single father. Relationships were hard enough in this business without the constant threat of the media or a fan taking things too far. Being a father meant Yadiel was and always would be his first priority. His family depended on him for everything, and Jasmine . . .

There was no way he could give her what she wanted. What she *deserved*.

She let out a soft sigh, something he'd noticed she did as she was falling asleep. It was utterly adorable.

And he should leave right now, before their emotions became even more deeply entwined.

Una noche más, he told himself, settling his head on the pillow. He'd take this one last night to cherish the comfort she'd freely given, and try to give back some of his own.

Then he'd figure out how to put some space between them before anyone found out, and before either of them got hurt.

Chapter 26

Jasmine awoke the next morning alone. She reached out a hand, patting the mattress to see if Ashton had shifted over during the night, and instead found a note he'd scrawled on the hotel memo pad. She squinted at it in the dim light edging around the room's thick curtains.

Jas—

Early flight to PR. Didn't want to wake you. Thank you for . . . everything.

XO Ash

The "thank you" made her smile. And while she missed morning cuddles, she did appreciate being able to sleep in. Last night had been a whole lot, emotionally speaking, and she wanted some time to process.

After what Ashton had shared with her, it was no wonder he hated being followed by the paparazzi and doing press events.

No wonder he kept others at arm's length. These aspects of his behavior made complete sense now; he wasn't a diva—he was guarded, and with good reason. But she couldn't help but wonder, had he always felt anxiety around crowds, or had it started after his home security had been breached?

She knew how it felt to have one's privacy violated, but having personal information made public was different than being made a target and then having your home attacked. That kind of experience changed a person.

The whole McIntyre fiasco had taken a toll on her, although it was still so recent, she didn't yet know what the long-term effects would be. Would she ever feel comfortable living in Los Angeles again? Would she be able to regain trust in her old friends and coworkers from the soaps?

She didn't have the answers yet. Thank goodness working on *Carmen* allowed her time to lick her wounds at home, in New York City, surrounded by those who loved her most. Her family was far from perfect, but at least they wouldn't betray her secrets to reporters.

That said, she was due in the Bronx that afternoon for a barbecue, so as much as she wanted to spend the day lazing around and thinking about Ashton, she couldn't.

The 6 train on a Saturday morning was her idea of a personal hell, so Jasmine took a taxi from the hotel to her grandparents' row house in Castle Hill, an extravagance she never would have made the last time she lived in New York.

Seven of the twelve Rodriguez cousins were there when Jasmine arrived, along with her parents, all of her father's siblings, and their spouses. The adults were scattered throughout the living room, kitchen, and backyard, while Jasmine's nephews and her cousins' kids played downstairs in the basement.

As was expected, Jasmine made the rounds, saying hello and dropping a kiss onto the cheek of every single relative. It took forty-five minutes. First she got roped into a ridiculous argument with her brother and sister about who had done the most chores when they were children, and then she actually enjoyed a quick chat with her tío Luisito's husband, Archer, about his book club. Her parents seemed happy to see her, but Jasmine ran away when she saw her mother set aside the tray of lumpia to reach for her phone.

When she was finally done greeting everyone, Jasmine grabbed Michelle from the basement video game tournament and Ava from the kitchen and locked them in one of the upstairs bedrooms with her.

"I had sex with Ashton," she blurted out the second the door was closed.

Ava's eyes went wide, but Michelle just smirked. "Knew it," she said.

"Don't be smug," Ava chided. Then she winced, and said, "But I knew it too."

Jasmine sighed and sat on the edge of the bed. "Am I *that* predictable?"

"You kinda are," Michelle said with a shrug. She leaned her butt against the old, ornately carved wooden dresser that displayed a statue of the Virgin Mary and a dish of rosary beads on top. "But can we blame you? No."

"There's also serious chemistry between you two," Ava added, taking a seat next to Jasmine. "Which is good, right? It'll come through on the show?"

Jasmine groaned. "Except it was supposed to *only* be on the show. Why am I like this?"

"Because you're an Aries," Michelle said matter-of-factly. "You love *love*."

Ava sighed and looked to the ceiling for help.

"Okay fine, you want a real answer? Look around." Michelle waved her hands, encompassing their surroundings. "The men in this family get away with acting like a bunch of babies. They sit around eating and talking while the women do everything. The Latinx gender roles run *deep*. Is it any wonder our generation has made such sucky romantic choices? I don't date." She pointed at Ava. "She's divorced. And you're a serial monogamist. We're like a freaking relationship bingo board."

Jasmine and Ava just stared at her.

"What?" Michelle threw up her hands. "Tell me I'm wrong."

Jasmine flopped back on the bed. "No, you're right. I just don't know how to navigate this. I've had so many relationships but this, somehow, feels way more real than any of the others."

"Why don't you talk us through it?" Ava suggested.

Jasmine thought back. "The first time he came over, yeah, we'd both been drinking, and it was hot and spontaneous. But we just fooled around. And he stayed the night, which—well, I didn't expect it, and I don't think he did either, but it was really nice, you know? And then the second time—"

"Whoa, hold on. Wait." Michelle stopped her. "There was more than one incident? When were you gonna tell us so we can live vicariously through your affair with the telenovela star? Which, by the way, would be a great title for a memoir."

Jasmine sent her a dark glare. "I'm telling you *now*."

"All right, sorry. Continue."

"Anyway, he came over the next night, and I think we were both kidding ourselves. He brought his script and we started off like we always do, rehearsing our lines, but then suddenly we were both naked and I was having the best sex of my life."

Ava sighed. "Jealous. Keep going."

"That night, he didn't stay, but since then, we've been . . . together. A lot."

How did she even explain what was happening between them when she didn't fully understand it herself? On the surface level, it was simple. They were two consenting adults having sex.

Okay, there was *nothing* simple about sex with Ashton, but she couldn't explain why. Aside from the fact that he was very, very good at it.

Jasmine stared up at the ceiling, trying to put her mixed-up emotions into words, when Ava interrupted with a question.

"Do you want a relationship with him?"

The answer was yes, and they all knew it. Jasmine wanted a loving relationship more than anything in the world. But for once, she didn't want to rush it or imagine things that weren't there. She'd never had this sort of open connection with anyone else before. But they hadn't discussed commitment or plans for the future, and her biggest fear was that Ashton would drop her like all the others had.

"I really like him," she admitted. "It's . . . I don't know. I think he's different?"

"Do you want to keep having sex with him?" Michelle asked in her typical blunt fashion.

"Well, *yes*, but . . . I don't know if I should." Jasmine sat up and sent them a pleading look. "I'm fucking up my Leading Lady Plan."

"Is that what this is about?" Ava asked gently. "Jas, you're not being graded on it."

"But I *am*. This is work. I don't want to screw this up."

"Then don't," Michelle said, as if it were that simple.

"Aaaaa-vaaaa," someone yelled from downstairs. "¿Dónde estás?"

Ava rolled her eyes. "Titi Nita wants my help with the lasagna. I asked why we're having lasagna at a summer barbecue, but they told me not to question the adults."

"We should go downstairs anyway." Jasmine got to her feet. "If we're gone too long, they'll start talking about us."

Michelle snorted. "They'll do that whether we're there or not."

While Ava got roped into helping with lasagna, Jasmine and Michelle escaped to the backyard and sat on plastic patio chairs, munching on chips. Someone moved into the sun, casting a shadow over them, and Jasmine looked up to see Sammy. She didn't like the joking grin on his face, but she tried to give him the benefit of the doubt.

"What's up, Sammy?" she asked. "How's Erica's new job going?"

Maybe if Sammy started talking about something else, he'd forget whatever bullshit he came over here to say. Erica was his seventeen-year-old daughter, and she wasn't at the barbecue because she'd just started working at the Gap on weekends to save money for college.

He shrugged. "She's happy to have the clothing discount."

"That's good."

Then Sammy waggled his eyebrows at her. "So, when's McIntyre gonna put a ring on it? Or did he just *mack* and *tire*?"

"Oh my god." Jasmine pressed her fingers to her eyes.

"Get it? Like he got tired of y—"

"Shut *up*, Sammy." Michelle shot back. "You're just jealous 'cuz you love that douchebag's music."

"Michelle! Language!" Esperanza shouted from inside the kitchen.

"The kids are all downstairs, Abuela!"

"This." Jasmine bolted up from her chair and jabbed a finger in Sammy's direction. "*This* is why I live three thousand miles away."

"Aww, Jas, I'm just messing with you," Sammy called after her as she stormed back into the house.

Jasmine didn't know where she was going—maybe upstairs, maybe the living room, maybe out the front door and back to the hotel where she could brood about Ashton in peace. Hell, maybe even all the way back to California. But Esperanza intercepted her on her way through the kitchen.

She placed her hands on Jasmine's cheeks and peered into her face.

"Muchacha, are you using that snail eye cream I told you about?" Esperanza sounded deeply concerned. "You look tired."

"Sí, Abuela," Jasmine replied through gritted teeth. "I use eye cream every day."

"And night?" Esperanza raised her eyebrows, waiting on Jasmine's answer.

Oh, for the love of— "Yes, every night."

"Bueno." Esperanza patted her cheeks and went back to stirring the rice on the stove.

Her grandmother was obsessed with skincare, and now that she'd discovered text messages and online shopping, she was forever sending Jasmine links to anti-aging products. Excessive nagging was how Esperanza showed she cared, but Jasmine couldn't deny she was feeling worn-out today, and it probably showed.

"Give la nena a break." Willie Rodriguez, Jasmine's beloved grandfather, eased up behind his wife and dropped a kiss to the top of her head. "Jasmine's eyes are beautiful."

"Thanks, Abuelo." Jasmine gave him a grateful smile. He was barely taller than Jasmine, with brown skin, a mustache that had gone white in recent years, and the kindest face she'd ever known.

The door behind Jasmine opened. Michelle entered the kitchen and signaled for Ava to get away from the oven.

Esperanza held up her hands like she was backing off, when in truth she never backed off from anything. "Yo lo sé, pero it's never too early to start fighting wrinkles."

Willie sent Jasmine a wink, and she took that as her cue to

beat a hasty retreat. Jasmine ducked out of the kitchen with the Primas of Power on her heels.

"Basement?" Michelle suggested. "I stashed two bottles of wine down there."

"Basement," Jasmine agreed. She'd take her chances with the children, who at least acknowledged that being on TV was a real job.

"Let's get day drunk." Ava grabbed plastic cups and they trooped downstairs to hide until the food was ready.

WHEN ASHTON DECIDED to put distance between himself and Jasmine, he hadn't meant miles. But talking about the Incident had triggered a deep need to see for himself that his family was okay. So after waking up early in her bed, he'd left her a note, gone back to his room to shower and change, then caught an early flight to San Juan.

Once again, his family had been surprised and happy to see him, although his father had pointedly remarked that it would be nice to know about these visits *in advance*. Abuelita Bibi fussed over him, as she always had, and Abuelito Gus had a lot of opinions to share about the latest *Mission Impossible* movie.

Being home was a relief. Seeing them safe and whole was a relief. But the restlessness that propelled him here refused to abate.

After they left for the restaurant, Ashton tried to lose himself in playing with Yadiel, like he'd done on his last visit, but all day long, one thought followed him.

He'd told her.

He still couldn't believe it. Aside from Yadiel, the Incident was his most closely guarded secret. He didn't even like refer-encing it with people who already knew. And while he wanted to blame his confession on gin or stress, those were lies.

The simple truth was that he trusted Jasmine.

And that scared him. If he'd trusted her with one of his se-crets, it made it too easy to think about trusting her with the other.

That secret was currently clomping down the stairs. Ashton looked up from where he sat on the sofa, idly watching a base-ball game while he waited for his son to "do something" in his bedroom. Yadiel approached him with an armload of books and dumped them unceremoniously and without proper warn-ing onto Ashton's lap.

Ashton jolted as the books—most of them hardcovers with sharp corners—landed on his thighs and groin.

"Papi." Yadiel's voice held a distinct tone of decree that im-mediately made Ashton suspicious. It was the same way the kid had announced that he wanted an Xbox.

"¿Sí?"

"I *want* to *go* to *New York*." Yadiel said it in English, like he was proving he was ready for the trip, placing emphasis on every other word.

Yadi had a bad habit of saying what he wanted with force instead of just asking in the form of a question and adding "por favor," so Ashton raised his eyebrows. "Are you asking me or telling me?"

"¿Puedo ir a Nueva York, pleeeeeeease?" The words spilled out in a rush as Yadiel clasped his hands together. "Look, I've been reading all these books about it."

Sure enough, the books scattered on Ashton's lap were a collection of stories like *Taxi Dog* and *A Walk in New York* mixed with photo-heavy travel guides for kids.

Ashton held up *Taxi Dog*. "I hate to break it to you, mijo, but I've never seen a dog in a taxi."

Yadiel rolled his eyes. "It's just a story, Dad."

Dad, huh? The kid must really want to go if he was breaking out "Dad."

On the one hand, Ashton loved the idea of showing his son around the city he was coming to enjoy. There were so many things Yadi would get a kick out of, from the museums, to the Broadway shows, to the architecture.

But the idea of his son wandering around the huge, crowded city made him sweat. He wouldn't be alone, of course, but what if something happened? There were so many things that could go wrong.

There were practical considerations, too, like where they would stay, and making sure Abuelita Bibi could get around, and whether Ignacio would want to close the restaurant, and—

And his son was looking at him with undisguised longing on his face. Yadi *wanted* this. And it was within Ashton's power to give his son something that would make him happy.

How could he say no?

Especially since the only real reason why he'd say no was fear. He couldn't let that get in the way of letting his son live his life.

So even though it terrified him, he said, "Okay, Yadi. You can come to New York."

Yadiel whooped and cheered, leaping all over Ashton and the sofa and knocking the books to the floor in his excitement.

Ashton laughed and tackled the kid to the cushions, sparking a father/son wrestling match.

In the end, Yadiel won, standing with one foot on Ashton's chest and crowing his victory. Ashton, sprawled out on the rug, wondered how the hell he was going to pull this off.

That night, after Yadiel y los viejitos had gone to bed, Ashton sat at the kitchen table and accepted the cold beer Ignacio passed him. It had been a long day—hell, a long week, a long *summer*—and he was tired.

Ignacio sat across from him. They clinked their bottles together and drank. "How's the production?" he asked.

Ashton scratched at the edges of the bottle's label, wet and peeling with condensation, to keep from picking at his own fingers. "I think it's going well."

Ignacio took a long swig. "Are you still keeping to yourself?"

Ashton sighed. "Not like I was before, no."

He didn't mention Jasmine, or how twisted up he was about her. His father was easygoing, and even when Ashton had suddenly found himself in the role of single dad, Ignacio had never been judgmental. But Ashton didn't know how to talk about Jasmine with him. Not yet.

Leaning back in the chair, Ignacio crossed his arms and sent Ashton an impassive look. "You can't be alone forever, mijo."

"I'm not alone." Ashton spread his hands to encompass the house, even though the rest of the family was sleeping upstairs. "I have all of you."

Ignacio just shook his head slowly, and when he spoke, the words were laced with a resigned sadness. "It's not the same."

Even though she'd never lived in this house—Ashton had grown up in Guaynabo—at times, the absence of his mother could be keenly felt, like he expected her to turn the corner into the kitchen at any moment. Sometimes the feeling of loss faded, more like a forgotten task nagging at his attention, or a misplaced item waiting to be found. But it never truly went away.

"I miss her," he said.

They didn't talk about his mother often. It had been ten years since she'd passed, after a quick and devastating bout with cancer, and they'd fallen into new rhythms. But Ashton still wished she could have met her grandson.

"I miss her too," Ignacio said, and then he polished off his beer. "But she would've wanted you to be happy."

"I'm fine, Pa. Really." Although lately, he'd been thinking more about what it would be like to have a companion on this parenting journey, and for Yadiel to have a mother figure in his life.

The fact that these thoughts popped up more since meeting Jasmine unnerved him.

"Well, if you say you're fine, you're fine," Ignacio said, but his face and tone implied he didn't believe it.

Ashton finished off his own beer and stood. "It's late. I'll let you get to sleep."

"Tomorrow?"

"I'll leave after Sunday mass."

"Fair warning, Yadiel wants to go to a baseball game in New York."

Ashton gave a brief smile. "I'll break out the hat and sunglasses."

"You sure you don't want a trench coat and a newspaper with two holes cut out, Señor James Bond?"

Ashton smothered a laugh so he didn't wake the others. "From your lips to God's ears."

Ignacio collected the bottles to dispose of them. "Buenas noches, mijo."

Chapter 27

Jasmine arrived at the studio the next morning in high spirits. The summit had been great press, the show was going smoothly, and Ashton . . . Well, she was trying to avoid examining her feelings too much, but it was safe to say she was happier than she'd ever been with a man. Real happiness, too, where she felt valued and like it was safe to open up to him, not performative happiness that relied on stuff like gifts or PDA. She was scared to hope for more, scared to identify where she was on the Jasmine Scale, and her conversation with the Primas of Power hadn't offered much in the way of clarity. But in all other regards, her Leading Lady Plan was on track. She'd even received some congratulatory texts from her family after Michelle sent them the video of Jasmine's Latinx in the Arts interview.

Abuelo Willie: good job nena

Abuela Esperanza: You looked so beautiful! Love you!

Followed by a link to a cream for neck wrinkles.

Most surprising of all, her parents had chimed in on their group text chain.

> **Mom & Dad**: Proud of you, honey!

Even Sammy had apologized for his behavior at the barbecue, and asked if he could get Lily's autograph for his daughter.

Jasmine was riding high when she strolled into her dressing room. She'd just set her purse down when the door flew open and Lily burst in.

"Jasmine, I'm sorry." Lily's face was flushed and she looked to be on the verge of tears. "It was taken out of context, I didn't mean to—"

"What happened?" Jasmine started to go to Lily, but then a jingle played from her bag. She stuck her hand in and pulled out her phone. Ava was calling.

Lily seemed to be in emergency mode, so Jasmine silenced the call without picking up and returned her attention to her on-screen hermana. "What's wrong? Are you okay?"

A text flashed from Michelle. Out of habit, Jasmine swiped to read it.

> **Michelle**: Turn off your phone.

With a dawning sense of dread, Jasmine turned to Lily, who held out her own phone. It was open to *Buzz Weekly*'s website.

And there, above a photo of Jasmine and Ashton taken at the Latinx in the Arts Summit, was the word, REBOUND.

Jasmine's heart sank as the world narrowed to the few square inches on Lily's phone. She took it and peered closer. Following the headline were two speculative questions: BEHIND-THE-SCENES ROMANCE? OR LOVE TRIANGLE?

Underneath those, a byline: Kitty Sanchez.

Of course.

"I was chatting with some bloggers at the summit," Lily said in a rush, tripping over her words. "One lady asked what it was like working with everybody on *Carmen*. I didn't think anything of it, you know? She asked other questions too. But she must have asked me about you guys, and all I said was—"

Jasmine didn't need her to continue. It was right there, a little ways down from the photo.

A source close to the couple tells us they get along really well and spend a lot of time together.

When Jasmine imagined Lily saying the words, they were innocuous. But taken out of context, as an anonymous quote? They were heavy with implied romantic meaning.

Fuuuuuck.

Jasmine continued to scroll, skimming past text and more photos from the event, both posed and candid. Farther down, another photo loaded under the word, *EXCLUSIVE!!!*

Her breath backed up in her throat. The picture was blurry, like it had been zoomed in too much and taken with an unsteady hand, but it was unmistakably the two of them. They stood close, with Ashton's arm around her while she smiled up at him, caught in a totally candid—and private—moment.

Somehow, Kitty Sanchez had gotten her claws on the photo taken by the grocery store employee.

"She twisted my words," Lily went on, sounding anguished. "I really didn't mean—"

At that moment, Ashton rushed in through the open door, eyes wild and hair disheveled.

"Look at this," he said, and held out a crumpled issue of *Buzz Weekly*.

They'd made the cover. The posed photo was largest, probably because it was higher quality, but off to the side were two boxes. One showed a paparazzi photo of Jasmine holding hands with McIntyre as they were leaving one of his concerts. The other was the grocery store photo. REBOUND was printed at the top in bright yellow, the word glaring at her just as accusingly as DUMPED had.

In a detached sort of way, Jasmine wondered why and how gossip rags still existed. Wasn't the print magazine industry dead?

Lily's face turned even redder and she slipped past Ashton. "I'll let you two talk," she muttered, and beat a hasty retreat, shutting the door behind her.

In Jasmine's hand, her phone rang again. It was Riley this time. She almost picked up, but Ashton was looking apoplectic, so she sent it to voice mail instead.

"All right," she said, trying to sound calm. "Don't freak out."

"Don't freak out? How can I not freak out?"

His accent had thickened, and she realized her own Bronx accent—kept under control, for the most part, except on the word "coffee"—was showing. Shit. They were *both* freaking out.

"It's not that bad," she told him. "It will be good promo for the show, and it will blow over quickly."

These were all things her agent and cousins had told her after her split with McIntyre had blown up, and they hadn't helped. But she didn't know what else to say. She remembered the first time she had made it onto the cover of *Soaps Monthly* magazine. She'd been thrilled. But this kind of exposure? It hurt, and there was no getting around that. For someone like Ashton, who was fiercely protective of his privacy, this had to feel nerve-racking and intrusive.

Ashton opened the magazine and flipped to the article about them. Before Jasmine could tell him not to read it, that it wouldn't help matters, he said, "I can't believe they would print this. People are going to think that we—"

"*Ashton.*" She waited until he looked at her. "We *are*."

"I know, but I don't need anyone else knowing that." He went back to the magazine, a look of disgust on his face.

Excuse me? Before Jasmine could find her voice to respond to *that* insulting statement, a sharp knock on the door interrupted them. "It's Tanya," said a muffled voice.

Ashton's gaze flew around the room, as if looking for somewhere to hide. His eyes locked on the bathroom door.

"Who cares if someone sees you here *now*?" Jasmine hissed at him, giving the magazine he held an irritated flick as she moved past him to open the door. Tanya stood on the other side. In her hands was another copy of *Buzz Weekly*. Shit, were the paps stationed near the studio's gates handing them out as people arrived for work?

Jasmine stepped aside to let Tanya in. "So you've seen it."

"Of course I have." Tanya handed it to Jasmine, who threw it directly into the trash. "I'm amazed they thought this was cover material."

Or Kitty Sanchez had been waiting to pounce on a new story about Jasmine, and the summit photos plus Lily's innocent quote had given her what she needed. Out loud, Jasmine said, "They're using me."

"That they are," Tanya agreed. "Ready to spin this?"

"What's the plan?" Jasmine asked.

"We have some interviews lined up," Tanya replied. "I won't lie, if you wanted to play this coy, it would be great for ratings. But I'm not about abusing my actors or making up stories that aren't there, so the simplest thing to do is say you're just friends and leave it at that. Good?"

Ashton looked like he was going to throw up, but he nodded. "We need to shut this down immediately."

Jasmine's heart ached for him, even as she wished he'd pull his head out of his ass. She understood where he was coming from, but she needed his support on this, damn it. She'd already gone through it once on her own.

Tanya headed for the door. "Ashton, you're going to need more prep. Come with me."

Ashton shot Jasmine an anguished glance, but he followed Tanya out the door.

Jasmine took a deep breath, then shut it behind them. Alone again, she went to her purse. Her phone buzzed incessantly with incoming calls and texts, so she took Michelle's advice and turned it off. After setting it aside, she pulled out her wallet and removed a folded piece of notepaper with her grandmother's name across the top.

She hadn't looked at the Leading Lady Plan since she'd written it, but this seemed like a great time to remind herself what was at stake.

1. Leading Ladies only end up on magazine covers with good reason.
2. Leading Ladies are whole and happy on their own.
3. Leading Ladies are badass queens making jefa moves.

And then there was the fourth mental item she hadn't dared write down: *Leading Ladies do not rebound with their costars.*

With a weary sigh, Jasmine dropped onto the dressing room sofa. Had she really thought she was on track? She was one for four, if she counted being honored by the summit as a "jefa move." But since it had led to her ending up on yet *another* magazine cover—specifically with the word "rebound" on it— it was hard to consider it a win. She might as well rip up the Leading Lady Plan and flush it down the toilet.

Was a man really worth potentially ruining all her plans for herself? Once upon a time, she would have said yes. Well, actually, she would have *said* no, but *thought* yes.

But that was before McIntyre had destroyed her self-image and then left her to fend for herself against the wolves in entertainment media. Sure, he'd said lovely, sweet things when they were alone, making her feel like the only woman in the world.

But when they were in public . . . Looking back, she could see he'd treated her like shit. Around his entourage, he would sit with his arm draped over her shoulders as if to say, *This is mine*, but he'd barely even looked at her. He certainly hadn't listened to her or cared about what she had to say.

At the time, it had felt like enough. She told herself it was enough. All she wanted was a little attention. To feel loved. Was that so much to ask?

The truth was, Ashton wasn't anything like McIntyre. She didn't even have to do the whole "compare the new guy to the awful old guy" thing, where the new guy looked better by comparison. Ashton made her feel valued. She could be herself around him without fear of judgment. And maybe part of it was that she was back in New York. The city felt like home in a way nowhere else did. She didn't have to put on an act to fit in, like she had in Los Angeles. But even so, she suspected she still would have felt okay being vulnerable with Ashton.

She knew it was a bad idea, but she retrieved the offending copy of *Buzz Weekly* from the garbage can and opened it to the article. Might as well know what was being said about her.

Despite the sensational headline, Kitty Sanchez had actually included information about Latinx in the Arts, along with quotes from Nino's and Lily's interviews and a group photo of all of them with a reminder to watch *Carmen in Charge* when it hit ScreenFlix. Unfortunately, the positive press was sandwiched between wild speculation about Jasmine's relationship with Ashton and how McIntyre played into it.

The photos themselves were mostly pretty benign. The article included another one of her with McIntyre, plus a different posed photo with Ashton. There was also a candid photo of them from the Latinx in the Arts Summit, but since Jasmine hadn't spent a second alone with Ashton while they were there, the picture must have involved some creative cropping to remove the others.

The grocery store photo, though . . . that was damning.

And fucking annoying, since it had been taken *before* they'd started sleeping together.

Jasmine left the magazine on the sofa and got up to make a cup of coffee, hoping the caffeine would jump-start her brain so she could wrap her head around what was happening here.

Because as much as she loved being with Ashton, she had to admit she was way off track with her plan. And this article? It was going to throw him into a tailspin.

Not that she blamed him. Ashton already struggled to let her in when it was just the two of them. Now, everyone's eyes would be on them. She wouldn't be surprised if the crowd of paparazzi outside the studio had doubled since *Buzz Weekly* hit newsstands that morning. Shit, they'd probably be around the hotel too. The Hutton Court staff and the local NYPD precinct were well-versed in keeping photographers and celebrity spotters away from the hotel entrance, but once the paps found out the photo was taken at the local grocery store, they'd be sniffing around the whole neighborhood.

Jasmine pressed her face into her hands, indulging in a moment of despair. She had a strong feeling she knew how Ashton was going to react to all of this—he was going to pull away from her again, like he'd done at the beginning. And it was going to hurt. A lot. More than before, because now she'd know what she was missing.

She'd miss his jokes and the questions he asked her about herself, as if the answer to each one was the key to unlocking the secrets of the universe. She'd miss the way he held her close as she fell asleep. The way he kissed her and touched her, as if she were a treasure to be adored.

She'd miss the way he said her name, like she was someone who *mattered*.

The single-cup coffee maker sputtered and filled her travel mug with Café Bustelo, thanks to the pods Ashton had gifted her. Jasmine checked her face in the mirror and dabbed at the corners of her eyes. She couldn't sit around all day moping. They still had scenes to shoot, and damage control interviews to fit in.

And then there'd only be one thing left to do. She would have to distance herself from him first. Just the thought of it made her feel sick with stress, like her stomach was full of snakes. It was the absolute last thing she wanted to do, but if she was right, he was going to go back to being the old closed-off version of himself anyway. For the sake of his own comfort, she'd give him space, and in doing so, she'd give her Leading Lady Plan another chance.

Time to get to work.

After ripping the magazine in half and tossing it back in the garbage, she headed to hair and makeup.

Her stylists were her ride-or-dies on set. Every morning after she arrived, Jasmine sat with them for hours while they worked their magic on her hair and face. Ashton usually had a slightly later call time than she did, since he required less beautification.

Today, Jasmine could sense her friends in hair and makeup were bursting with curiosity, but thankfully, no one asked her outright, "Are you and Ashton . . . ?" And since no one asked, Jasmine didn't have to lie.

When it was time to film the interviews, Tanya had negotiated every aspect in advance, so all Jasmine and Ashton had to do was smile charmingly and repeat, "No, we're just really good friends," in twelve different ways. It was hard to pretend he meant nothing to her, but they were actors. It was just like playing any other role.

Or so she kept telling herself.

After the last interview, Tanya pulled them aside to debrief. "I think that went pretty well, don't you?"

Jasmine smiled, even though her heart was a shattered shell inside her chest. "Absolutely."

Ashton grimaced, and Jasmine was pretty sure he'd been screaming internally for the past forty-five minutes. The final reporter had asked a ton of questions, and while Jasmine had tried to field most of them, many had been aimed directly at Ashton.

"It was bound to happen sooner or later," Tanya said. "Romance rumors pop up on every show. This should satisfy their cravings, and hopefully they'll drop the story soon and focus on the whole show."

"Let's hope," Ashton muttered darkly.

Tanya patted his shoulder. "Get some rest, you two. It's been a big day."

After Tanya left, Jasmine turned to Ashton. Better to get this over with.

He surprised her by speaking first. "So, this week . . ."

She raised her eyebrows. "Yeah?"

"I won't be around," he said, not looking at her. "I'm going to be at a music studio for the next few days, recording Victor's songs, and in the evenings they want to get B-roll footage of me singing in a few clubs—"

"Ashton, it's okay." He was pulling away, as expected. What she hadn't expected was that it would hurt quite so much. She forced herself to smile like everything was fine. "I'll see you in a few days. Have fun recording."

He nodded, the movement jerky, and slipped away. Just like he used to. Jasmine held back a sigh. If she let it out, tears would come next. And they might not stop.

Distance. Distance was good. Maybe it would give her some much-needed perspective and answers.

Like how to stop being in love with him.

Chapter 28

Ten minutes. That's all Ashton wanted. Ten minutes alone with Jasmine. But when he knocked on the door of her side of their double-banger trailer, there was no answer.

They were on location in front of the building that posed as the Serranos' brownstone in Spanish Harlem, prepping to film a kissing scene they'd practiced with Vera a week earlier. This kiss would be deeper than the others they'd shared on camera. After all they'd done together, they'd both assured Vera they were comfortable taking it up a notch. For the sake of the show, of course.

But that had been before the *Buzz Weekly* cover story. Before he'd convinced himself he needed time away from her. Now, he just wanted a chance to talk to her before the camera started rolling. It had been four days since he'd last seen her. With him in the recording studio and her at the production lot, their paths hadn't crossed.

But she had been on his mind. Often.

Okay, a lot.

Okay, *constantly*. He hadn't been able to stop thinking about her. She was in his dreams when he slept, in his memories when he worked out, and in his thoughts when he recorded Victor's songs.

The production had moved him to a different hotel for a few days so he could get away from the media circus and be closer to the music studio and the tiny downtown clubs where they'd shot footage of him singing live as Victor. After the agonizing "just friends" interviews and the increased presence of photographers on the way to ScreenFlix Studios and near the hotel, a change of scenery should've made him happy. That magazine article had been a wake-up call, a reminder that he didn't have room in his life for a romantic relationship. His family was arriving on a plane that very night, and he had to be more careful than ever. There was no way he could sneak around to see them while also sneaking around with Jasmine. It was begging for trouble.

Except that was exactly what he was doing now—sneaking around the set, looking for her. He didn't even have a good reason for wanting to see her—the excuse he'd made up was that he wanted to tell her about the recording studio. While he'd trained with vocal coaches in the past, working in a sound booth was another thing entirely. He wished she could've been there, to discuss the artistic challenges of recording, to cheer him on from the audience while he sang live, or even to join him on stage for a duet, like they'd done during karaoke.

He'd thought being apart from her for a few days would help him get his feelings in check so he could be around her without fantasizing about getting her naked. But deep down, he *just wanted to see her*. His anxiety had reached new heights as of late, and her presence soothed him. He was falling for her, and it was incredibly inconvenient.

He'd tried to cancel his family's trip to New York, but Ignacio had chewed him out. Yadi would be crushed, and for what? Because of some bochinche magazine? Unacceptable. And so, the trip was on.

Another reason to see Jasmine now, before all his free time was given over to a travel itinerary written by an eight-year-old. Jasmine would have loved Yadiel's plan. It had not one, but *three* pizza places on it.

He swung by the makeup trailer to see if she was there, but when the stylists caught him poking his head in, they dragged him inside to touch up his face powder and hair spray.

"Stop scowling," the makeup artist scolded him, echoing the words Tanya had said at the Latinx in the Arts Summit. She tapped the space between his eyebrows with a sponge. "You're getting a crease."

"Sorry," he mumbled, then held his breath before getting blasted with a cloud of hair spray.

When they released him, he headed over to check craft services next. Jasmine wasn't there, but as he was grabbing a carton of water, Marquita pulled him aside.

"The music engineers are thrilled with the results of your sessions," she told him, grinning. "These songs will be a great addition to the show soundtrack."

Ashton inclined his head. "I'm glad they turned out well."

Marquita made a few more comments about the music, and once Ashton was able to get away, he resumed his search for Jasmine.

Had he really wanted more space between them? Fuck that. This space thing wasn't working for him. To make matters worse, not being able to find her was activating the same irrational fears that popped up when he couldn't reach his father, the worry that *something bad had happened*.

Nothing had happened, of course. They were on a set, with tons of people around. Nothing was going to happen. Jasmine was somewhere, and wherever she was, she was safe.

So why couldn't he find her?

She finally appeared on set at their call time and gave him a breezy smile. "Hey, Ashton. Long time no see."

"Where were you?" His tone was harsh, and she blinked in surprise. He couldn't blame her—he had no right to make such demands.

Before he could apologize, she said, "I was in Nino's trailer with Lily, playing cards. Why, what's up?"

"Quiet on the set!"

"Nada. Está bien." Ashton shook it off. He'd catch up with her after they finished shooting.

Before sneaking off to ensure that his family had settled in okay.

Anxiety still simmered, but he let it stay. He could use it in this scene. Climbing the steps to his mark, he let Victor take over.

Chapter 29

CARMEN IN CHARGE

EPISODE 7

Scene: Victor and Carmen debrief after a series of
    talk show appearances.
EXT: East Harlem, Serranos' brownstone stoop—NIGHT

The sky was dark, lit by yellow streetlights, and the neighborhood was quiet. Victor sat beside Carmen on the stoop of her parents' home, close enough for their shoulders to brush. They had just returned from a whirlwind day of Victor spilling his guts on one talk show after another. He'd admitted to struggling with depression and anxiety, and self-medicating with alcohol, all of which had led to pushing people away, the downfall of his marriage, and canceling a tour.

"You did great today." Carmen's voice vibrated with genuine pride, and her lips curved in a small, private smile. Just for him.

"Thanks." Victor exhaled and leaned his elbows on his

knees. "Do you think anyone is going to want to buy my new album after all that?"

Carmen placed a hand on his back and rubbed it in soothing circles, her touch gentle but firm. "I would. Vulnerability is sexy."

"Vulnerability is *exhausting.*"

After a pause, she said in a quiet voice, "I never knew."

She was referring to all the things he'd confessed. He closed his eyes. "I didn't want you to know."

"But I should have known something was going on. I should have tried to help—"

"There wasn't anything you could do."

"I still could have tried."

Victor lifted his head and gave her a rueful grin. "I didn't make it easy."

The corner of her mouth tipped up in response. "No. But neither did I."

Since the moment seemed right, he took her hand in his, lacing their fingers together and resting their joined hands on her thigh. "We both made mistakes, Carmencita."

She leaned into him, placing her head on his shoulder. "We did."

He swallowed hard and looked up to the sky for guidance, then back down at her. And took the leap. "So what do we do now?"

She lifted her chin and gazed into his eyes. Then, with her free hand, she cupped his face and kissed him.

This kiss was slow, languid. As if they had all the time in the world. As if they weren't sitting on the stoop of her parents' home, where anyone could see them. As if they were just two normal people . . .

As if his own family weren't on their way to New York that very minute, as if they were in charge of their own lives, as if they weren't surrounded by crew members, as if this kiss hadn't been choreographed down to each touch and sigh . . .

When they slowed to catch their breath, Victor looked at her with a question in his eyes.

"I don't know what we do," Carmen said in response, her voice husky. "But this—opening up, letting people in, even if it's just to carry the burden of the knowledge—it's a start. You're not alone, mi amor."

The tension in him eased. He wanted to kiss her again, but it wasn't in the script. So he just nodded, and got to his feet. He helped her up and together, they ascended the steps, hand in hand.

"Cut! Go again!"

Chapter 30

Jasmine locked the trailer door behind her and let her shoulders droop with exhaustion. Keeping her distance from Ashton was *killing* her.

She'd given him the out and he'd taken it, like she'd known he would. Old Jasmine would have called him multiple times during the last few days, but New Jasmine was sticking to the Leading Lady Plan.

And if she'd had to enlist the Primas of Power to help her hold strong, well, sometimes change took time.

She moved to the mirror and started to remove her makeup with wipes, taking extra care around her eyes. Esperanza had sent her an article about how makeup wipes were terrible, and while Jasmine wanted to sneer at it, the information had stuck in her mind.

When she got to her lipstick, she paused. Part of her didn't want to wipe away the feel of Ashton's mouth on hers. What if this was the only way she'd get to be close to him? They only had one episode left, and a second season wasn't assured.

Sangana. She was acting like a teenager with a crush vowing never to brush her teeth again after being kissed for the first time, not a Leading Lady who was whole and happy on her motherfucking own.

Screw it. She scrubbed at her mouth with one of the wipes, harder than strictly necessary.

When she was done, she stared at her reflection. Her lips were slightly swollen and dark pink from the friction. She could just imagine what her grandmother would say, and pictured Esperanza slipping a tub of Vaseline into Jasmine's purse.

The image made her smile, and she held on to that while she changed out of Carmen's outfit and into her own clothes. Esperanza's party was coming up soon, and while Jasmine had given up all hope that Ashton would show up—especially now that she knew how much he hated big crowds—she was still looking forward to it. She and her cousins had been busting their butts to make it an event the Rodriguez family would remember forever.

There was a light tap on the door, and Jasmine opened it to let Nino and Lily in. They'd planned to meet in her trailer, since it was largest, before hitting up a nearby taqueria for drinks and a late dinner.

"Ready to go?" Nino asked.

"Almost. Make yourselves comfortable." Jasmine rubbed moisturizer onto her face while her friends sat on the small sofa looking at videos of Nino's dog. Just as Jasmine was applying lip gloss, there was another knock on the door.

Jasmine met Lily's and Nino's eyes in the mirror. "Did you invite someone else?"

When they shook their heads, she shrugged and went to open it. It was probably a PA with script updates. The writers on *Carmen* made more changes than Lady Gaga at an awards show.

Opening the door, Jasmine gave an involuntary gasp. Ashton stood on the metal steps, and even though they'd just been on set together, the sight of him there caused an answering tug in her solar plexus, some combination between desire and yearning. He was so handsome, with his own face freshly washed, dressed in a simple T-shirt and jeans. But it wasn't his sex appeal that made her gasp. It was the recognition and surprise, the feeling of *there you are, I've been waiting for you.*

But she hadn't been waiting, because she didn't think he'd come. Except he had. And what was it he'd said earlier? *Where were you?*

Had he been looking for her?

"Jasmine, I . . ." He trailed off and his gaze drifted past her to where Nino and Lily sat on the sofa, waving cheerfully at him.

"We're going for margaritas," Lily called out to him. "Want to come?"

"No. Thank you." Ashton gave them a brief smile, then looked back at Jasmine. "Just . . . saying good night."

As he turned to leave, she caught the slight creasing of his brow, the tightening of his features, and before she knew what she was doing, she whispered, "Ashton."

He paused and glanced over his shoulder, something wistful in his eyes. "Good night, querida." Then he jogged down the stairs, away from her.

Jasmine inhaled, ready to shout for him to come back, but this time, she held the words in, even though they suffocated her.

He *had* been looking for her. Before and after they'd filmed.

Seeing the others in her trailer had clearly thrown him off. Was he looking to get her alone? And if so, why?

Hope bloomed in her chest, and she didn't know whether to nurture it like a flower or squash it like a roach. Either way, it pained her to see Ashton reverting to his old ways and turning down invitations to hang out with the cast. She wanted better for him. But she'd resolved to give him space, so she closed the trailer door and addressed her friends.

"Let's go," she said. "There's a margarita out there with my name on it."

AFTER LEAVING THE shoot, Ashton headed to the short-term rental on the Upper East Side that he'd booked for his family. He would have loved to have had them closer, but with all the paparazzi roaming around, he couldn't chance it.

The irony of filming a scene about opening up to people and then turning around to go visit his secret family wasn't lost on Ashton, but what could he do?

Although even Ashton had to admit nothing about this was normal.

It was late when he got there, and his father was the only one still awake. Ashton chatted with him briefly, peeked in on Yadiel's sleeping form sprawled out on a twin bed, and left.

By the time he got back to the Hutton Court, Ashton was practically dead on his feet. He picked up his bag from the front desk, which production had retrieved from the hotel he'd stayed in the last few days, but when he stepped onto the elevator, he found himself pressing the button for Jasmine's floor instead of his own. Then he found himself at her door, and before he could question his motives or talk himself out of it, he knocked.

It was late. She was probably sleeping, or still out with the others. He should go back to his room and go to bed. But just as he took a step back, the door opened.

He'd spent what felt like all night looking for a moment alone with her. And now here she was.

She wore a simple black tank top and gray shorts. She looked tired, but her eyes were alert.

He didn't say anything. What was there to say when you showed up at a woman's hotel room in the middle of the night? But she stepped back and let him in.

"Were you asleep?" he asked quietly.

She shook her head. "Couldn't."

And then he saw the TV was paused, and a lone glass of red wine sat on the coffee table.

"Come on." She led him to the sofa, which had one of the hotel's extra fleece blankets bunched up on it. She shoved the blanket aside and sat, leaving room for him to sit beside her. "Wine?"

"No, thanks." He glanced at the TV. "What are you watching?"

"*Real Housewives.*" She looked at the screen, which was paused on a frame of two women shopping. "It's what I watch when I can't sleep."

She picked up the remote, and just when he thought she was going to press play, she put it down again and turned to him.

There was a wary look in her eyes, and he knew she was going to ask him what he was doing there or why he'd come to her trailer. Slight panic rose in anticipation—he didn't know what he was doing there. He didn't know what he was *doing*, period. Everything was a mess.

Except this. With her, things seemed to make sense, even though they shouldn't. So before she could voice the question in her eyes, he slid his hand around the back of her neck and sank his fingers into the warm mass of her hair.

She didn't move toward him, but nor did she pull away. They hovered like that, his intention clear, and her—waiting? So he leaned in and kissed her. Until their lips touched, he still wasn't sure if she'd stop him, but she met his mouth with open enthusiasm, and he had a flash of kissing her earlier on the stoop. The two experiences merged—then, wanting to kiss her more deeply, but needing to stick to the agreed-upon choreography—and now, feeling a jolt at the touch of her tongue on his, craving the heat but worrying he needed to pull back.

Except they weren't Victor and Carmen now. It was just the two of them, alone. He shut everything else out and lost himself in her. In her touch, sure and confident as she stroked his chest. In her taste, so sweet and with faint fruity notes from the wine when her tongue teased his.

He tugged at her clothing, needing to be closer, to touch more of her. She helped him strip away her pajamas before tossing them to the floor. Then he stretched her out on the sofa, taking a moment to gaze down at her body, cataloging her curves in his memory and feeling a deep sense of contentment. How lucky he was, that this amazing woman let him be close to her, let him touch her, let him—

He cut off the thought before it could go too deep and bent to kiss her breasts. She let out a long sigh, holding his head closer to her, but he had another destination in mind. Shifting lower, he spread her legs, draping one over the back of the couch. When her hips rocked toward him in invitation, he lowered his mouth to her and worshipped her.

Her response delighted him. She gripped his head, pulling his hair and urging him on as he licked her. When he stroked her and tongued her clit, a litany of "yes, yes, yes" fell from her lips. She writhed and shook beneath his touch, kneading and pinching her own breasts, the most beautiful sight he'd ever seen. And when she climaxed against his mouth, around his fingers, he knew bliss.

As he eased back, to take in the sight of her naked body reclined in sated pleasure, a smile curved his lips. His dick was rock hard, and he was still fully dressed, but her pleasure was everything to him. Absently, he caressed her thigh, just happy to touch her after so many days apart. But she surprised him by rearing up and scrambling into a position at his feet.

After tucking a throw pillow under her knees, she yanked at the fastenings on his jeans with hurried moves.

"Jasmine, you—"

"Shh." She reached into his boxers and gently withdrew his cock. At her touch, he groaned and dropped his head back. In a smooth move, she took him in her mouth. Her hot, wet mouth.

This is it, he thought. *This is how I die.*

It was too good. Too absolute. No one could feel this good and survive, could they? Maybe not, but he was willing to test it.

She worked him with her mouth and hand, getting him

slick with her lips and tongue, squeezing his hardness within her fist. He sank his hands into her hair and rocked his hips, panting her name as she took him for a ride.

He was almost there, so close, but he didn't know if—

"Jasmine, *por favor*," he ground out, not knowing what he was even begging for. Stop? Keep going? He didn't know. She was in total control.

She must have guessed he was close, because she pulled her mouth off him with a smacking kiss, then climbed up to straddle his lap.

He filled his hands with her as she kissed his mouth. Her lips wet and soft, and his still carrying the lingering taste of her. He couldn't get enough. All the reasons why this could never be fled from his mind, or seemed inconsequential in the light of his burning need for her. She'd gotten under his skin, so quickly and easily, it should have been impossible. And yet here she was. Here *they* were.

Her busy fingers undid the buttons of his shirt and she pulled back enough to whisper against his mouth, "Dime qué quieres."

The words sent shivers through his body. Her utter confidence, the latent sensuality, the fact that she now felt comfortable enough with him to try dirty talk en español. This woman was already everything he could ever want. How was he supposed to put it into words?

"I want"—*I need*—"you."

She let out a husky chuckle and kept undressing him. "Which part of me?"

All of you.

He couldn't say that. Some shred of self-preservation remained. Instead, he reached between them and stroked her, finding her wet and open. She let out a sigh as he slipped his fingers into her, pumping back and forth. She rocked her hips, riding his hand, looking so fucking beautiful he could barely stand it, but after a moment she eased back.

"Condom," she whispered, getting to her feet and yanking at his jeans to pull them off. "I want you inside me."

"Fuck yeah," he ground out. He grabbed his wallet out of his back pocket before she could toss the pants away and took out the foil condom packet. While she opened it, he went to the bedroom and came back with the bottle of lube, because he knew she liked it. Squirting some into his hand, he waited while she rolled the condom down his cock, which was exquisite torture in and of itself. Then he greased himself up, resumed his seat on the sofa, and leaned back.

He didn't know what the hell they were doing here, but as she sank down and sheathed him in her heat, he didn't fucking care. Everything felt different—no, *better*—with her. *He* was better, just for being in her presence. Her patience and emotional responsiveness allowed him to explore how it felt to let someone in and be truly seen—something he'd forgotten how to do. It was a gift he could never repay.

The lamp in the corner was turned on low, the light caressing her skin and gilding her curves with gold as she rocked on top of him. He followed the light with his hands, touching her, memorizing the shape of her. This couldn't last—good things never did—but for right now, he would live in the moment with her while he could. Her full breasts swayed in front of him, and he leaned forward to suck her nipple into his mouth, rolling it with his tongue and loving the way she cried out in immediate response. He wrapped one arm around her waist, holding her close, then reached his other hand between them to slide his fingertips over her clit. She shivered at the touch, her thrusts becoming shorter and more insistent.

"Ashton," she said on a gasp. "Oh god. Don't—don't stop."

He wouldn't have dared. While he couldn't give her much, *this* he could give her. He pumped his hips, grinding against her as he urged her to climax.

He knew she was close when her nails sank into his shoulders, and he grinned against her breast and increased the pace, thrusting up and into her soft, wet sheath.

"Ashton!" He rolled his eyes up to look at her, soaking in the ecstasy etched on her gorgeous face, the urgency in her voice, and the way her mouth fell open when she came. Pleasure wrung broken, staccato gasps from her throat, and he loved the sound of them. God, he was falling for this woman so hard, and he couldn't even lie to himself about it. He held her through her orgasm, squeezing his eyes shut to hold back his own as her pussy squeezed his dick in an almost irresistible rhythm.

She sighed and melted against his chest, her arms twining around his back as she pressed her face to his neck.

"More," she whispered.

The soft command unleashed something in him. Keeping their pelvises locked tight, he shifted them so she lay on her back, propped up by throw pillows, the blanket bunched underneath them. Ashton braced himself on his forearms, gave her a quick kiss, and surrendered to hot and fast fucking.

Their bodies grew slick with sweat as he pounded into her, their skin slapping together as she met each thrust with one of her own. He ground out curses in English and Spanish, and she panted what would have been benedictions in any other setting.

He didn't want it to end, but it was too good to last forever.

As Jasmine came apart in his arms again, Ashton lost the battle. With his face pressed into the curve of her neck, breathing in the sweet citrus scent of her hair, he drove into her one last time. The orgasm ripped through him. He shuddered hard, heart pounding, breath heaving.

In the aftermath, his mind emptied and his body went numb. They were a joined tangle of sweaty limbs, and he couldn't even begin to figure out how to separate himself, so he didn't. He just listened to the sound of her breathing, counting the rise and fall of her chest under his cheek.

And in the pure clarity following a climax, he knew, finally, what he wanted.

This. He wanted *this.* To come home to this woman, to be with her, to love her, and to let her love him back.

But the world returned to him in bits and pieces, along with all the reminders of why this would never work between them.

His career.

Her fame.

His *son.*

He didn't want to move from this sofa. If he didn't move, he didn't have to face the consequences of his actions, and he could pretend, for just a little longer, that this was possible.

But it wasn't. And he was softening inside her. In a second he was going to have to dispose of the condom and—

She shifted, breaking the spell. He climbed off her and grabbed the box of tissues on the end table. As he was cleaning up, she pulled the blanket off the cushions and wrapped it around herself.

It pained him to see her cover herself, as if shielding herself from *him*, the way she had their first night together before she'd asked him to stay. He shouldn't have come here. He was just getting in deeper, starting something he couldn't finish.

"I didn't think I'd see you tonight," she said softly.

The postcoital quiet called for truth. "I was trying to stay away."

She sighed. "And I was trying to let you."

He blinked in surprise. "You were?"

She nodded and gave him a little smile. "I was doing a pretty good job of it, too, but then you came to my trailer tonight looking ten kinds of delicious, and it took all my self-control not to run after you."

"You—really?"

This pleased him to no end, even though it shouldn't.

He'd told Jasmine about the Incident, and she'd understood. What would happen if he told her about Yadiel? She valued family as much as he did. He thought—hoped—she'd understand about that too.

The full truth burned on the tip of his tongue, but by now he was so used to keeping secrets, it was easy to swallow it down.

There was still time.

Jasmine picked up the wineglass and drained it. Then she turned off the TV and stood.

"Are you . . . going to stay?" she asked.

He caught the slight, hopeful lilt in her voice, the way she chewed at her bottom lip, like she expected him to leave.

He should leave. But he didn't want to.

"I'll stay."

She nodded, then reached out her hand to him. "Good."

He took her hand and let her lead him into the bedroom.

Chapter 31

"Cut!"

Ashton stood in the middle of the Serrano PR office set with Jasmine and Nino, shooting a brainstorming session about Victor's career. When Ofelia, the first AD, let them know the scene was good, they trooped off the set, ready to hit catering for lunch.

Marquita approached before they'd even gone ten paces.

"Ashton, can we . . . talk?"

The hesitation in her voice and posture made him instantly wary. But she was the showrunner, so he nodded and gestured to Jasmine and Nino that they should go on without him. Jasmine shot him a worried look, but then Marquita drew him over to a quiet corner—or as quiet as the corner of a sound stage at lunchtime could be. She stared at him, her eyes round and uncertain, holding her phone to her chest, like she wanted to show him something, but was worried about his reaction.

Immediately, Ashton assumed the worst. Was it another picture of him and Jasmine? Had they been discovered? Or shit, was he being fired again? He'd thought he was doing well as Victor, but maybe—

"Do you . . ." Marquita shook her head, like she wasn't sure what to say, then blurted out the rest of the question in a rush. "¿Tienes un hijo?"

Ice flushed through his veins, chilling him from the inside out as he tried to keep his expression bland.

Do you have a son?

If she was asking, it meant she already knew.

Ashton swallowed hard and continued. "¿Qué están diciendo?"

"They're saying that you have a child." Marquita glanced down at her phone, then faced it toward him. "There's a picture."

The sight of Yadiel's innocent and unsuspecting face on Marquita's phone screen had Ashton curling his hands into fists. Rage swept through him, burning away the ice. *How. Dare. They.*

He took the phone carefully and zoomed in to see the details. The first photo had been taken two days earlier at the Yankees game Ashton had brought Yadiel to, but there were others, including one of Ashton at the airport as he returned from his latest trip to Puerto Rico. He hadn't seen anyone who looked obviously like a paparazzo, but someone had seen him. Seen him and recognized him, despite the baseball cap and sunglasses.

What the hell? Did *Buzz Weekly* have spies everywhere?

The headline read: TELENOVELA STAR'S SECRETS REVEALED! SEX, STALKERS, AND A SECRET CHILD!

It was certainly comprehensive, he thought bitterly. The writer, Kitty Sanchez—why did that name sound familiar?—

must have been researching him for some time to uncover *everything*.

Ashton wasn't violent or prone to fits of anger, but now, terror mixed with fury within him. These people—these paparazzi and gossip columnists—had dug into his past, tracked down his family, and *spied* on him. All because they thought he was screwing his costar.

Which he was. Pero carajo, why couldn't that remain his own business?

The spotlight focused on Jasmine had now trained itself on him and uncovered a story too juicy to ignore. The "just friends" campaign had failed. As careful as he'd been, he'd made mistakes—like bringing his family to New York because he missed them.

He should have known this would happen. Indeed, it was a low-grade fear he carried daily. But he'd hoped, naively, that he'd done enough to keep his family safe from all this.

Now everything was ruined.

Even worse, Yadiel's mother was bound to see this. His stomach dropped as he recalled how she'd handed their infant son over to Ashton. In exchange for full custody, she'd made it clear she didn't ever want to deal with the media fallout over a "secret lovechild," as she'd put it. What would she do if the tabloids traced Yadiel back to her?

He scrolled farther. Somehow, this Kitty Sanchez bruja had also found out about the stalker, the attempted break-in, and— coño, carajo, there was even a picture of him kissing Jasmine from the exterior scene they'd shot in Spanish Harlem the other night. Presented without context, of course.

As he stared at the photos, the words accompanying them blurred. His chest and throat grew tight, and he got a hot, claustrophobic feeling, like the walls were closing in on him. His worst nightmare was coming true. Every single one of his secrets was being revealed for public consumption.

"Ashton?" Marquita's brow creased with worry.

He'd been holding her phone for too long. Passing it back to her, he grated out, "Sí. Él es mi hijo."

He would *not* deny Yadiel's existence outright. He had never been ashamed of his son—he just wanted to protect him.

Marquita sucked in a breath, but Ashton's attention was drawn to movement across the sound stage.

Jasmine stood, staring at him with hurt in her dark eyes.

He recalled Carmen's words from the scene on the steps. *Opening up, letting people in, even if it's just to carry the burden of the knowledge.*

"I have to call my lawyer," he said. If there was any possibility of getting the photos pulled—for Yadiel's safety—he had to try.

As for Jasmine, he didn't know how to make this right. Didn't know if he could. But he had more important things to deal with at the moment.

She found him in his dressing room just as he was hanging up with his agent.

He froze when he saw her at the door, all the things he wanted to say backing up in his throat.

He knew her well enough now to know her moods, and she was *furious*. Her eyes blazed, and she stormed past him into the room.

He quickly shut the door behind her. "Jasmine, I—"

"First step: context." She cut him off and held up one finger, as if counting. "You had sex with me. You told me something that made me think you trusted me, and then I had to find out *yet again* from a *fucking magazine*"—she shook a copy of *Buzz Weekly* at him so violently the cover tore—"that a guy I was screwing had lied to me."

"I didn't lie to you." The words tasted sour in his mouth. All the times he'd omitted Yadiel from their conversations flashed in his mind. Fuck, he hated that she was right. Hated that he'd done the same thing to her as that pendejo McIntyre.

"Well, you sure didn't tell me the whole truth, did you?" Her tone dripped with sarcasm and she held up a second finger. "Step two: communication. Your turn."

She tossed the magazine at him and he caught it by reflex. The cheap paper crumpled in his hand. If he hadn't already ripped up a copy earlier, he would have done so now.

She wanted communication? He didn't even know where to begin, and he was too stressed out from the calls with his lawyer, his agent, his former boss in Miami, and his father to figure it out.

He'd kept everything related to Yadiel locked inside him for so long. The revelation should have been like opening a dam. Instead it was like pulling teeth.

Then, before he could think of what to tell her, she gasped. Her jaw dropped and she said, in a hushed voice, "Oh my god. This is why."

"Why what?" he repeated irritably. Unable to stand holding it any longer, he tossed the magazine into the garbage can under his desk.

"This is why you don't fuck your costars." Jasmine's eyes widened as she put it all together. "You worked with her, didn't you? On a telenovela."

The reference to Yadiel's mother had his stomach dropping like he'd just fallen ten stories on a roller coaster. Panic made his voice tight. "I'm not telling you who—"

"Did I ask?" Her voice was sharp with anger. "No, I didn't. And while I do respect your privacy, I also think someone who is *allowing you to enter their body* deserves a modicum of respect and trust as well. We got close, and you hid a major aspect of your life from me. And don't even try to tell me this was *just sex* because you and I both know goddamn well it was more than that."

Her words were like a kick in the gut, because she was right. Nothing between them had been "just" anything. But he couldn't tell her that now.

He shoved a hand through his hair, ruining forty-five minutes of the stylist's work in half a second. "I wasn't just hiding it from *you*."

"Is that supposed to make me feel better?" Her voice was high with outrage and disbelief, and something else. Coño, he'd hurt her. "Ashton, I've dated enough guys who didn't care about me to know that you do. And honestly? That only makes it worse."

On that, she spun on her heel and left, but not before he heard the crack in her voice, or saw the tears in her eyes.

All of his instincts screamed at him to go after her, to beg her to come back and let him explain. Her pain cut him to the core, made worse by knowing he'd caused it, however inadvertently.

This was so much worse than dumping a coffee on her. And it couldn't be fixed with a simple apology and a few cups of Café Bustelo either.

But what was there to say? She was right. He'd had his chance to tell her about Yadiel on his own terms, and he hadn't taken it.

Whatever hope they'd had as a couple was gone now. And it was all his fault.

WHEN THE DAY from hell finally ended, Jasmine called Riley on the ride to the hotel. Her agent said all the right things about how *all press is good press*, but Jasmine could barely take it in.

Tanya sent a slew of texts to schedule interviews to capitalize on the media attention and do damage control, but Jasmine couldn't focus on them.

Michelle and Ava waited for her in the hotel lobby when she arrived, with bottles of wine and fancy chocolate and a giant margarine tub full of their grandmother's arroz con pollo. They took her upstairs to her room, hid her phone, and said all the right things about how *he should have told her*, but as soon as they left, Jasmine crawled into bed with her phone and kept searching for what people were saying about them.

It wasn't healthy, and she knew it, but she couldn't stop.

Sure, she got that celebrity gossip could be fun and intriguing, but god, did people have to be so *mean*?

Even after Jasmine shoved the phone under a pillow, the headlines and quotes plagued her.

When sleep eluded her, she went back to scrolling social media for commentary about Ashton. Both their names were trending, but she already knew her own baggage. Ashton, on the other hand . . .

After so many years of secrecy, everyone wanted to know about his son, and by extension, who the boy's mother was. Apparently it was the best-kept secret in the world of teleno-velas, and everyone was dying to know.

Jasmine cared less about who the woman was and more about why Ashton had kept it from her.

He couldn't fucking tell her he had a child?

She was tempted to text him and ask for the real story. But he would have told her if he'd wanted her to know.

If she were being honest with herself, that was the part that hurt the most. She'd shared so much of herself with him, and he hadn't trusted her enough to do the same.

And after the way they'd left things, she didn't think he'd want to hear from her right now anyway.

According to the *Buzz Weekly* exposé, his son—Yadiel, that was his name—lived in Puerto Rico, which explained why Ashton had flown down there a few times during production on *Carmen*. But one of the photos revealed that Ashton's son had been in New York City that very weekend, at a Yankees game in the Bronx.

Ashton had slept in her suite the night before, which meant he had left her bed and gone to the game. Which meant his family had been, and maybe still was, in New York City.

And he hadn't told her. Angry tears burned her eyes but Jasmine refused to let them fall. Instead, she turned her phone off and finally fell asleep.

Chapter 32

ScreenFlix security was pretty good about keeping photographers away from the gates of the studio, but being located in Queens, with one-way streets, there were only so many routes off the lot.

The crowd down the street from ScreenFlix Studios had grown. There'd always been a small but loyal group of guys sitting on camp chairs inside a pen of metal police barricades, but after the Latinx in the Arts Summit, their crew had tripled in size. Now, in the wake of Ashton's "scandal," that number had doubled over the course of the day.

The paparazzi yelled and jeered, their gigantic cameras snapping and flashing as Ashton's car rolled through the gates. They shouted questions at him about Yadiel, about Yadiel's mother, about Jasmine, about the ridiculous rumor of a love triangle, even about Puerto Rican politics. That last one he *did* have a lot of thoughts on, but he wasn't falling for the bait.

Inside the SUV, Ashton slumped in the back seat and attempted to ignore them, immeasurably grateful for the vehicle's dark windows. He'd tried to close his eyes to block them out, but that only made it worse. He felt more in control with his eyes open. If something was going to get him, at least he'd see it coming.

Rationally, he knew they couldn't hurt him. Probably. Most likely. Okay, he didn't really believe that. All the media attention had ratcheted up the paranoia he kept tamped down, and every time he tried to talk himself out of it, his brain reminded him that someone had already *tried*. So no, he couldn't convince himself he was safe, because when the police had finally found the would-be intruder, the man had a hunting knife in his possession.

Aside from the police, Ignacio was the only other person who knew this detail. Ashton prayed it remained that way.

He finally closed his eyes when they got on the highway. And didn't open them again until the SUV rolled up in front of the apartment where Ashton's family was staying.

Ashton waited inside the vehicle while Drew—his new bodyguard friend, courtesy of Tanya—checked the sidewalk and vestibule. Ashton guessed the coast was clear, because Drew headed back over to the car. Ashton climbed out and they went inside. And although he felt weird about the whole thing, he asked Drew to wait in the lobby and make sure no one snuck up on the building.

Drew didn't seem to think any of this was weird, because he just said, "Sure thing," and took up a post by the door.

In his line of work, Drew had probably seen some shit Ashton didn't even want to know about—his nightmares were bad enough already.

Upstairs, Ashton assembled his father and grandparents for a family meeting while Yadiel, up past his bedtime and riding high on his second wind, climbed on every piece of furniture in the living room.

"No veo cuál es la gran cosa," his father said for at least the tenth time.

Ashton gritted his teeth and tried, once again, to explain why the entertainment news media dragging his name through the mud was a very big deal.

"I want Yadiel to have a normal life," he began in Spanish, but Abuelito Gus cut him off.

"What's normal, anyway?" The older man shrugged and gestured at the energetic boy. "He's fine. Kids are growing up with all sorts of new concerns that we didn't have. This is just one more."

The memory of glass breaking echoed in Ashton's ears. "I'm not talking about something like too much screen time. Most children don't have photographers stalking them and printing pictures of them in magazines."

"I *don't* get enough screen time," Yadiel muttered under his breath, and Ashton regretted bringing up what was already a sore topic in their household.

"How do you know?" Abuelito Gus held up his smartphone, challenging Ashton's assertion. "Everyone has one of these now. Anyone could be taking pictures of him at any time."

That argument did *not* make Ashton feel better. "That's my point—"

"Verdad." Abuelita Bibi nodded and cast on a new color of yarn to her needles. She was taking advantage of the "cooler temperatures" of New York City to get some knitting done.

It was eighty-five degrees outside.

Then Abuelita Bibi turned on Ashton with that eagle-eyed *dime el bochinche* expression she wore when she sniffed out gossip. "¿Y la mujer?"

"¿Qué mujer?" Did she mean Yadiel's birth mom? The only people who knew her identity were sitting in this room. Ashton had given Yadi a choice, and the boy had decided he would wait until he was ten to be told. He viewed ten as some magical age where all sorts of information and skills—mostly regarding video games and skateboarding—would be unlocked for him.

"La nena de las telenovelas americanas," Abuelita Bibi clarified. "Jasmita?"

"Jasmine." Ashton corrected her before he could stop himself. The last thing he needed was his family making up nicknames for her.

"Sí." Abuelita Bibi gave him a look like, *¿Eres estúpido?* "¿Pues? ¿La mujer?"

Ashton heaved a sigh. "We're just . . ." The word *friends* turned to ashes on his tongue. "No sé."

He had no idea. In all likelihood, Jasmine would never want to speak to him again. Regret hung like a lead weight around his neck, but it was an emotion he didn't have the bandwidth to indulge.

Abuelito Gus wiggled his eyebrows. "Ella es muy hermosa."

It was on the tip of Ashton's tongue to extol her other virtues. Yes, Jasmine was beautiful, but she was also so much more than—

Ashton sighed. They were trying to change the subject and get him to come clean on the truth about his tryst with Jasmine, but he wasn't ready to do that yet. The wounds were too fresh, hastily bandaged so he could get through the current crisis. But sometime soon, he'd have to poke at them, and then he'd become fully aware of everything he'd sacrificed. He'd been fooling himself, thinking he could make room for her in his life.

You're fooling yourself if you think you can live without her, a little voice whispered in the back of his mind, but Ashton slapped it away. He should have stuck to his policy.

Just in case he needed the reminder, he'd received a text that evening from a number with a Miami area code that read *Leave me out of this* in Spanish.

It could only be from Yadiel's mother.

Thoroughly exasperated, Ashton blurted out, "Am I the *only* one who remembers what happened before?"

Yadiel leaped off an armchair and crashed to the floor with a resounding thud that rattled everything on the coffee table. "What happened before?"

Carajo. Yadiel didn't know about the attempted break-in. How could Ashton have been so careless? The weight of all these secrets was going to bury him.

Ashton wiped a hand over his face and said, again, "Mijo, this is an apartment. People live downstairs."

Yadiel ignored him and bounced to his feet. "Papi, quiero visitar tu trabajo."

This conversation was going off the rails. Just the thought of bringing his son to the studio now, when it was swarming with photographers and reporters and who knew what else, was enough to make him sweat. "No, mi amor. I'm sorry, but it's not a good time for you to visit."

"¿Por qué no?" Ignacio cut in. "Everyone knows about us now. Why can't we visit the set?"

Ashton nearly choked. "*We?*"

"Sí, let's all go." Abuelita Bibi looked up from her knitting with an excited smile.

Yadiel cheered while Ashton panicked at the image of his worlds colliding. What would the cast and crew think? And, coño, what if they met Jasmine? His father would absolutely try to meddle.

Not to mention the potential for exposing them to the public, to the press, to . . . anyone with nefarious purposes.

"Espérate," he began, but Ignacio got up and patted him on the shoulder.

"We'll come tomorrow, okay?" Then he leaned in and said in a low voice, "The person you're worried about is back in jail."

The person—did he mean the stalker? "How do you know?"

Ignacio shrugged and gave him a crooked smile. "I check with my friends at the policía every month."

Some of the tightness in Ashton's chest eased. Of course Ignacio hadn't forgotten what had happened. He'd been there that night. While Ashton had grabbed Yadiel out of his crib and called the police, his father had run outside with a baseball bat to chase the intruder away. What's more, Ignacio had also been the one to file all the reports and follow up with the Miami PD while Ashton made immediate plans to sell the house and move Yadiel to Puerto Rico. Without his father's help, Ashton never would've gotten through the experience.

Looking around at their smiling faces, at Yadiel high-fiving Abuelita Bibi, at Ignacio and Abuelito Gus discussing what they were going to wear to the studio, Ashton couldn't deny them this. Even though it scared him.

He nodded. "Fine. I'll ask the producers."

God help him.

Chapter 33

Some small part of Jasmine hoped Ashton would have reached out while she slept, to offer an explanation, an apology, *something*. Instead, she got radio silence.

Oh, she had *plenty* of texts and voice mails, but not a single one from Ashton.

Everything about her . . . fling? Affair? She didn't even know what to call it. But everything about her time with Ashton had been different from all her other relationships.

Except this part. The part where she ended up alone. Again. Shit had hit the fan, and he'd bounced. Left her hanging. Ghosted her.

Okay, so he was probably dealing with some shit over on his end. After everything he'd told her, she could understand why he'd gone to extreme lengths to protect his child. It was admirable, if misguided. No one could work in the public eye and expect complete privacy. She knew that all too well. Especially since the news about Ashton's son had unleashed renewed interest in Jasmine and her love life.

The "love triangle" rumor had picked up steam, and now a lot of outlets were carrying the story. Jasmine indulged in an epic eye roll. Of all the ridiculous notions. There was no *jealousy on the set* or *secret text messages*, but the tabloids would write anything they could dream up to make the story more salacious.

They even unearthed Seth Thomas, Jasmine's ex from *Sunrise Vista*, from whatever rock he'd been living under after a cocaine bust and multiple DUIs, to prove that Jasmine had a pattern of messy breakups.

As if she weren't 100 percent aware of her own romantic failings.

Also, those things had happened to Seth long after they'd broken up and had nothing to do with her.

It hurt, being made out to be some kind of wild woman who threw herself at every man she worked with. Especially since, deep down, she worried it might be true.

She was just looking for love. What was so wrong with that? Granted, she was clearly looking in all the wrong places. But the headlines cut her to the core. Gems like HERE ARE 8 OF JASMINE LIN'S MOST MEMORABLE BREAKUPS, JUST IN TIME TO MAKE YOU FEEL BETTER ABOUT YOUR OWN MISERABLE LOVE LIFE. Jasmine didn't think any of her breakups were particularly memorable, and she declined to go down memory lane with the photo slideshow. Or SOAP SLUT? JASMINE LIN'S ON THE PROWL WITH HER LATIN LOVER COSTAR AND HIS SECRET BABY. Slut-shaming *and* an offensive stereotype, all in one headline? Real classy.

And another by her good friend Kitty Sanchez that made an old quote from Seth sound like it was from McIntyre: DESPERATELY SEEKING JASMINE: EX SAYS "SHE WAS OBSESSED WITH ME."

So much for her Leading Lady Plan. Clearly all anyone cared about was who she was fucking. Why bother trying to do more?

Anger flared—at Ashton, but also at herself.

She'd done it again, given her heart and her body to someone without any kind of assurances that they felt the same way.

Even she couldn't ignore the patterns anymore. She'd seen them during that horrific brunch with her family, as if there were glaring neon signs over the heads of her parents and siblings that read, HERE IS THE SOURCE OF YOUR EMOTIONAL BAGGAGE! UNPACK ME!

She didn't want to. She wanted to leave it all bundled up and locked away. But once you knew, you couldn't unknow.

This was it, then. The final straw that would break a lifelong pattern of looking to men for external validation, for proof of her worth.

No. More.

The Leading Lady Plan, written in a mix of her handwriting and Michelle's, flashed in her mind, reminding her that she was a *badass queen* who was *whole and happy on her own.*

Old Jasmine would have tormented herself with what-ifs and all the ways she might have done something to cause this.

New Jasmine refused to take the blame for the actions and choices of others. This was *not* her fault. She had not forced the media to obsess over her. She had not made Ashton hide his son. And she certainly hadn't done anything to warrant the kinds of headlines being written about her.

From now on, she would never again allow anyone to make her feel like her worth came from the man she was attached to.

Not her parents, not the media, not goddamned Kitty Sanchez, and not herself either.

Fueled by fresh resolve, Jasmine threw back the covers and stalked to the bathroom mirror to check her eyes. Not puffy, despite her restless night. Maybe her grandmother was on to something with this snail stuff.

Instead of waiting until she got to the studio for her first hit of caffeine, she padded into the suite's tiny kitchen and brewed herself a cup there. Maybe it would help her get her head on straight before she got to work.

She spent the morning filming opposite Peter Calabasas on the sound stage outfitted as the Serrano PR office. Ashton was nowhere to be found, but then, he wasn't in that scene. After that, Jasmine was booked for an interview, thanks to Tanya, the hardest working publicist in the business.

A PA had set up two chairs off to the side of the sound stage, along with some lights. Jasmine took a seat opposite a pale, gangly man with short dark hair. The first few minutes of the interview were fine, mostly questions about *Carmen*, but then he blindsided her.

"In a recent interview, McIntyre let it slip that he misses you and wishes things had ended differently. Do you have a message for him?"

What. The. Fuck.

Behind the interviewer, Tanya squeezed her eyes shut and slapped a hand to her face in disbelief.

Out of sheer habit, Jasmine's smile remained fixed to her face. But inside, anger rumbled like a volcano about to erupt. All of her hurt feelings about Ashton, McIntyre's betrayal, and the stress of watching the career she'd busted her ass to build devolve into clickbait, churned like burning lava ready to spew . . . and incinerate the smug asshole sitting across from her.

Little did he know, he was dealing with New Jasmine.

She smiled sweetly, and while her tone dripped with honey, she let the Bronx out. "I will not be answering questions about anything related to my love life, at this time or any other. Let's keep this interview focused on *Carmen*, 'kay? Now, do you have any other questions?"

The interviewer stumbled over his words as he shuffled the cards in his lap. What the hell, were *all* of them about her ex-boyfriends?

So she did something Old Jasmine never would have had the guts to do, but Carmen sure the hell would. She stood and waved Tanya over to deal with him.

"We're done here," Jasmine said, and with a toss of her hair, strode away without looking back.

Once she was out of sight, she resisted the urge to high-five herself for drawing a clear boundary and sticking to it. But the pride was tempered by sheer annoyance. The absolute fucking *nerve* of McIntyre. Oh, he missed her, did he? He wished he hadn't broken up with her via tabloid while gallivanting around Cabo with a model half his age? That was fucking rich.

Old Jasmine would have taken that as proof that she was worthy of a man's attention and run back to him for validation. New Jasmine just wanted him to take her name out of his damn mouth.

Still, the adrenaline rush from the confrontation left her a little shaken, so she made her way to catering for lunch. She hadn't felt up to eating breakfast that morning, and she needed food and more caffeine. As she was fixing a cup of coffee, a squeaky voice behind her shouted, "¡Comida!"

Jasmine abandoned her cup just in time to catch the tornado of elbows and knees that crashed into her.

It was a little boy with sandy blond hair and familiar brown eyes. She immediately recognized him from the photos she'd seen online. His wide, gap-toothed smile won her over instantly, and she couldn't help but grin back, even as her heart twisted.

"Yadiel!" Ashton's voice came from around the corner, not sharp, but concerned. When he stepped into view and saw them, he froze.

"Like father like son," Jasmine said wryly, helping Yadiel back onto his own two feet. Then she picked up her coffee and raised it in a mocking toast.

Ashton's lips pressed into a straight line and he didn't reply.

"¡Papi, mira!" Voice full of glee, Yadiel gestured expansively at the array of food. "Hay mucha comida aquí."

"Sí, mijo," Ashton said gravely. "But you just ate."

"Pero quiero comer *eso*," Yadiel replied, pouting.

Since Ashton still hadn't even deigned to acknowledge her presence, let alone make introductions, Jasmine picked up a plate and addressed Yadiel directly. "¿Qué quieres comer?"

As Yadiel turned starry eyes on the trays of food and snacks, Ashton moved closer. "Inglés, Yadiel," he said, when Yadiel started chattering about the food in Spanish.

Jasmine rolled her eyes and muttered, "I do know some Spanish." Enough to talk to children, at least.

Ashton finally met her eyes. "He speaks English too. It'll be good practice for him."

The mention of practice made her recall her own Spanish lessons with Ashton. He'd been unfailingly patient with her . . . almost like he was used to teaching a reluctant learner. At the time, she hadn't given it much thought. But now, after meeting his son, things were starting to fall into place. His kindness, the bad jokes—holy shit, they were *dad* jokes not *bad* jokes—and how he was always texting with his father.

He wasn't just a caring son, as she'd thought. He was a caring son and *dad*.

Once Yadiel and Jasmine had plates piled high with food— arroz con pollo, pastelitos, tostones, and fruit on the side—she led him to the dining area to eat. She had a feeling their eyes were bigger than their stomachs, but they'd had fun selecting the food and talking about their favorite dishes. Yadiel revealed that his abuelo y bisabuelos owned a restaurant, which Jasmine had already known, so the kid had lots of opinions about Puerto Rican food.

Ashton followed, stiff and silent, while Jasmine's conversation with Yadiel shifted to the Avengers. In the dining area, Jasmine and Yadiel sat at a round table with four chairs around it, but Ashton remained standing by the door. She tamped down her anguish and got a bunch of napkins for Yadiel, in case he was anything like her nephews. Despite Jillian's best efforts, the boys ate like monsters.

"How do you know about superheroes?" Yadiel asked her through a mouthful of rice.

"I have nephews," she told him. "I think you'd get along with them. They like superheroes and LEGOs too."

Yadiel was an easy kid to talk to, but Jasmine couldn't ignore Ashton hovering like a nervous shadow in the doorway. His eyes were cold and distant, his expressive mouth set in a firm line. Everything about him was aloof and unapproachable . . . just like how he'd been when they first started working together.

It hurt her heart to see him this way. He'd come so far over the past few months, opening up and letting people in. Not just her, but the rest of the cast. Nino looked up to him, Peter sought him out daily to discuss baseball, and Lily had named him her official dominoes nemesis. Watching Ashton retreat behind the mask he'd worn at the beginning made Jasmine sadder than anything else that had happened between them.

If she thought about it further, she was going to weep, so she focused on Yadiel, who'd pulled a LEGO mini-figure from his pocket and was enumerating the toy's many cool features.

Jasmine looked up as a man wearing a pale blue guayabera shirt strolled into the dining area. He was shorter than Ashton, his skin darker and more lined, but he was unmistakably Ashton's father. They had the same jawline, the same stride, and the same taste in shirts.

As he approached the table where Jasmine and Yadiel sat, his face creased into a smile and he held out a hand. "Hola, Jasmine. Soy Ignacio, el padre de este cabrón aquí." He jerked his chin to indicate Ashton.

Yadiel let out a delighted giggle at hearing his grandfather call his dad a dumbass. Over by the door, Ashton muttered something under his breath and his scowl deepened.

Jasmine grinned and took Ignacio's hand, leaning in to kiss his cheek. "Hola, Ignacio. ¿Cómo está usted?"

He winked and took a seat on the other side of Yadiel. "Call me Nacho."

Ashton let out an audible sigh.

Ignacio picked at the food on Yadiel's plate as he talked to Jasmine about the show, her family, and where her grandparents had been born in Puerto Rico. He was a sweet, charming man, with as many opinions about food as his grandson. Jasmine had a flash of a younger Ignacio sitting and eating with Ashton when he was Yadiel's age. But no, Ashton would have still been Ángel Luis then. She imagined Ashton as Ángel Luis at different ages. Lighter in demeanor and more carefree, before the stress of protecting his family amid the chokehold of fame had worn him down, compelling him to erect walls around himself. Part of her wished she could have known him then, but she'd grown to love the man he'd become, the man who expressed the depth of his emotions through other characters. The one who'd finally cracked open the door and given her a glimpse inside. Having seen what was within, she could even love the walls for keeping him safe, even though she thought he was being a royal jackass for locking her out again.

Finally, Ashton checked his watch and stepped forward. "I'm due on set soon. Pa, can you take Yadi back to my dressing room? Hang out there for a little while, and then I'll finish giving you the tour."

Yadiel turned big, irresistible eyes on Jasmine, the same shape as Ashton's but a lighter brown. "Will you come with us?"

Her heart felt torn in two. Yes, she absolutely wanted to take Yadiel on a tour of the studio. If Ashton had kept him away from this world, it was probably the boy's first time on set. She'd offered to give Jillian's kids a tour, but her sister had implied they might be exposed to something improper, so Jasmine hadn't asked again.

But it wasn't just that. She was also dying to see Ashton interact with his son. She wanted to observe the back and forth, how Yadiel pushed boundaries—because that's what kids did—and the ways Ashton enforced them or capitulated.

Except the look on Ashton's face made it clear that he didn't want her to join. After being his scene partner, and his lover, she was an expert at reading his expressions. If it were a college degree, she'd have graduated with honors.

"Maybe," she hedged. "I might have to film something else."

It wasn't just the forbidding set of Ashton's mouth that made her decline—it was the sheer panic lurking in his eyes. He was scared of her being around his son. She could see that, she just didn't know why.

"Okay." Yadiel sounded disappointed, but then, without warning, he launched himself at Jasmine, catching her around the neck in a tight hug and landing a smacking kiss on her cheek. "Bye! Maybe I can meet your nephews someday."

"Maybe." She couldn't help smiling at him as he clambered down and skipped over to take his dad's hand.

Ignacio rose and picked up the remains of their lunch.

"Un placer," he told her. A hint of humor twinkled in his eye.

"Igualmente." She waved as they left the dining room, but at the last second, Ashton looked over his shoulder at her.

Pure anguish burned in his gaze, so intense it stole her breath.

For whatever reason, Ashton was utterly conflicted about how well Jasmine had gotten along with his father and son.

Well, he wasn't the only one. Ignacio and Yadiel were *delightful*. But she couldn't keep doing this—pretending to be into him on camera, and pretending not to be into him behind the scenes, where her stupid self had gone and fallen in love with him. For the sake of her heart, she needed to draw a clear line in the sand. And this time, she would *not* cross it.

It was incredibly weird to see his family on set. He'd texted Marquita to help him smooth the way with the producers, and she'd come through. Security was so high on a film lot, it was rare to bring guests, but after attaining permission, Ashton had dutifully taken his son and father and grandparents around the interior areas of the lot and introduced them to a few people. And despite Ashton's own anxiety about driving through the swarm of paparazzi, Yadiel had thought it was "awesome." On the upside, Yadiel had *loved* his first studio tour. Ignacio and Peter had hit it off, and Nino had been totally enamored with Yadiel.

And of course, Ignacio and Yadiel had *loved* Jasmine. Yadiel asked about the "pretty lady" every day, and Ignacio had become insufferable, winking and nudging Ashton at every opportunity.

Standing by the door like a creep while they hit it off gave him plenty of time to wallow in regret. She'd been *perfect* with them. Listening to Yadiel chatter on about LEGOs and comics, talking to Ignacio about her family. It was all Ashton could do not to throw himself at her feet and beg her to forgive him. Her kindness to his family was more than he deserved. And he was *so fucking pissed* at himself for not telling her about them sooner.

After sitting through hair and makeup, Ashton was on his way back to his dressing room when a PA intercepted him to hand over the script for episode eight.

Ashton accepted with some trepidation. This was it—the season finale. And depending on whether they were renewed for a second season or not, it could end up being the *series* finale.

The way viewers—and potential casting directors—felt at the end of a season was the emotion they would always associate with the show. It would be the last image he left them with. The rest of his career depended on nailing this episode.

He tore through the pages, skimming scenes of Victor filming a TV special, being approached about writing a memoir, and performing an outdoor pop-up concert, and then . . .

Ashton groaned out loud.

More kissing. They were ending the season on an optimistic note for Victor and Carmen, and of course, that involved a heavy make-out session. He should probably be glad it wasn't a full-on sex scene. Ashton had done plenty of those in his career, but to go from kissing on set, to kissing and fucking behind the scenes, to only screwing on-screen, would have broken him. He needed to clear the air with Jasmine, but he had no idea how, and really, he hadn't had time. When he wasn't on set, he was spending every waking minute with his family and navigating calls from his agent, Tanya, and interviewers wanting to know why he was such a terrible father. Words like "negligent" and "abandoned" got thrown around a lot, tapping into all of the guilt Ashton already carried from living apart from his son.

He hadn't heard from Yadiel's mother again, which was a small blessing, and so far no one had uncovered her identity. Yadiel had been born in Orlando, and his birth certificate listed his parents' birth names, not their stage names. Ashton was on there as Ángel Luis Felipe Suarez Bonilla. He hoped this would make it harder to find, or that people would lose interest before digging that deep.

Jasmine was angry and Ashton couldn't blame her. Still, he didn't like leaving things open-ended like this, and he didn't want her to think he'd used her, or that he was like her pendejo ex. He couldn't tell her he loved her. What would be the point? But he could find a way to apologize. Somehow. She might not forgive him, and that was her choice, but he loved her too much to leave her hurting like this.

In the meantime, he'd suffer through a choreography session directed by Vera and make the most of his last intimate moments with Jasmine—on camera. When it was all over, he'd mourn the loss of what could have been. If he were different. If his life were different.

But it wasn't. And there was nothing he could do about it.

Chapter 34

CARMEN IN CHARGE

EPISODE 8

Scene: Victor pulls Carmen up on stage.
EXT: Pop-up concert at Rumsey Playfield in Central
  Park—DAY

From the center of the stage, with a full band behind him
rocking out with his signature blend of pop and Latin beats,
Victor sang his number one hit single, "Hola, mi amor," with
renewed energy and emotion, his rich voice ringing out across
the concert arena in the middle of Central Park. The crowd
loved him, cheering and clapping and singing along.

But Carmen was the only one who mattered. No one else
knew it, but Victor had written this song for her.

Across the heads of a thousand people, his gaze sought hers
where she stood with her father next to the tent. Pride shone
in her eyes as she watched him perform, making him feel like a
million bucks—or a million records sold. Her faith in him had

made this possible, her strength had seen it through. And—he hardly dared hope—her love had given him his life back. He'd gotten the tour spot, beat out Dimas del Valle, and even been approached about writing a memoir—with a sizable advance payment. He owed her everything.

At Carmen's side, her father crossed his arms and nodded approvingly. The script flashed in Victor's memory, mapping onto what he knew they were saying.

"You did it, mija." Ernesto gave Carmen a warm smile. "Serrano PR is back on top. Tío Fredo would be proud."

When Ernesto dabbed at the corner of his eye, Carmen leaned in to give him a hug. "We did it. Together. Serranos do it better, remember?"

The sentiment gave Victor a pang. One of the things that had broken them up before was Carmen prioritizing the family business over their future together. Would the same thing happen now?

Maybe. But he wasn't giving up without making his feelings clear.

The song ended. Victor struck his ending pose and yelled, "¡Gracias, New York!"

The crowd went wild.

Sweating and breathless, with no filter left on his emotions, Victor leaned into the mic. "I wasn't sure I'd get to do this again. Thank you for being a wonderful audience and for making my comeback concert so special."

More screams. When the audience quieted down, Victor zeroed in on Carmen again. His heart leaped at the way her eyes lit up and the encouraging smile she sent him. He felt the warmth of it all the way up on stage, but he needed more. He needed *her*. He held the mic close and said in a low growl, "Come up here, Carmencita."

Carmen's eyes went wide and she froze as everyone turned to stare at her.

Her father took her elbow, urging her up toward the stage, and Victor counted his blessings that Carmen's parents were on his side.

Still, Carmen only ever did what she wanted to do, so he wasn't sure if she'd turn and bolt. He didn't know what he'd do if she ran; there was no plan B. So he waited with nervous expectation as she climbed the steps, looking slightly dazed by her surroundings. Victor extended a hand out to her and she gripped it like he was her anchor in a storm. Warmth washed over him at her touch, and he drew her closer.

"Did you plan this?" she hissed, but he smiled gently and shook his head.

"No. But you deserve to be up here. This is your victory too."

Once she was with him in front of the mic, he put his arm around her and turned back to the crowd.

"None of this would have been possible without the amazing Carmen Serrano." He paused, then added in a soft voice, "My wife."

And then he kissed her full on the lips, right in front of everyone.

Chapter 35

CARMEN IN CHARGE

EPISODE 8

Scene: Carmen and Victor get intimate in his tour
  bus.
INT: Victor's tour bus—DAY

Carmen and Victor burst into his trailer, buoyed by exhilaration. They couldn't keep their hands off each other.

"Victor, you were amazing," she said. All the love she felt for him reverberated through her voice. "The crowd adored you. And now there's the book deal, the tour, the new album— you've done it. I'm so proud of you."

Victor took her in his arms and held her close. "It's all because of you, Carmencita. You always believed in me. You saw the best in me, even when I didn't see it in myself. Everything I've done, I owe to you."

"You sure know the way to my heart," she said, blinking

back tears. "Complimenting my work will get you every-where."

"There's only one place I want to be." With a husky laugh, he leaned in and kissed her. It was the hottest, most sensual kiss they'd shared since his return, deeper and more intense than all the others. Their hands roamed each other's bodies as he backed her into the vanity and helped her perch on the tiny counter.

When Victor broke the kiss, Carmen started unbuttoning his shirt, desperate to touch him, but Victor had other ideas. Dropping to his knees, he pushed her skirt up and parted her thighs. Carmen leaned back on the mirror, eyes closed, one hand clutching his hair as he pressed his face between her legs. She fought to catch her breath, repeating his name over and over until her voice broke on a low moan and she shuddered.

He rose and pressed his forehead to hers. They were both breathing hard.

She fought back tears. *You're breaking my heart, Ashton Suarez.*

"Carmen," Victor said softly. "I—"

Someone knocked on the door.

Carmen jumped to her feet, only a little unsteady. "Who could that be?" she whispered. "My father? I thought he already went home."

Turning to the mirror, she quickly straightened her clothing and swiped at her smeared lipstick.

"I'll check." Victor fixed his hair and adjusted his pants before he went to the door. When he opened it, he froze, staring at the person on the other side for a long beat. Behind him,

Carmen gasped and pressed a hand to her throat in shock. Then Victor's brows creased, his expression turning as hard and impenetrable as granite.

"What are you doing here?" he demanded.

"Cut! And that is a *wrap*!"

Chapter 36

With that, the last episode of *Carmen in Charge* was complete.

Jasmine let out a long breath and pressed her hand to her solar plexus. Her legs shook, and she wanted to weep, but all around her, cast and crew members were cheering. A few feet away on the tour bus interior set, Ashton turned to her. It was hard to look him in the eyes, considering he'd just had his face between her legs and they were barely on speaking terms.

She'd been surprised that the writers had included Victor going down on Carmen, but hell, after putting up with so much of Victor's nonsense, Carmen deserved some spontaneous cunnilingus on a tour bus. It had been a painful melding of worlds, since Jasmine knew from experience just how it would feel and how Carmen should react. But it was over now.

She couldn't wait to get the fuck out of there.

When Ashton raised his hand for their post-take ritual, the corners of his eyes were tight with unexpressed emotion. Jasmine refused to look deeper. She was past caring how he felt.

No, that wasn't true. She *did* care. She just couldn't turn off her feelings as easily as a faucet, and she was trying to steel herself for what she planned to do later. That line in the sand was begging to be drawn.

He was still waiting, so she lifted her hand and smacked his palm in a half-hearted high five. The last one they'd ever share.

Before she could talk herself out of it, she grabbed his elbow and leaned in. "Meet me in my room," she told him, fighting to keep her voice steady. "When you get back to the hotel tonight."

His gaze searched hers for a long moment. Just when she thought he was going to flat-out refuse, he nodded.

Without another word, she pasted a smile on her face and leaped into the fray. Someone handed her a glass of champagne, which she accepted gratefully and downed in one go. She hugged everyone and pretended to be happy, but inside, she was a wreck.

The day had been hot and long, with New York City's particularly disgusting brand of humidity. When Jasmine got back to the room that night, she took a shower and changed into a summery dress that accentuated all her best assets. She needed to wash the stress of the day off her, and while she knew it was petty, she wanted to look gorgeous when she confronted Ashton.

But the longer she waited, the more her stomach tied itself into knots. She hated confrontation, hated hurting people. But being in limbo with Ashton while filming episode eight had destroyed her. To go from being in love with him to only connecting through their characters had taken a toll, and the only thing she could think to do was enforce the strongest boundaries possible.

Leading Ladies are whole and happy on their own.

When she'd first written down the Leading Lady Plan, she hadn't believed it. But now, she understood that being whole and happy on her own was the only way the other two things—getting recognition for positive reasons and making jefa moves—could happen.

She didn't know what she was going to do next, but whatever it was, it would be on her own terms. For now, she was getting the hell out of dodge and going back to her apartment in LA that didn't contain any pesky memories of Ashton. She was going to put her head down and work while she waited for the reaction to *Carmen in Charge*. *No dating.* And then . . . they would see.

Too nervous to eat, she rummaged around in her suite's kitchen and found a bottle of Patrón that Michelle had left behind. Jasmine was more of a wine drinker, so she didn't have shot glasses on hand. Improvising, she poured two fingers' worth into one of the drinking glasses, then knocked it back.

Oh, lord. The tequila hit like a sledgehammer all the way down. But it had the intended effect of strengthening her resolve, hardening her heart, and incinerating the tears building in her throat.

Before she could resort to turning on a playlist of breakup songs, Ashton knocked on the door.

She opened it, and all the witty, sarcastic greetings she'd practiced fled from her mind. Did he have to be so handsome? Or smell so good?

Or look so solemn?

"Come in," she said quietly, stepping aside.

He went through the little hallway into the living room, but didn't sit down.

"Do you want something to drink?" she asked, unnerved by his silence.

"I'm fine," he said. "I can't stay long. I have to check on my family."

He could barely look at her, and the awkwardness was killing her slowly. Bracing herself, she got right to the point.

"I won't drag this out," she said. "But I want to be perfectly clear. We're done."

Jasmine balled her hands into fists. Apparently breakups felt awful even when you weren't on the receiving end. Who knew?

Eyes downcast, Ashton nodded. "Understood. If there's a season two—"

"There won't be a season two."

His eyes shot up at her interruption. "How do you know? Did you hear something?"

She shook her head. This would be the final nail in the coffin. "If it gets picked up, I'll fight it. I'm done with *Carmen*."

And you. She didn't say it, it was too mean. But it was implied.

The look on his face was horror-stricken, like she'd broken his heart.

But she knew she hadn't. She was the one with the broken heart.

ASHTON FELT LIKE she'd slapped him. His entire body prickled, but it wasn't anger—it was panic.

"Are you kidding me?" He ground out the words, too taken aback to articulate more.

She shook her head. "I'm perfectly serious."

She couldn't be. Desperation welled up inside him. This show was his big break, but Jasmine played the title character. If she quit, the show was over.

"Jasmine, think about this. Why would you do that?"

"Why not?" Her eyes flashed, whether with anger or pain, he wasn't sure. "Why would I want to put myself through this again?"

Coño, she was right. He'd known better. He never should have gotten involved with her in the first place, and once he had, he should have told her about Yadiel. He hadn't, and that was on him.

But the rest? With the show? That was business. He *needed* this show. For one thing, it paid more than telenovelas, and he had a lot of people relying on him to pay the bills. And the exposure was the next step on his road to that Best Actor nom. He wasn't getting any younger here. He was certainly too old to have made a stupid mistake like having a fling with his co-star and sabotaging his career. Yet here they were.

In the back of his mind, he felt bad thinking about it as a fling, and he felt bad about being angry at her. It took two to tango, and he'd been right there with her, diving headlong into a love neither could afford.

But anxiety and a sense of betrayal sparked his anger and came flowing out of his mouth. "I cannot believe you are sabotaging me this way."

Her eyes went wide. "Excuse me?"

"You know what a good thing we have going here? Screen-Flix is the number one streaming service in the world. We might never get the chance to work on a Latinx-driven mainstream production like this again."

His phone buzzed in his pocket. He pulled it out to glance at the screen. His father was calling.

But Jasmine wasn't taking his accusation quietly.

"Don't act like you care about this show," she scoffed. "It was like pulling teeth to get you to connect with the rest of the cast. And look, you're not even paying attention now. My cousins were right. You are full of yourself."

With an angry move, he sent the call to voice mail and tossed his phone across the room, onto the sofa cushions.

"There," he bit off. "Happy now?"

"Do I *look* like I'm happy?" she snapped, brow furrowed in exasperation.

He didn't answer that. Instead, he tried to reason with her. "We're both contracted for three seasons."

She shrugged and looked away. "So?"

"Jasmine, this show is a great opportunity—for *both* of us. Don't make a—"

"A what?" She fisted her hands on her hips and stared him down.

"A . . ." What was he going to say? Something with "emotional," but he realized that was a bad idea. "Don't make a decision from . . . from your feelings . . ."

"Are you calling me *emotional*?" She narrowed her eyes at him and he knew he was in trouble.

"No. You—" *Use "I" statements, idiot.* That's what Vera always reminded them during their rehearsals, although she'd never called him an idiot. "I mean, *I* feel that this is a rash decision. A mistake."

Jasmine let out a strangled laugh. "Of course you do. Because this is all about you. You never once considered me, or my feelings, or thought that I would want to know—" She snapped her mouth shut.

"Is this because of Yadiel?"

She shot him an impatient glance. "No, it's because you didn't *tell me* about Yadiel. Please tell me you understand the difference."

He pinched the bridge of his nose. "I haven't told *anyone* about him."

"Well, I'm not just *anyone*." Her voice rose in anger. "Don't treat me like I'm some random person on the street trying to get a picture with *the famous Ashton Suarez*."

The way she said his name, the sarcastic air quotes were clearly implied.

"Jasmine, I gave you more than I've given anyone else in . . . in a long time." *Ever.* "And with the way the press is always on your ass, can you blame me for not wanting to reveal everything?"

She sucked in a breath, and her eyebrows dipped in pain. It was a low blow, and he felt terrible, especially since he knew she didn't enjoy all the attention the media heaped on her.

Jasmine let out a shaky breath, and in a severe voice, said, "Ashton. You *can't* have it both ways."

His brow creased. "What do you mean? I've been in this business a long time, and I managed to keep Yadiel hidden until now."

She shut her eyes against his words, and he knew he'd hurt her again. He couldn't seem to stop. The stress of the last couple weeks had worn him raw.

"You know, I sometimes think, 'I never asked for it,'" she said in a quiet voice. "But the truth is, the second I signed a contract to be on *television*, I made a deal with the public. They would get part of me in exchange for knowing my face and connecting with the characters I play. And so did you. You can't have it both ways, Ashton. You can't be a public figure and have a completely private life. You think the actors who make it to the Oscars have *privacy*? Don't be naive."

He felt like the walls were closing in on him. "I was doing pretty well at it until I met you."

She sucked in a shocked breath, and the hurt that crossed her features made him feel like absolute shit. It had been another low blow, and he opened his mouth to apologize, but the hotel phone interrupted him. They both stared at it, startled by the ringing of an actual telephone.

"Don't say another word," she ground out, her voice hoarse and brittle. She moved to the desk to answer it.

"Hello?" She listened for a moment, then sent Ashton a worried look. "Sí, él está aquí."

Ashton's surprise at hearing her speak Spanish meant he wasn't thinking about who was on the phone. When he lifted the receiver to his ear, he was shocked to hear his father's voice on the other end. He listened to Ignacio with growing horror, guilt and fear roiling in his gut. With frantic movements, he grabbed the pen and paper on the side of the desk and scribbled down the information.

"Ya salgo para allá." Ashton replaced the phone in the cradle and stalked over to the sofa. Digging around in the cushions, he retrieved his cell phone and checked the screen. Five missed calls from his father, and a series of texts, telling him what he now already knew.

"Yadiel fell," he said harshly.

Behind him, Jasmine gasped. "Oh my god. Is he okay?"

The concern in her voice was genuine, but Ashton was too fired up to be kind. "He broke his collarbone. They're in the ER and my father has been trying to reach me."

"Oh no. I hope—"

"Jasmine, don't you see?" Ashton didn't want her trying to make him feel better. His child was *hurt*, and he hadn't been there. Never mind that Yadiel was *always* climbing and falling and hurting himself. Ashton had years' worth of guilt stored up, and for the first time, he had somewhere to direct the pain.

Even if, in the back of his mind, he knew she didn't deserve it.

When she didn't respond, he whirled on her, ignoring the hurt look on her pretty face.

"I don't have time for *this*." He waved a hand, vaguely gesturing at them and everything between them. "Any of it. I should have been with my family. If I had—" Guilt stabbed at him. "My family and my career are the most important things in my life, and now you've managed to sabotage *both*."

He ignored her sharp gasp and headed for the door. When

he got there, he paused, and gave her his most painful truth. "I'm sorry, Jasmine. I just don't have room for *you*."

He left without looking back and caught a taxi to the emergency room where his family waited. The whole time, he replayed the horrible things he'd said. The guilt of hurting her mixed with the guilt of not being there for his son, until he felt like he was going to vomit. Or maybe it was the cab driver's heavy foot on the brake. Either way, by the time he got to the ER, he was sick with worry.

He found Yadiel sitting in a hospital bed playing with Star Wars LEGOs. A sling kept his left arm mostly still. Ignacio sat on a chair next to the bed reading a murder mystery in Spanish.

"Mijo, are you okay?" Ashton rushed over, checking his son for any other signs of injury or distress.

But Yadiel simply received him with a sunny, gap-toothed smile. "Hi, Papi. Can we go home now? To the apartment, I mean."

Ignacio closed the book and stood. "We're all done here," he said in Spanish. "They patched him up sooner than expected. We would have met you back at the rental, but you were already on your way, so we figured we'd wait. Your grandparents already went back in a taxi."

Ashton felt like the floor had rocked under his feet. Yadiel was . . . *fine*. *Everyone* was fine. Without him. He'd built up all this anxiety and fear—for nothing. And now the emotions had nowhere to go.

Ignacio gathered the LEGOs and his book into Yadiel's Spider-Man backpack and hoisted it over his own shoulder. "Vámonos, Yadi."

"Okay, 'Buelo."

Ashton moved to help, but Yadiel slid off the bed on his own and skipped out of the room.

Feeling useless, Ashton walked beside his father. "I'm sorry I wasn't here sooner."

Ignacio shrugged. "No es nada. You know this happens to Yadiel all the time. Since we were in the same city, I figured you could come deal with the insurance and everything. But I handled it. No big deal."

As Ashton followed his father and his son out of the ER, an unpleasant feeling simmered in his gut.

His own family didn't need him. They managed just fine, functioning as a cohesive unit whenever he wasn't there . . . which was most of the time. Everything he'd done had been for their safety and well-being. But as much as he wanted to protect his son from everything, maybe he couldn't. And maybe . . . that was okay.

If that was true . . . he'd been tremendously unfair to Jasmine.

He wanted to run back to her. To apologize, to spill all of his hopes and fears where Yadiel and his family were concerned.

But after all he'd said, he had no right to ask her for any more emotional labor on his behalf. They were done. And it was better this way.

He was on his own.

Chapter 37

The wrap party was held at an event space in Chelsea with a trendy, industrial vibe. Exposed pipes, neon pink and purple lighting, gray concrete floor, and a circular bar in the center manned by two overworked bartenders.

Jasmine hated it. The air-conditioning was cranked to eleven, and she was freezing in a strapless red minidress. Her feet hurt, thanks to her strappy stilettos, and because she was scared that she'd get sloppy if she let herself drink, she was knocking back glasses of seltzer instead of champagne.

Which meant, on top of everything else, she had to pee every half hour.

But she needed to grin and bear it. There were members of the press everywhere, along with some actors from other ScreenFlix shows and a few local celebrities.

And as much as Jasmine tried to avoid Ashton, *everyone* wanted pictures of them together. The whole show hinged on their chemistry, and they'd done too good a job convincing everyone they were in love.

Including themselves.

"Another seltzer." Lily tottered over from the bar on sky-high heels and passed Jasmine her drink. "I swear, these vodka tonics are the only thing keeping my shoes on. How much you wanna bet I'll be barefoot in the next hour?"

Jasmine snorted. "I'm not taking that bet."

She saw Tanya heading toward them and shoved her drink back at Lily. "Be right back," she said. "Gonna hit the restroom again."

Before she could get far, a firm hand gripped her elbow. Jasmine turned, and Tanya shot her a wide grin. With her other hand, Tanya held Ashton's wrist in a death grip. "You two are wanted for another interview."

Jasmine bit back a groan and tried to smile. "Of course."

Tanya positioned them in front of a backdrop covered in the *Carmen in Charge* logo. It also happened to be located right under an air vent, and Jasmine clenched her teeth to keep them from chattering. The saving grace was that she'd left her hair loose, and it provided a slight bit of cover on her neck and back.

A perky interviewer from an entertainment news channel stepped up to them with a mic. The camera guy turned a bright light on them and gave a thumbs-up.

Jasmine flashed what she thought of as her red-carpet grin—big enough to make it obvious that she was smiling, but not so big that she couldn't talk—and tried to ignore the blinding light and freezing air.

The interviewer asked the same questions they'd already been asked countless times that night.

What can audiences expect from Carmen in Charge?

How different is it from working on soaps/telenovelas?

How does the show resonate for you as Latinx actors?

And then, of course, *What is it like filming romantic scenes together?*

To the last, Jasmine would joke, "It's a tough job, but someone's gotta do it." Every single time. Let them all have the same sound bite—she didn't care.

Ashton, the big jerk, was as handsome as ever, dressed in a sleek charcoal gray suit with his hair curling freely. He answered questions with his particular brand of cool charisma, but Jasmine could tell he was dying inside.

They stood next to each other for interviews and photos, and he put his arm around her when he had to, but he held himself stiffly, his hand hovering over her skin, not touching her.

Finally, Jasmine couldn't take the cold anymore, and her fifth—sixth?—seltzer and lime was testing the limits of her bladder. "If you'll excuse me," she murmured to Tanya, then made a beeline for the restroom.

She passed Lily, who was chatting with Nino and his boyfriend.

"I drank your water," Lily called, and Jasmine waved her off.

In the gender-neutral restroom area, Jasmine caught sight of her reflection in the mirror over the sinks. Shit, she looked awful. Not her hair and makeup—those were perfect, thanks to a team of stylists—but her eyes were wide with anxiety, her jaw rigid, and she looked . . . skittish, almost. As if she were ready to leap out of her skin at any moment.

Damn it. No, she knew just what she looked like—that damned picture on her grandmother's refrigerator! She could almost see the word "DUMPED!" hovering over her head.

Not this time, Kitty Sanchez, Jasmine thought. *This time, I dumped him.*

Except that didn't make her feel any better. And it didn't exactly feel true.

After leaving the restroom, she sent Lily a text.

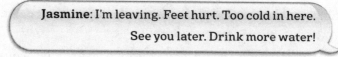

Jasmine: I'm leaving. Feet hurt. Too cold in here. See you later. Drink more water!

And then she ducked out a side entrance and took a taxi back to the hotel.

The whole way, she fought back tears. This was the wrap party for a show *she* had starred in. She should be happy!

She was miserable.

This is why you don't date costars, dummy, her brain shouted at her. *So much for being a Leading Lady. Go back to soap operas where you belong.*

At her hotel room, Jasmine let herself in and turned on all the lights. After kicking off her shoes and shimmying out of the dress, she went to her shoulder bag, pulled out her wallet, and removed the Leading Lady Plan she'd created with her cousins. She stared at her grandmother's name on the top of the paper for a moment, then with deliberate, decisive motions, she tore the paper into tiny pieces and left them scattered on the dining table that was haunted by memories of Ashton.

Still clad only in a strapless bra and shapewear, she dragged out her suitcases and began to pack.

Goodbye, New York City. Jasmine Lin was going back to Los Angeles.

So what if she'd never truly been happy there? Who cared if she felt betrayed after people gave quotes to the press about her breakup with McIntyre?

She didn't care anymore. It was what she deserved. How stupid to think she could have more.

Her Leading Lady Plan had been hopeless from the get-go. She would never be all the things she aspired to be. And she had once again ruined a good thing.

If ScreenFlix offered her a second season, she would see what she could do to get out of her contract. She just couldn't be around Ashton anymore.

When the first suitcase was full, she stopped packing long enough to call Riley. The call went to voice mail. She kept the message short and to the point.

"Hi, it's Jasmine. I'm done here. I'll be catching the red-eye back to LA tomorrow night. Get me back on *The Glamour Squad*, please. I don't want to have anything else to do with *Carmen*."

Her voice broke on the last word and she quickly ended the call. Then she ignored the calls and texts that came through in response as she booked her flight. As much as she wanted to leave right that minute, her cousins would kill her if she missed the party tomorrow.

Besides, she'd worked too damn hard on it, and she wanted to see her grandmother's reaction.

Too bad she couldn't manage the one thing that would have truly made Esperanza's day. Just another thing she'd failed at. Jillian would always rank higher. And Jasmine . . . would always be alone.

Tears streamed down her face as she tossed the phone aside

and resumed packing. Might as well be alone in LA, where the summers were dry and the winters were warm.

When she was done, she put her suitcases next to the door, laid out her outfit for the next day, and popped an over-the-counter sleep aid to knock herself out.

One more day. She just had to get through one more day, and then she could put all of this behind her.

ASHTON WAS HALFWAY through packing the next morning when someone knocked on his hotel room door.

For a brief, wild moment, he both hoped and feared it would be Jasmine. But after the way she disappeared from the party last night, he was sure it wouldn't be her.

Still, he hoped.

When he opened the door, his father stood on the other side. Ignacio took one look at the open suitcases in the room beyond, and gave Ashton a bland smile.

"Going somewhere?"

Ashton rubbed the back of his head and ducked his gaze. That look and tone always got him, never mind that he was rapidly approaching forty. "Ah . . . just packing. There's no reason to stay in New York."

"Back to Miami?" Ignacio strolled through the chaos in the living room, eyeing the piles of unfolded clothing, multiple pairs of running sneakers, and scattered bottles of cologne. Ashton grabbed some stuff off a chair so Ignacio could sit.

"No. I'll go to Puerto Rico with you. I don't have any jobs lined up, so . . ." Ashton trailed off, and his father pinned him with a hard look.

"You're running away," he said.

"No, I'm taking the next steps for my life and my career."

Ignacio actually laughed at that. "Really? Because from where I'm sitting, it looks like running away."

Ashton paused with a bundle of folded gym shorts in his hands. Coño, his father was right. Ever since the Incident, Ashton had let fear control his actions. He'd been reactive instead of proactive.

Until he'd met Jasmine. She'd coaxed him out of his shell. With her, he'd made his own choices from a place of wanting something and going after it, instead of being afraid of something and avoiding it.

Someone else knocked on the door.

"Ah." Ignacio braced his hands on his knees and stood. "They're here."

Ashton's brow furrowed as his father made his way to the door. "Who's here?"

In response, Ignacio opened the door and stepped back to admit Abuelito Gus, Abuelita Bibi, and Yadiel.

Ashton bit back a sigh and resisted the urge to scrub his hands over his face. Or hide in the bathroom. He knew an intervention when he saw one.

He met his father's grin with a grimace. "This is an ambush," he said in English.

Ignacio shrugged and shut the door. "You had it coming. Now, siéntate."

Ashton hurried to clear space so his family could sit comfortably. Yadiel immediately tried to climb over the back of the couch, but stopped at his great-grandmother's stern glance.

"¿Quieres volver al hospital?" she asked, eyeing the sling he still wore on his left arm.

"No, Abuelita Bibi." Yadiel pouted, but he sat his butt on the sofa.

Once Ashton sat too, his father got right to the point. "I'm going back to Puerto Rico."

Ashton nodded. "Okay. We'll all go back together."

But Ignacio was shaking his head. "No. You're staying here. And so is Yadiel."

Ashton's brow creased, but he opened his arms when Yadiel bolted to him and climbed in his lap. "I don't understand."

"You're not done here," Ignacio said. "And I want to put more time into the restaurant, get it back to what it used to be before Maria."

"I am done. There won't be a season two of *Carmen*."

Ignacio shrugged. "So what? There will be something else. You'll either be here or in Los Angeles. You're not going back to Miami or telenovelas."

Ashton resisted the urge to roll his eyes, tamping down the petulance his father still sometimes managed to bring out in him. "You can't know that."

Abuelita Bibi spoke up then, without looking up from her knitting. "*I* know that."

Abuelito Gus nodded, a firm believer in his wife's "feelings." Ashton, who'd been down this road before, didn't bother to argue.

"So why is Yadiel staying here?" Ashton asked, and a grimy little hand pressed to the side of his face.

"Because I *want* to," Yadiel replied, like *Duh, most obvious answer in the world.*

"Yadi, you have school—" Ashton started, but his son interrupted him with a shrug that was so much like Ignacio's, Ashton fought a grimace.

"School is overrated," the boy said. "I want to be homeschooled. You know, you can do it all online now, and in fewer hours of the day. It sounds like a way better deal."

Clearly this argument had been rehearsed. "Won't you miss your friends?"

"Well, yeah, but I can still go visit them, right? And make new ones."

Ashton swallowed hard. How had he ended up with such a well-adjusted kid? He looked to his father, who likely deserved all the credit.

"This isn't a normal life for a child," Ashton warned. "Are you sure?"

"Daaaaad," Yadiel said, which was how Ashton knew he was being outmaneuvered. Yadi had picked up the drawn out "Dad" habit from some Nickelodeon show, and he used it whenever he wanted to imply Ashton was being an idiot. "I'm not a baby anymore."

"Everyone already knows about him," Ignacio pointed out. "Your career is about to take off, and you won't have time to fly to Puerto Rico every weekend. You can get tutors and a nanny. And if I can spend more time at the restaurant, we won't need help."

He meant financial help. Ashton knew it pricked his father's pride to accept money.

But his family was bigger than just his father and son. Ashton turned to his grandparents. "And you?" he asked them. "What do you two want?"

They exchanged a glance, then Abuelita Bibi announced, "We'll be staying with you."

"Part of the time," Abuelito Gus amended. "We've spent our whole lives in Puerto Rico, and we like traveling. But we also want to be around Yadi while we can."

Ashton's heart constricted. They meant *while they were alive.*

"What do you say, Papi?" Yadiel pulled on Ashton's neck with his good arm. "Can I live with you?"

And as Ashton looked down into his little boy's dark, shining eyes, he was hit with the realization that Yadiel wasn't a little boy anymore. He was almost nine. Ashton had missed a lot during those years, and he didn't want to miss any more.

Jasmine had been right. He couldn't have it both ways. If he wanted the fame, he had to come to terms with being more visible. If he wanted to keep his private life completely private, then he couldn't be a celebrity. The two just didn't mesh.

He'd blamed her unfairly. She'd handled her rising fame far better than he had, with clear eyes and a thick skin.

And he couldn't continue to live in fear because of one terrible incident. He deserved better too. He deserved to feel free and happy . . . the way he felt when he was with Jasmine.

He owed her a whole lot more than an apology. And he finally knew how to make it up to her.

With a jolt, he checked his watch. Good, it was still early. Maybe there was still time to salvage . . . something. If he was about to change everything about his life, he might as well go all in.

"Yes, you can live with me," he said. Yadiel cheered and pumped a fist into the air, narrowly missing Ashton's nose. He shifted Yadiel off his lap so he could stand up. "One more thing. The woman I'm in love with asked me to attend her abuela's eightieth birthday party today."

Ignacio raised an eyebrow. "Well, you'd better get there then."

"Stop sitting around blabbing," Abuelito Gus teased.

"Why didn't you tell me?" Abuelita Bibi tossed her knitting aside and leaped to her feet as fast as the arthritis in her knees allowed. She began to rummage in the clothing Ashton had strewn about the room. "What are you going to wear? Where's that nice blue suit?"

Yadiel stood on the chair Ashton had just vacated. "Is it the pretty lady who likes superheroes? Can I come too?"

Ashton caught him before he jumped off. "Of course, mijo. From now on, where I go, you go."

Yadiel cheered.

"We'll all go," Ashton added, hoping Jasmine would recognize the magnitude of the gesture. He was willingly revealing his family to the world.

And also maybe using them as a shield so she couldn't chew him out. She wouldn't do that in front of a kid and three old people, right?

"¡Caramba!" Abuelita Bibi straightened and looked down at her purple sweat suit. "I can't go to a party dressed like this!

And Yadiel needs to look nice. We have to go back to the apartment to change."

Ashton took charge then, sending them out the door and promising to meet them in an hour.

When the door shut behind them and quiet returned, he had a moment of clarity.

This was the last time it would be just him. After this, he'd have Yadiel with him full time, and sometimes his grandparents too.

He looked around at the empty, messy room, and felt like the luckiest guy in the world to have a kid who wanted to be around him.

And like the biggest idiot for letting his own misconceptions and fears ruin something good with the sweetest woman he'd ever met.

He grabbed his clothes and headed for the shower. Hopefully it wasn't too late to fix things.

Chapter 38

Ava and Michelle were waiting outside the venue when Jasmine rolled up in an SUV. When the driver began to unload all her suitcases, her cousins immediately gave her the eye.

They at least had the decency to wait for the car to drive away before starting in on her.

Michelle spoke first. "All right, spill it. What's up with the bags?"

Ava checked her watch. "And we don't have time for you to give us the runaround so just tell us a straight answer the first time, 'kay?"

Jasmine blinked, feeling mildly taken aback. She was used to this level of directness from Michelle, but not Ava. They wanted an answer? Fine. She was owning her choices. Raising her chin, she said, "I'm going back to Los Angeles and rejoining *The Glamour Squad*." Okay, so that wasn't a done deal yet, but she was about 87 percent sure they'd take her back.

Ava's eyes widened but Michelle's narrowed.

"Shut. Up." Michelle's tone was flat with disbelief and a tinge of anger. "You're moving back to LA? Just like that?" Her dark eyes flicked to the small mountain of suitcases. "Today? What, are you gonna leave directly from the party?"

That was exactly what Jasmine was planning to do, but she didn't want to say so. Luckily, Ava jumped in.

"What about your Leading Lady Plan?" Ava sounded personally hurt by Jasmine's decision to give up.

"I ripped it up." Jasmine gave a nonchalant shrug. "Clearly wasn't working out that well for me."

Michelle rolled her eyes. "Oh, please. You loved working on *Carmen.* And you hate LA. You're just too much of an actress to admit it. You're going to trash all the progress you've made because things didn't work out with a man? Really?"

"It's not just that it didn't work out." Jasmine's voice held a defensive edge, but she was too tired to soften it. "I can't keep being intimate with Ashton on-screen while pretending I'm not in love with him. And when shit got hard, he disappeared. Everything related to this show is tied up in him, and the bottom line is, he didn't trust me. I can't keep working with someone like that."

"Ah." Michelle nodded sagely. "Point four on the Jasmine Scale."

Ava's voice was gentle. "Sweetie, is it so unreasonable that he didn't tell you he had a son? It sounds like he was used to keeping that secret under wraps. And you . . ."

"Are a paparazzi magnet," Michelle finished bluntly. "Now get inside, we have flower arrangements to prep."

Between the three of them, they dragged Jasmine's suitcases into the venue and set to work.

"How many magenta flowers again?" Michelle asked.

"Two," Ava replied between her teeth. "For the fifth time, it's *two* ginger alpinias, *one* yellow rose."

"Got it." Michelle yanked all the delicate tropical flowers out of her vase and started over. "So he didn't trust you with his kid. So what? You trust people too easily."

Jasmine huffed as she lined the inside of a rectangular glass vase with large leaves. They looked crooked, so she pulled them out and did it again. "I know I do."

"My point is, you can't measure another person's willingness to trust against your own. For example, you'd never have a secret baby because you can't keep a secret. I'm kind of impressed he managed it for—how old is the kid?"

"Eight," Jasmine replied, finally satisfied with the leaves. "Yadiel is eight."

Wait. There was something about numbers . . .

Jasmine's hands stilled on the leaves as her stellar memory supplied a missing piece of the puzzle. After the Latinx in the Arts Summit, Ashton had told her about the attempted home invasion. What had he said exactly?

Around seven years ago, someone tried to break into my house.

Seven years. According to *Buzz Weekly*, Yadiel was eight. That meant . . .

Oh, shit. Yadiel had already been born when it happened. He would have been just a baby, but god, no wonder Ashton was so overprotective about his son's safety.

"That is impressive," Ava agreed, referring to how long Ashton had kept Yadiel a secret. "And you're both right. These centerpieces *are* too complicated."

Michelle held up a finger threateningly. "Oh no you don't. You designed them and insisted they would be 'easy' to assemble at the venue. We had our doubts, but now we have committed to these centerpieces and goddamn it, we are *making* these centerpieces."

Ava sighed and kept sorting palm leaves.

Jasmine's mind continued to turn over this new realization. Ashton had left out mention of Yadiel when he'd told her about the break-in. But still, he'd shared it with her, one of his biggest secrets. That couldn't have been easy for him.

Michelle was right. Jasmine did trust easily, and look where it had gotten her. She could see now it was a direct response to feeling ignored and misunderstood by her parents and siblings. It was why she'd readily given her heart to every semi-attractive man who'd even shown her an ounce of attention. She sought her parents' love by securing romantic relationships, because in her family, that was what made you a success.

But that wasn't healthy. And trust wasn't meant to be given in one lump sum. It was earned, little by little. And hadn't Ashton been doing that? Little by little, he'd let her in. Who was she to say he wouldn't have told her about Yadiel eventually? Kitty Sanchez had forced his hand, and Jasmine had made herself the victim.

It occurred to her that maybe, just maybe, packing her bags and leaving a frantic voice mail on her agent's cell phone was just a tiny bit rash.

Jasmine's mind wandered back to something else Michelle had said earlier. "You're right about another thing," she murmured.

"Of course I am." Michelle shot her a grin to show she was joking. "What am I right about this time?"

"I do love working on *Carmen*." Jasmine set down the shears and tried to put the feeling into words. "Working on a show with so many Latinx cast and crew members? It was an incredible experience. I got so caught up in the drama of Ashton that it didn't fully sink in while I was there. But when I compare it to working on, well, every other show I've worked on . . . god, it was like magic."

Ava nodded, her eyes full of understanding, and touched Jasmine's hand. "Keep cutting the leaves," she said in a mock whisper. "And I'm sorry it wasn't picked up for a second season."

"Oh, we still don't know," Jasmine said absently as she measured and cut.

"Wait, what?" Michelle stared at her, then at the suitcases in the corner. "You don't even know if you're getting a season two but you're still going back to *Glamour Squad*? What about your contract?"

Before Jasmine could answer, someone called out, "Hello?"

Ava let out a panicked squeak. "Oh god, one of the tías is early."

"Worse than that," Jasmine murmured, spotting a familiar freckled face in the entrance to the ballroom. "It's my agent."

"For real?" Michelle dropped the roses and raised a hand, waving Riley over. "Hey, come over here and help us talk some sense into your client."

Riley Chen rushed into the room, her dark shoulder-length bob mussed and her freckled cheeks flushed. She dragged a rolling suitcase behind her with a laptop bag slung over one shoulder, making her petite frame slightly lopsided.

"I'm so glad I caught you," Riley said. Her eyes widened as she took in Jasmine's pile of suitcases.

"Did you just come here from California?" Jasmine asked in disbelief.

Riley shot her an exasperated look. "I got on the first flight this morning, which I wouldn't have had to do if you'd answered your phone."

Jasmine grimaced. "I swear I was going to call you when I got back to LA."

Riley shook her head. "I don't need you in LA. I need you here."

Jasmine pursed her lips as something else occurred to her. "Speaking of, how did you know to find me here?"

"I follow Michelle on Instagram."

Michelle looked up from where she was taking a picture of the flowers from an artful angle. "What, you didn't know Riley and I are mutuals?"

Ava retrieved a bottle of water and a donut for Riley, who took them gratefully. "So, since you're here," Ava began, and glanced meaningfully at the still-unassembled centerpieces. "Want to help us with these while we help Jasmine make a decision?"

"I've already made a decision," Jasmine said, although she was feeling less decisive by the minute.

"Your decision sucks," Michelle told her. "Make a new one."

Jasmine shot her a glare, but didn't reply.

Riley wiped the donut crumbs off her fingers with a napkin,

then took the cut ribbons Ava handed her. "While I would never tell you that you've made a bad decision," she began, "it is my duty as your agent to remind you that you signed a three season contract, and to ask that you hold off on deciding anything just yet."

"I guess this means you didn't call Ben at *Glamour Squad*?"

"Ah, I did not, no. Because I was waiting for you to wrap *Carmen* before telling you I've had a lot of inquiries come in. People want to work with you, and they're trying to get you on their schedules before *Carmen* gets picked up for another season."

"We don't know if it will," Jasmine pointed out, but Riley cut her off.

"Oh, it will. Trust me, with the amount of buzz the show has been getting, they'd have to be stupid not to film more episodes."

Jasmine frowned. "You mean all the stuff about me and Ashton? That's not good buzz."

"All buzz is good buzz. Haven't you—oh, shoot." She slapped a hand to her forehead. "I forgot you deleted all your social media apps. You really haven't seen."

"Seen what?" Bewilderment mixed with apprehension. *Now* what were people saying about her on the internet?

Riley pulled out her phone and navigated to Jasmine's Instagram profile.

Jasmine blinked. "Holy shit. Since when do I have one hundred thousand followers?"

"Since the publicist for *Carmen* has been working her butt off to generate early buzz for the show." Riley took her phone back. "Tanya's been posting pictures and videos from the set since the beginning, playing up the Latinx angle and the rom-com angle. Rom-coms are huge right now."

Jasmine shook her head in awe. "I had no idea. After McIntyre, I've been completely ignoring all that."

"Stop saying 'after McIntyre' like he was some kind of natural disaster that destroyed your home," Michelle snapped, slapping a rose on the table and sending petals flying. "He was one douchebag who broke your heart. He just happened to be a household name."

"Michelle . . ." Ava raised her eyebrows in warning.

Michelle shook her head. "No, I'm tired of it. She needs to know."

Ava sent Michelle a look and soon the two were having a whispered argument while Riley stuffed palm leaves into glass vases like her life depended on it.

But Jasmine ignored them because . . . Michelle was right.

What was next? "After Ashton"? While it had a nice ring to it, this wasn't what Jasmine wanted her life to be. All it did was play into the myth society wanted her to believe, that her love life was the most important thing about her. And it wasn't, damn it. She was a fully rounded person with hopes and dreams and fears—and a hundred thousand Instagram followers, apparently.

She could still be the Leading Lady in her own life.

What would that look like? How did she want it to look?

Your decision sucks. Make a new one.

What if it were really that easy?

Jasmine dug in her bag for her phone.

"What are you doing now?" Michelle's voice was heavy with suspicion.

"Canceling my flight."

Riley let out an enormous sigh of relief.

Some part of Jasmine's brain must have known she was overreacting, because she'd gotten travel insurance on the flight. While she navigated the cancellation on the airline's app, her mind whirled with everything her cousins had said, including some wise words from Ava . . .

Is it so unreasonable that he didn't tell you he had a son?

At the time, yeah, it had seemed *completely* unreasonable. How dare he keep something like that from her? She'd shared openly with him about her own life.

But the truth was, she didn't have any secrets nearly as big as his. Hell, her business was already splashed all over magazine covers. And Yadiel was a secret Ashton had fought hard to protect for good reasons. As much as it stung to admit, it made sense that he hadn't told her. She shouldn't feel entitled to every part of him, especially not so early.

They'd said some awful things to each other, but all relationships had ups and downs, right? She had minor tiffs with her cousins and siblings all the time.

Make a new decision.

What if she did things differently this time around? What if, instead of throwing herself in headfirst, they took things slow? She'd get to know his family, since they were clearly so important to him, and he could . . . well, he could meet hers, but she wouldn't be offended if he didn't want to spend a lot of time around them. She sure didn't.

But as she looked over at her cousins arguing over the flower arrangements, she knew that wasn't entirely true. Sure, Ava and Michelle were her best cousins, her Primas of Power, and she trusted them in all things, but when it came down to it, she knew the rest of her family would have her back. And her parents loved her, even if they didn't always understand her.

She would get through the party and try to enjoy herself. Then, when it was over, she'd have a meeting with Riley about next steps. It was time to let her agent in on the Leading Lady Plan. Knowing Riley, she'd happily turn it into a spreadsheet.

And after that . . . she'd call Ashton. She'd apologize, and then . . . well, she'd see where it went from there.

She picked up the flowers Ava dumped in front of her and got to work.

Chapter 39

Ashton's nerves were out of control by the time he arrived at the party venue in the Bronx. He'd imagined a small gathering at someone's casa, maybe a community center, but this was . . . *grand.*

Marina Del Rey sat right on the water, overlooking the Long Island Sound. The exterior was all sand-colored stone, with fountains and archways and columns, and lined with trees and well-trimmed shrubs.

"Is it a wedding?" Abuelita Bibi asked as Ashton helped her out of the rental car.

"They must have weddings here," Abuelito Gus replied, then he elbowed Ashton and winked. "In case you really want to make this a spectacle."

"Is there gonna be *cake*?" Yadiel leaped out of the car and bounced on his toes.

"I'll park," Ignacio said. "Wait for me."

They all walked in together. A few people in the entranceway gave them odd looks, but Ashton channeled Victor and strode forward, Yadiel's hand tucked into his.

"Are you going to stand on a stage and tell everyone how you feel?" Yadiel asked in a mock whisper.

Ashton remembered how Victor brought Carmen up on stage in the final episode. But Ashton wasn't like Victor. If anything, Jasmine was more like Victor, and he was more like Carmen. And Carmen . . . she'd do this differently.

"No, mijo. I don't think so. I only need to tell *her*."

Abuelita Bibi patted his arm approvingly and whispered, "Tengo un buen presentimiento."

Taking heart in Abuelita Bibi's good feeling, Ashton led his family into the main hall. His mouth immediately went dry.

Ignacio came up beside him. "Now this is what I call a party," he said, sounding impressed.

There had to be at least two hundred people packed inside. Salsa music blared, and the central dance floor was alive with movement. Couples danced, children ran around underfoot, and people sat chatting and eating at the round tables interspersed around the room.

Everyone was dressed to the nines, and Ashton sent up a silent prayer of thanks for whatever "feeling" had led Abuelita Bibi to pack Yadiel's suit "just in case." His son was looking sharp, even with his sling.

The color scheme of the party was magenta and yellow, and it showed in the flowers, table settings, and even in the neon lights lining the ceiling and arches on the walls. People browsed a buffet table along one end of the ballroom, and there was an enormous cake on its own table at the other end.

Yadiel spotted it at the same time.

"Cake," he said reverently, and Ashton choked back a laugh.

Then the whispers started, and he knew he'd been spotted.

A week ago, they would have sent him running for the hills. But not today. His parents had always shown him that when you cared about someone, you showed up for them.

Besides, he had a grand gesture to make.

Squaring his shoulders, Ashton gave Yadi's hand a squeeze.

The crowd on the dance floor parted. An older woman in a yellow sequined dress with a full skirt stood in the center, dancing with a young man.

For a second, the whole room held its breath. Then the woman in yellow screamed.

Shouts broke out. People leaped over chairs to reach her, but all she did was point wordlessly at Ashton.

Others found their voices, though. And suddenly, from all throughout the ballroom, he heard the name of every character he'd ever played on a telenovela.

"It's el matador!"

"El diablo más sexy!"

"El duque de amor!"

And then Jasmine's voice. "Ashton? Is that you?"

He turned to her like a dying plant seeking the sun. She was radiant in an off-the-shoulder red dress, her dark hair spilling in shiny waves over her bare shoulders. Everything else fell away, and he felt a tug in his gut, pulling him toward her. He saw the look of shock on her face, but there was something else there too. Something like gratitude.

All he wanted to do was take her in his arms and steal her

away, or—more appropriately—drop at her feet and beg her to forgive him.

But this was her grandmother's birthday. And while he was here to give his heart to Jasmine, she had originally asked him to make it a party no one in the family would ever forget.

It was time to uphold his end of the bargain.

Channeling the confident gallantry of el matador, Ashton turned to Esperanza. "May I have this dance?" he asked in Spanish.

Esperanza seemed to have recovered from the shock of seeing him. She drew herself up, grabbed a fistful of her full skirt, and struck a pose. "Can you salsa?"

Ignacio snorted. "Of course he can salsa."

Ashton strode forward and caught the older woman up in a fierce, fast dance. She was good—really good—and soon everyone around them was dancing and cheering. Cameras and phones were out, recording them, but for once, Ashton didn't care. The happiness in Esperanza's eyes was enough to put him at ease. When was the last time he'd felt that?

Before Yadiel was born, maybe. Since then, he'd been keeping a secret, constantly worried someone would uncover it or that something terrible could happen to the people he loved and that he wouldn't be there to protect them. While he was still pissed over the invasion of his privacy, he had to admit he felt lighter than he had in a long time. He'd kept himself isolated, except from his own family, which was small. But Jasmine's . . . reminded him of home. Of big parties with his mother's relatives before they'd all eventually moved to the

States. He hadn't realized how much he'd missed the feeling of community.

He desperately wanted Yadiel to have this.

When the dance ended, Esperanza beamed at him. Everyone around them broke into applause and raucous cheers.

Jasmine's abuelo, Willie Rodriguez, stepped in to shake Ashton's hand and thank him for coming. Others streamed onto the dance floor to tell him which of his characters they loved or hated. He smiled and chatted easily in a mix of Spanish and English, but his eyes searched the room until he spotted Yadiel running around with some of the other kids and his father and grandparents sitting at a table with Ava. They had full plates of food in front of them.

At the edge of the dance floor, Jasmine waited with two people who could only be her parents. Her mother's skin was a smooth golden brown like Jasmine's, and they had the same sparkling eyes, but Jasmine's smile was all her father's, a handsome older man of medium height.

When Ashton finally made it over to her, she began the introductions.

"Ashton, this is my mother, Lisa, and my father, Julio."

"I've heard so much about you both," Ashton said, and bit back a laugh at Jasmine's alarmed expression.

They both hugged him and told him to feel welcome. Remembering how Jasmine spoke about her family, Ashton took the opportunity to talk her up to them, as he'd once planned.

"I'm sure you already know how talented and hardworking your daughter is," he said, walking off the dance floor with them.

Lisa sent an indulgent smile her daughter's way. "She's always gone after what she wants."

"Being an actor's not an easy life," Julio added, and Ashton resisted the urge to say, *Yeah, no shit.* "But it makes her happy, so what can we do?"

Behind them, Jasmine rolled her eyes, but her lips curved in a smile.

Michelle came up and elbowed Ashton in the side. "Didn't think you were gonna make it, Golden Lion."

Ashton spoke in a hushed voice while Jasmine was busy with her parents. "Thanks for sending the invitation."

Michelle winked. "Don't fuck it up."

As she wandered away, Ashton tried to subtly shift Jasmine aside.

"We should talk," he said.

Her eyes were big and serious, but she nodded. "Not here. Let's make the rounds, introduce you to everyone, and then we'll sneak away."

And so Ashton began the greeting ritual of every Puerto Rican family event—walk around and say hello to *everyone*. Hug, kiss, handshake, fist bump—and in many cases, a photo.

Normally this was the kind of thing he hated. But despite his fame—in this particular crowd, especially—everyone treated him like family. They complimented his salsa moves, teased him good-naturedly about his telenovela roles, and asked him questions about himself and his family. And for the first time, he was able to answer those questions truthfully.

For his part, Ashton made a point to tell everyone how great of an actress Jasmine was, and how much he couldn't wait for them to watch the show—especially when he got to her brother and sister.

"Yeah, Jasmine got all the creative genes," her sister, Jillian, said wryly. "No one at my office can believe my sister's an actress, since I'm so boring."

Ashton shot a glance at Jasmine, who appeared to have swallowed her tongue.

As they finally finished their circuit of the room, Jasmine nudged him with her elbow. "This isn't a press junket, you know," she said out of the side of her mouth.

"Are you kidding?" Ashton grinned. "This is tapping directly into the Boricua grapevine. If we get them watching, we'll really be a hit."

She took a deep breath. "Speaking of . . ."

"Yes." Time to talk. Nerves simmered, but like Abuelita Bibi, he had a good feeling.

She tilted her head toward the doors that led outside. "Let's do this."

Ashton held the door for her, then followed her out to the walkway that overlooked the water.

It was now or never. He'd give her his heart, and then they would see where they stood.

Chapter 40

So." Jasmine crossed her arms and leaned back against the railing. "First things first, I appreciate you stopping by. It meant the world to my abuela."

She'd been so sure he wouldn't show up. Why would he? After all the horrible things they'd said to each other? She almost texted him multiple times to beg him to come—not for her, but for her grandmother—but that was Old Jasmine behavior. She was done doing anything out of desperation, or fear, or a sense of lack.

Leading Ladies are whole and happy on their own.

Damn right.

But then he'd shown up, casually sexy in a tailored blue suit with his white shirt open at the neck, revealing a hint of that hard chest. Her heart had leaped at the sight of him. And when she realized he'd brought his family with him, she understood it for what it was—the biggest proof of trust he was capable of giving.

"Her smile was all the thanks I need," he said quietly. "Truly, her response, and the rest of your family . . . it reminded me why we're in this ridiculous business. I've missed this."

Jasmine's brow creased. "You miss it? But you brought your family with you. Which, I wanted to add, I also appreciate. I know how hard it is for you to expose them to the public."

He ducked his head. "It is, but . . . I trust you."

She was melting inside. "Thank you."

"But I didn't mean them. Before my mother died, most of her family still lived on the island. We did big parties like this for all the holidays, birthdays, you name it. But it's been a long time and . . . I didn't realize how much I missed them. Since Yadiel was born . . ." He trailed off and shrugged, looking a little helpless, so Jasmine threw him a bone.

"I'd imagine . . . it's hard to talk about him to other people."

The relief on his face broke her heart.

"*Yes.*" He said the word with a rush of gratitude, like she'd hit the nail on the head. "I wanted to tell you, Jasmine. So many times. But . . . keeping secrets becomes a habit. And I think I fell out of the habit of trusting other people. I'm a single dad, but I don't know how to talk about it. I don't know how to date anymore. My life . . . it's complicated. And it might have just gotten more complicated, or less. I'm not exactly sure."

She wanted to go to him, to hug him, touch him while he talked. This was the Ashton she'd gotten to know during their time alone—the sweet, earnest, uncertain man behind the telenovela hero. But she had to hold out, to give them both space to speak. "What do you mean?"

He let out a sigh and rubbed the back of his head. "My father is going back to Puerto Rico and Yadiel is going to live with me. Full time."

Jasmine scrutinized his expression. "You seem pleased."

"I am." A grin tugged at his lips. "I know it will take some adjusting, but this is all I've ever wanted."

"I'm glad."

He opened his mouth, paused, then spoke. "Could you date a guy who already has a kid?"

A shaky laugh burst out of her, a release of the tension winding her up as she'd waited for him to speak. "Of course I could."

"Good, because anyone I get involved with . . . it's not just me. I'm a package deal."

"I know," she said quietly. "I would never expect otherwise."

He took a deep breath. "Jasmine, I'm in love with you."

Her heart stopped. Everything in her went still as she stared at him, slack-jawed. Her eyes searched his face, seeking out any hint that she'd misheard, or that he was joking, or . . .

Sincerity shone in his eyes. And a deep well of steadiness. She knew the curves and lines of his face, the subtleties of his expressions, the emotions radiating from his eyes. And his voice . . . He'd said the words with matter-of-fact seriousness.

"Really?" Her voice squeaked, and they both let out a nervous laugh.

"Sí, querida."

She threw her arms around his neck and kissed him, breathlessly, with all the love in her heart. He held her close, and in his arms, she felt . . .

The same. She felt happy, but she no longer felt the sense of completion she used to feel when she was with a guy.

No, she felt the same because . . . she was already complete. And wasn't that a lovely feeling?

"I don't know how we'll make it work," Ashton was saying, his face pressed into her neck. "God, you smell good."

"Make what work?" she asked, still riding the high from his kiss.

"Us. I don't know where I'm going to live, and I'll have Yadiel with me—"

"Yadiel is an amazing kid," she said, pulling back to look him in the eyes. "Don't feel like you have to hide him from me. You know I want a family. Not because it will give me value, but because I have a lot of love to give. I want to be loved, too, but I also just want to *love* someone. And I don't know why, but something about that scares everyone—"

Ashton took her hands in his and looked her deep in the eyes. "I'm not them."

She pressed her lips together, holding back the flood of emotion threatening to overwhelm her. "I know."

"And I'm not scared."

He wasn't. She could see the difference in him now. Despite the crowd and the attention and revealing his family to hers, there was a sense of calm and contentment in him that hadn't been there before. And it made her so fucking happy to see it.

"I love you," she whispered, and the words were like a release. Lightness infused her heart, and a tear spilled over her cheek.

Ashton pulled her close and kissed her, then he was mumbling apologies against her lips as he held her tight.

"I'm sorry I blamed you for . . . a lot of things. My son falling—when really, he's *always* falling off things. And the tabloids, and—"

"I forgive you. You were scared. And I was hurt. I understand why you didn't tell me about him."

"I should have. I'm sorry I didn't."

"I know. But I get it. And I'm sorry I called you selfish."

"Speaking of . . ." His lips curved. "I'll have to get Yadi to call you by name."

Her brows creased. "Why, what does he call me?"

"Pretty lady."

She laughed. "In English?"

"Yes."

"Okay, maybe we should correct that."

For a long moment, they just looked at each other, smiling. Jasmine tried to note every detail, so she never forgot this moment.

"We'll make it work," she said in a quiet voice. "And we'll take it slow. I think . . . I think we both need that."

He nodded. "You're the most amazing person I've ever met," he whispered, kissing her again.

Just then, the door from the main hall swung open. They broke apart and turned to see Riley running over to them.

Riley's eyes were wide and she waved her phone excitedly. "Season two," she cried. "ScreenFlix has already ordered a second season!"

ASHTON'S HEART POUNDED in his throat. Despite everything they'd just shared, he and Jasmine hadn't yet talked about the show. And he didn't want her to think he'd manipulated her into making a decision.

Jasmine's brows shot up. She released Ashton and grabbed her agent.

"Oh my god!" Jasmine said on a gasp. "That was so fast!"

"I told you!" Riley shrieked.

The two women jumped up and down, hugging, then Jasmine was hugging Ashton too.

"We got it!" she whispered in his ear.

"Does this mean you'll agree to film another season?" he asked.

"Of course she will," Riley said. "Your agent will probably be calling you any minute, by the way."

Sure enough, Ashton's phone buzzed in his pocket.

"I'm getting a drink!" Riley ran back to the ballroom.

"You should answer," Jasmine told him, but Ashton shook his head.

"You're Carmen," he said. "This decision is yours. And I want you to feel free to decide however you want, regardless of me. This is your choice."

He'd been so scared before, when she told him she would turn down a chance at a second season. His life was falling apart—or so he'd thought. He'd put too much pressure on this one show to be everything he needed it to be to achieve all his hopes and dreams.

Now . . . he still had those dreams, but he could see that the journey there would be better if he let people in, if he trusted that there would be more opportunities.

Jasmine sighed. "No, you were right, and so was Michelle. I was running away because I felt rejected. It's what I always do. But the truth is, I love playing Carmen. I love our cast and crew, and I love the stories we get to tell. There are so few roles for Latinx actors outside of the maid, the gang member, or the sexpot—why would I run away from that? I'd be shooting myself in the foot. And for what? To prove a point to Kitty Sanchez?"

His brow creased. "Who's Kitty Sanchez?"

"The gossip columnist who seems to have it out for us."

"Oh, *that* Kitty Sanchez." Ashton waited to see if she said more. When she didn't, he prompted, "So is that a . . ."

She laughed and hugged him hard. "It's a yes! We're doing season two!"

"There's just one thing I don't understand," Ashton murmured against her hair. "How did your grandmother not know we were working together?"

"Oh, Michelle threatened to spill everyone's secrets if they told her. It would have ruined the surprise if she knew, and if you didn't show up, it would have disappointed her. So the whole family was working to keep her from finding out."

"Wow. I'm impressed."

Jasmine nodded. "Michelle has dirt on *everyone*, so it was an effective threat. Luckily, she uses her powers for good."

Yadiel came running out then, looking left and right. When his eyes landed on Ashton, his face lit up. Chocolate was smeared around his mouth.

"Papi!" He ran over and Ashton scooped him up, hoisting him on his hip.

With a glance at Jasmine, Yadiel spoke in English. "I like New York, Papi. Can we stay here? Or come back to visit?"

Ashton raised his eyebrows. "Are you sure it's not just because you got chocolate cake?"

"Not just that." Yadiel grinned. "The kids are really fun. They all play *Minecraft*."

Jasmine's smile was heartbreakingly sweet as she looked at Yadiel's little chocolate-covered face.

"We'll discuss it later," Ashton told his son. "But I think we can."

"Yay!" Yadiel threw his good arm up in victory, then wriggled down. He paused a moment, looked at Jasmine, then quick as lightning, he hugged her around the waist. Before Ashton could say anything, Yadiel had already scampered back inside.

Taking a page from his kid's book, Ashton put an arm around Jasmine and hugged her close to him. "We'll make it work," he said quietly.

"No more hiding?" she asked.

"No more."

He kissed her, and when someone cleared their throat, he eased back. Riley stood before them with an open bottle of champagne and a stack of clear plastic cups.

"Are we celebrating?" she asked, sounding hopeful.

Jasmine reached for the bottle. "Yes. But I want producer credit."

Riley cheered, pumping her fist in the air as Jasmine popped the cork.

After she was done pouring, Riley held up her cup for a toast. "To success."

"To family," Jasmine added, with a look at Ashton.

He raised his cup and met her eyes. "To love."

Epilogue

They were once again on a red carpet, but this time, it was real.

Jasmine clung to Ashton's arm as they walked, stopping to chat with interviewers and pose for photos, showing off her red Carolina Herrera gown and his navy blue Tom Ford suit.

The whole thing was surreal. She'd never imagined *Carmen in Charge* would hit so big, but apparently the story of a woman trying to balance career, family, and love was universally relatable. Who knew?

Well, now *she* did. Jasmine was finally, for the first time in her life, successfully balancing all three.

It was definitely work, in a way she'd never expected. But through open communication—thanks, Vera!—growing trust, and practicing intentional vulnerability, she and Ashton were making plans for the future. With more episodes of *Carmen* on the slate, they'd rented an apartment together in Brooklyn. Yadiel was being homeschooled by a team of tutors. Ashton had appeared in a bilingual Off-Broadway production of *Cyrano* that was in talks for a Broadway run the next year and an early contender for a Best Actor Tony Award, and he'd won a "Villano Favorito" telenovela award for his role in *El fuego de amor*. Jasmine was putting those stage combat classes to good use as the lead in a ScreenFlix comedy about a Latinx superhero squad. She'd also started attending weekly therapy sessions, which were helping her cope with her need for external validation and her tendency to self-soothe with alcohol. Ashton was also in treatment for anxiety and PTSD from the home invasion, and there was a lightness to his demeanor that hadn't been there when they'd first met. Although Jasmine suspected having Yadiel close by helped too.

And just when she thought things couldn't get any better, *Carmen in Charge* had been nominated for a Golden Globe.

She cuddled against Ashton's side and gave a happy sigh. "I love you," she whispered just for him. Saying it never got old.

He smiled down at her, eyes soft. "Te amo."

Hearing it back never got old either.

Behind them, Ava and Michelle walked the carpet with Yadiel between them, holding his hands so he didn't run off.

"You have your speech prepared?" Ashton murmured.

"Yeah." She sent him a cheeky grin. "I'm going to thank your evil twin, Hector."

He chuckled at that. Viewers had loved the reveal at the end of *Carmen in Charge*, when Victor opened the door to find his estranged identical twin brother, Hector—played by Ashton with a beard.

A very sexy beard, in Jasmine's opinion.

Just then, a handler caught their attention and brought them over to a woman with a mic. But as they got closer, the woman turned, and it was—

"Kitty Sanchez!" Jasmine said on a gasp.

Kitty shot Jasmine a wide smile and even bounced a little on the tips of her toes.

"Jasmine Lin!" She grabbed Jasmine's hand and shook it vigorously. "I'm so excited to meet you. I'm a *huge* fan."

Jasmine struggled to keep from gaping at Kitty in shock. Wait, she was a *fan*? Then why had she been terrorizing Jasmine via gossip column for a year?

"I've been following your career since the beginning," Kitty went on. "And as a fellow puertorriqueña, I really wanted to make sure you were highlighted, so people would know your name and you'd keep getting roles. Congratulations on the Golden Globe nomination. I'm unbelievably happy for you!"

Unbelievable was right, but Jasmine couldn't help smiling back. Kitty's enthusiasm was genuine. And while she wanted to ask, *Why the mean articles and headlines, if you're such a fan?*—she didn't. Because in that moment, she looked at Kitty and saw herself a few years back, struggling to make it in an industry that didn't value her contributions, fighting to make her voice heard and her work visible. In reality, Kitty probably didn't even write the headlines. There was likely an editor or someone in marketing who chose them based on SEO. And it was true, Kitty had helped make Jasmine a household name.

Besides, hadn't it all worked out for the best anyway?

Jasmine leaned in and gave Kitty a hug. "Thank you," she whispered. "I know it's hard."

When she leaned back, Kitty had tears shining in her hazel eyes. She pointed the mic toward the carpet and said in a soft voice, "You're an incredible actress, and I just really want you to go far." She sniffled, then turned to Ashton. "You too. We need more Latinx actors breaking new ground in this industry."

Ashton nodded. "We're trying."

Kitty pulled herself together and held up the mic again. "Okay, I do have some real interview questions, if you have time?"

When they were done, Ava and Michelle wandered closer. Yadiel dropped their hands and grabbed Ashton's, reporting back on all the actors he'd seen and recognized. He was over the moon at how many superheroes had shown up.

"What was that about?" Ava asked lightly.

Jasmine sighed. "That was Kitty Sanchez. Turns out she's a huge fan."

Michelle barked out a laugh. "'Course she is." Then she linked her arm through Jasmine's. "Thanks for bringing us. Maybe I'll hook up with an Avenger while we're here."

Jasmine smiled, but she knew Michelle was joking. Michelle didn't date.

Ava slipped her arm through Jasmine's other arm. "I just saw Rita Moreno. Now I can die happy."

"We've come a long way," Jasmine murmured, remembering their days watching the red-carpet broadcast in their grandparents' living room. She knew everyone back at home was watching tonight, and while she wanted to win, it would be okay if they didn't.

This was only the beginning.

And she was just happy to share it with the people she loved.

Acknowledgments

First, I want to send my love to Puerto Rico. While I've never lived there, I feel a deep connection to the island. I still have family there, which makes that bond even stronger. Over the last few years, the people of Puerto Rico have weathered one blow after another. But Puerto Ricans are resilient and compassionate, and I am inspired by their strength every day. With these stories, I hope to show mi gente living our best lives—with success, happiness, and, most of all, love.

This book would never have happened if not for the unwavering support and enthusiasm of my agent, Sarah E. Younger. At every step, she goes above and beyond, and I'm so grateful to have her on my team.

I also owe tremendous gratitude to my editor, Elle Keck, for her guidance and encouragement. She built me up during low moments in the creative process and cheered me on during the highs.

Sarah and Elle, I can't thank you both enough!

I also give my thanks to the publicity team at Avon, including Rhina, Pam, and Kayleigh; to the art department, especially Elsie; to my copyeditor, Cecilia; and to the production team, Rachel W., Rachel M., Pamela, Lizz, and Diahann. It takes a village! Thanks for all you do.

Special thanks go to Bo Feng Lin for creating a cover illustration beyond my wildest dreams. It's perfect and I love it more than I can say.

I have a lot more people to thank, so please bear with me. Books may be written by the writer, but the support system is huge.

To my fellow #LatinxRom authors—Adriana Herrera, Priscilla Oliveras, Mia Sosa, Sabrina Sol, Zoraida Córdova, Lydia San Andres, Angelina M. Lopez, Diana Muñoz Stewart, Natalie Caña, Liana De la Rosa, and more—you remind me why I'm doing this, and I'm so honored to be part of this vibrant and growing community with all of you.

To my Golden Heart Rebelles, you are an endless source of encouragement and love. Special thanks to Evi Kline, Scarlett Peckham, Laurel Kerr, and Sarah Morgenthaler for providing early feedback.

To my friend Susan Lee, who, at times, served as my writing babysitter, and who also made sure I took breaks to see Broadway musicals.

To my Team RWchat mastermind group, thank you for being with me every step of the way—Kimberly Bell, C. L. Polk, and especially Robin Lovett, who read each scene as I wrote it and assured me it was fine and to *just keep going*.

To my cousins Kathryn, Lisa, and CarlyAnn, who championed this book when it was just a glimmer of an idea scribbled in a notebook.

To my fellow New York City romance writers, who always remind me to celebrate. Cheers!

To my beta readers, who provided invaluable insights: Ana Coqui, Audrey Flegel, Elizabeth Mahon, Marianne Robles, and Amber Friendly. This book is better because of your help. And to Laura Clifton, who gave me details and encouragement early on.

To Kate Brauning, my excellent writing coach, who asks the best (and toughest) questions, and to her Breakthrough Writers community for the accountability.

I also have to thank my parents, who encouraged my artistic pursuits, and my boyfriend's parents, for their unfailing support.

And as always, I give thanks for my boyfriend, who refills my mug with tea and refills my confidence with impromptu pep talks. Thank you for believing in me when I don't always believe in myself.

And last but most certainly not least, I am grateful for my readers. Thank you for giving this book the gift of your time, your attention, your feelings. It means the world to me.

About the Author

ALEXIS DARIA is a native New Yorker and an award-winning author writing stories about successful Latinx characters and their (occasionally messy) familias. Her debut, *Take the Lead*, was a 2018 RITA® Award winner for Best First Book and was named one of the Best Romance Novels of 2017 by the *Washington Post* and *Entertainment Weekly*. Her superpowers include spotting celebrities in NYC, winning Broadway ticket lotteries, and live-tweeting her favorite TV shows at @alexisdaria.